P9-DGG-978

THE *KO* CONSPIRACY

Hands shaking, Matt pushed the button for rewind, and then ran it again in slow motion, frame by frame.

It was all there on the screen. The missile entering the hardened-glass viewing window, shards of glass flying back from the impact. Then it was all the way in, out of sight, a split second before the flash and boom, a wave of light and dust wiping out everything on the screen for a moment, and then, when the noise stopped, the dust and sand settling back to reveal—

Nothing. A cloud of shrapnel and debris settling slowly back to earth now, but no trace of the building or its occupants.

The camera continued to film, soaking up the silence. Matt sat rooted to his chair, his pulse pounding in his ears. Finally, Marty's voice. "Ah—I hope the camera caught all that. Dead! They must all be dead! Oh, my God, what happened? Oh, sweet Jesus, I don't believe this."

THE K⊕ CONSPIRACY

A NOVEL

RIALL W. NOLAN

A DELL BOOK

Published by
Dell Publishing
a division of
Bantam Doubleday Dell Publishing Group, Inc.
1540 Broadway
New York, New York 10036

If you purchased this book without a cover you should be aware that this book is stolen property. It was reported as "unsold and destroyed" to the publisher and neither the author nor the publisher has received any payment for this "stripped book."

Copyright © 1995 by Riall W. Nolan

All rights reserved. No part of this book may be reproduced or transmitted in any form or by any means, electronic or mechanical, including photocopying, recording, or by any information storage and retrieval system, without the written permission of the Publisher, except where permitted by law.

The trademark Dell® is registered in the U.S. Patent and Trademark Office.

ISBN: 0-440-21250-2

Printed in the United States of America

Published simultaneously in Canada

January 1995

10 9 8 7 6 5 4 3 2 1

RAD

This is for William

THE RULE OF *KO*

From Gō, the Japanese game of territorial conquest. In situations where two warring pieces are deadlocked, the *Ko* rule requires one of the players to move elsewhere and begin an attack on another part of the board.

Using the Rule of *Ko* a seeming defeat in one sector can often be a means of securing a decisive advantage elsewhere. An almost certain loss can sometimes be changed into a victory, even in the very last moments of a game.

Although the ideograph for *Ko* is sometimes translated as "talent" or "skill," its real meaning is "threat."

1

Animal noises came from the shadows at the end of the alley. An animal in pain.

Matt McAllister stopped, balancing on his toes. Brushing his dark blond hair out of his eyes, he turned, listening. Georgetown lay quiet, twilight's coolness settling like a cloak over the fading heat of the day. Not five minutes earlier Matt had left his narrow town house on S Street, heading for the Safeway on Wisconsin Avenue to pick up a quart of ice cream. He was due at Marty Larsen's apartment in half an hour, and she'd promised him a surprise. If he didn't get a move on, he thought, he'd be late.

There it came again. Small noises, a kind of whimpering, coming from far back in the alley. From around the corner, where Matt couldn't see.

And the whisper of something scuffling on the concrete. Claws? Paws?

Then Matt saw the coat.

Almost at his feet a woman's cloth coat lay heaped carelessly on the damp, dirty concrete. Matt bent, picked it up. Nearly new, he thought; good quality.

He glanced up the alley again, into the dimness at the far end. What the hell was a coat doing here?

He stood stock-still, thinking. Spring's promise filled this early April evening in Washington, but the night was still chilly. Nobody, Matt thought, would toss a coat like this away.

Not these days; not in Washington. The homeless and the destitute, once confined mainly to the downtown areas, had multiplied in recent years, and in the district there were thousands who would appreciate something warm across their shoulders as they trudged from one trash can to the next, even here in staid Georgetown. A serviceable coat lying out in the open, Matt knew, wouldn't last an hour.

He walked a few feet into the alley and stopped again, his eyes moving from side to side, probing the shadows. Relax, he thought. It's America. You live here, remember? Not like the old days, in strange places where death could move into your peripheral vision before you knew it. Lighten up, he told himself; the old days are over.

The alley ran between two wings of an old school, a classic structure of weather-beaten brick wedged between Thirty-fifth Street and Wisconsin Avenue, an island in a mainly residential sea. The alley walls were smeared with the unintelligible graffiti that passed for urban art in these last years of the twentieth century. Bars and wire lay across the ground-floor windows, which stared blankly out at the gathering darkness. Toward the end of the alley Matt could make out a narrow alcove let into the wall, a sort of corridor with steps leading down, presumably to the basement or the boiler room.

The sounds came from there.

Matt had passed the old school hundreds of times, never really noticing it. Not exactly the cheeriest of places, he thought. Although the sun had not yet set, shadows lay in the spaces between the walls and the buildings, spreading across the concrete like dark puddles. To the left a sagging and torn cyclone fence enclosed a grassless sports field, a place where you might easily imagine a drug deal taking place. Or a gang fight.

But Matt had never seen either event, and he had never been remotely apprehensive crossing the schoolyard at night. After all, Wisconsin Avenue was only a few yards away, and the all-night Safeway supermarket was a constant hive of activity.

The noises came again. Low moans, almost like a baby's cry. It's not an animal, he thought. It's a woman.

He began to run down the alley, the narrow walls echoing his footsteps, his heart thudding as the adrenaline kicked in.

Three people stood in the alcove. One man held the woman from behind, his free hand clamped over her mouth. The other man stood in front of her, legs spread in a half crouch, working on her clothes. He had the front of the woman's jeans open, pulling them down her legs with short, savage tugs. A handbag lay open at her feet, its contents scattered across the damp concrete.

Matt's eyes moved to the woman. Tall and slim, she had Asian features and long black hair, now in disarray. Her bruised face was streaked with blood, her eyes puffed almost shut. Her blouse and bra hung in shreds from her shoulders. She struggled weakly and moaned, trying to push sound past the hand at her mouth.

She caught sight of Matt and gave a convulsive jerk, almost pulling free. The man holding her cursed and cuffed her hard. His partner turned, showing Matt hooded reptilian eyes above a hawk's nose. "Butt out, motherfucker," he rasped.

Matt drew in his breath, holding it for a beat. "Let go of her," he said quietly. "Now."

The hawk-nosed man laughed, baring crooked teeth. He said something to his partner in a language that Matt did not understand. Then he stepped forward, reaching into his jacket pocket.

The switchblade appeared suddenly, the *snick* of the opening blade sounding unnaturally loud in the sudden silence. "Make me, asshole."

Matt let the woman's coat fall to the ground. "You got it," he said softly.

He shifted his stance, balancing his weight evenly and slowing his breathing, narrowing his concentration and focus. He kept his knees slightly flexed, one foot forward. Elbows bent, arms up in front of him, he sized up the two men.

Young and vaguely Mediterranean looking they wore the standard inner-city uniform: baggy jumpsuits, puffy high-top sneakers, and oversize team jackets with wide leather shoulders. They looked tough and capable, Matt thought, and they'd probably used their looks to frighten many people into giving them their purse or wallet without a struggle.

But not this time.

"Let her go," Matt repeated. His voice echoed in the alley.

Hawk-nose stared defiantly back at Matt, moving the point of his switchblade in slow, tight arabesques. His partner, slightly older and sporting a thick Emiliano Zapata moustache, kept his hand firmly clamped across the woman's mouth.

Matt watched Hawk-nose's eyes, not the knife. He remembered his instructor's words from years ago: "Guns and knives don't kill people. Assholes kill people. The weapon won't do anything by itself."

Forget the knife, he told himself. Go for the man, do him damage. Get his attention centered on pain, and away from you. He shifted position so that his feet were comfortably far apart, his hands up in front of him, one slightly higher than the other, as if describing a fish he'd caught.

Hawk-nose glanced at his companion, who nodded. A second later he charged.

Dropping into a crouch Matt crossed his wrists and raised his arms, blocking the man's downward slash. Turning his right hand he grasped his assailant's knife hand firmly and rolled himself backward, adding his own motion to the man's forward momentum.

They fell backward, Matt keeping a firm grip on the knife hand. Matt hit the concrete first and twisted sideways, forcing the knife out of the man's grip. He heard it clatter on the concrete, and with his free hand he pushed it away.

He rose to his feet smoothly and stepped back. Hawk-nose scrambled up, rubbing his wrist, the first wisps of uncertainty beginning to cloud his eyes as he searched for his knife. He spotted his weapon and started toward it, only to find Matt blocking his way.

Time to finish this one, Matt thought. He had only seconds before he would have to deal with the second and far more dangerous threat—the Zapata look-alike who held the woman's neck in a stranglehold.

It almost *was* like the old days, he thought. Coyote days. He had been one of an elite, hand-picked unit of the Defense Intelligence Agency, dealing with the tiny brushfire wars that seemed to be a Third World growth industry. Called Coyotes after the men dropped in to battle forest fires in remote areas, their work was far more dangerous, and Matt had been trained in unarmed combat, weapons and explosives of all kinds, and the fine points of helicopter piloting.

He'd spent ten years poking through the world's back alleys, sniffing out the smoke, sifting through the rubbish heaps, looking for the little, glowing coals. He had concentrated on the Middle East and Africa, working on the fringes of the empires. To play the Great Game, Matt found, one must play a series of little games, getting down close to the ground and listening to the small sounds, the sounds that others, from their loftier perches in Whitehall, Foggy Bottom, or the Kremlin, hardly heard at all. And he had proved to be very good at that.

But as he quickly learned, the Great Game is hard on the players. No matter how good the Coyotes were, it wasn't always possible to put out the fires in time.

Even today Matt still occasionally dreamed of those days, memories flickering across his mind in the night like frames from a grainy horror film. He dreamed of Kolwezi in Zaire, his first big assignment, and of the hot deadly days in May when foreign troops had patrolled the ruined town, shooting stray dogs to keep them from eating the corpses. He dreamed of vultures wheeling high over the burning *quartiers,* while below, the dead lay stacked like cordwood on street corners, under clouds of buzzing flies. Of the bodies gutted like fresh fish and lined up neatly on the lawn outside an African bungalow, and a French paratrooper vomiting into a drainage ditch. Of the faces of the European children as they'd led them out under armed guard to the giant Starlifters for evacuation.

Compared to *that,* he thought, the man standing in front of him now was less than child's play.

He looked Hawk-nose up and down, remembering the lessons of his training. There were at least three ways he could think of to kill the man, but he rejected all of them in favor of a simpler, nonlethal approach. He would go for the center.

Years earlier, on the Agency's training fields, Matt and his classmates had toiled under the watchful and highly critical eye of a diminutive Filipino instructor named Bert Ramos, as he explained to them about balance and centering. Matt and the other Coyotes had spent long hours on the training ground, practicing Bert's eclectic and deadly repertoire of fighting techniques.

Bert taught his pupils about *chi,* the center of being located approximately two inches above and behind the navel. First, you found your own center. Then, you found your enemy's.

And destroyed it.

Matt filled his lungs with air, finding his own center and holding it, letting his breath out slowly. He sighted in on Hawk-nose, turned halfway to the left, and lashed out with his right foot, striking just below the sternum, trying to punch a hole through the man's solar plexus.

The powerful blow lifted Hawk-nose six inches off the ground, slamming him back against the brick wall with a grunt and whoosh of expelled air. Matt was on him instantly. Using the sides and heels of his hands he drove repeated hammer blows into the man's face and neck, battering him to the ground. It was ugly, crude work, but the point of fighting, Matt knew, was to win.

In seconds the hawk-nosed man lay unconscious at Matt's feet, bleeding from the nose and ears. Although Matt's heart was thudding, his breathing had hardly quickened. One down, one to go. He straightened, turning.

Only to face the muzzle of an automatic pistol, pointed straight at his chest.

The man with the Zapata moustache pushed the woman aside and stepped around her, keeping the gun straight out in front of him at arm's length. "You wanna play games, shithead?" His voice crackled with tension. "Okay, play with this."

Instead of retreating Matt moved forward two steps, watching the man's eyes carefully, noting the fear and uncertainty there. The weapon was no problem. He just needed to be closer. He took another step forward, and as he did so, Zapata backed up, meeting the brick wall of the school.

"Stay away, motherfucker." The man's voice had become a croak now, heavy with panic.

"Drop it," Matt said, speaking softly, keeping his voice calm and even. "Drop it now and you can leave." As he spoke, he extended his left hand, palm up, toward the gun. Matt's main concern was the possibility that the man would use it to kill the woman before Matt could take it away from him.

Zapata cursed, shook his head, and, as Matt had expected, tracked the outstretched hand with his eyes. Inevitably, the gun barrel followed. Matt kept his hand moving to the left, and then suddenly followed it with his body, spinning around, the smooth fluid movement almost a blur. In less than half a second his heel connected with the man's jaw, snapping his head back against the bricks in a spray of sudden blood and tooth chips.

The weapon clattered to the concrete, dropping from numb fingers.

Matt grasped the man's collar and pulled him off the wall, driving his fist up hard into his groin. As he doubled over, Matt's knee connected with his nose, making a noise like a walnut being cracked.

Matt wasn't through. He grasped the man's right wrist with his two hands and bent it down, hard. Zapata gave a brief shriek of pain as the wrist broke with a grinding, popping sound. Then he sagged to the ground, unconscious from the pain and shock.

Matt stepped back and surveyed the damage. Both men lay on the concrete, the first one still retching uncontrollably from Matt's blow to his solar plexus, the second one unconscious. Elapsed time, less than two minutes.

Matt bent and picked up the gun. A Ruger automatic, .38 caliber, in good condition. Pulling the slide back he saw a bullet in the chamber, and underneath it a full clip of hollow-nosed Magnum shells. He whistled softly. Any one of them could have blown him—or the woman—almost in half.

The woman. He'd almost forgotten about her. He turned and knelt beside her where she lay slumped against the concrete, her eyes puffed almost shut from the brutal punishment she had received as a prelude to rape. Her cotton blouse had been ripped to shreds by her attackers, her jeans spotted with blood. She had been badly beaten about the head and upper body, the bruises beginning to show.

Cradling her face gently in his hands, Matt

wiped the blood away as best he could. He checked her pulse, finding it at last, weak but steady. He scanned her pupils for signs of awareness, but got no response. She had clearly entered shock.

Matt glanced at his watch and swore softly. He was going to be late for his dinner with Marty. He tucked the .38 automatic into his waistband and wrapped the woman carefully in her coat. Then he picked her up and began to walk out of the alley.

She couldn't weigh much more than a hundred pounds, Matt thought, as he scanned Wisconsin Avenue for a taxi. Maybe hospital food would put some weight on her.

2

"So what happened then?" Marty Larsen's dark eyes shone with excitement and curiosity. "This is more fun than a late-night movie. And stop hogging all the ice cream." She turned, her dark-brown skin glowing in the light of the overhead lamp, and took the spoon away from him.

They lay stretched out comfortably on Marty's big leather couch beside her "office"—two large doors set on sawhorses, serving as a combination workspace and dining table.

The one-room loft apartment in Washington's Adams Morgan district was pure Marty, a veritable reflection of her personality, disordered and fascinating at the same time. A king-size mattress lay on the floor at the far end of the room, covered with a colorful Bedouin spread. Bookshelves ran from floor to ceiling across most of one wall, containing a wide range of fiction, political commentary, and poetry, most of it from the sixties and seventies. The record and tape collection below it was similarly dated.

Hanging plants, posters, and photographs filled up most of the rest of the wall space. Marty's taste in posters—as in most things—ran to the political. The three that Matt liked best included an early photograph of Angela Davis in Berkeley, a rare framed copy of the MEESE IS A PIG poster, and a cartoon of a grinning Lenin, saying, "An' just remember, kids, when yer smashin' the state, keep a smile on yer lips and a song in yer hearts!" In one corner, almost hidden, were half a dozen framed clippings from national newspapers and magazines carrying her byline.

"Here." He passed across the quart of Häagen-Dazs, almost empty now, that he'd picked up after his visit to the hospital. They'd been passing it back and forth across the wreckage of an excellent dinner, which Marty claimed to have just thrown together at the last minute. Clamshells and shrimp tails were all that remained to tell the story.

Marty spoke around a large mouthful of maple walnut, her favorite. "So come on, babe, finish the story. What happened to the two scumbags?"

"I left them there," Matt replied. "The woman was in shock, and it seemed more important to get her to the hospital than to call the cops." He shrugged. "Anyway, they'd been taken care of."

"I'll bet. What'd you do with the gun?"

"Threw it in a trash can," Matt said. "And

dropped the clip down the sewer." He paused. "Fewer questions to answer that way."

Marty gave a dry chuckle. "There's your spooky past talking." She took another spoonful of ice cream. "So who was the mystery woman?"

Matt shrugged. "Nobody knows. I brought her into the emergency room at George Washington and told them I'd found her in the street." He reached forward, took the spoon from Marty, and scraped out the bottom of the carton. "Did you know they call that place the Ronald Reagan Institute of Emergency Medicine?"

Marty snorted. "You never noticed that before? Goodness, how unobservant white men are. It's carved right into the stone over the damn door." Marty shifted, turning so that she nestled farther back in Matt's arms. She felt warm and firm, and smelled faintly of apples. She'd done her hair with cowries and small wooden beads, and they clicked as she settled back against him. "But who *is* she? What did they find out about her?"

"Nothing. They were going through the stuff in her purse as I left, but everything seemed to be in Japanese. She was unconscious, with bruises all over her face and upper body." He slid his hands up under her blouse, feeling the taut warm skin, silky smooth to his fingertips. "They were getting X rays when I left. I'll check back tomorrow before I go to work."

"Those assholes rape her?" Her voice was quiet.

"No, but they tried hard. She must have been tougher than they thought. They knocked her around quite a bit and were in the process of getting her pants down, ready to start on the main course, when I showed up." He paused. "If she's a tourist, she'll have one hell of a set of memories of Our Nation's Capital when she wakes up tomorrow."

"Well, babe, she's seen it like it is." She stretched, a graceful feline gesture. "Hell, maybe there's a story in it for me. People get mugged and raped every day around here, but a Japanese tourist sounds a little unusual. Maybe I should do an interview with her; write it from a foreigner's perspective."

Matt moved his hand down to the top of Marty's jeans, found the top button, and popped it open. "Well," he said, moving to the second button, "maybe tomorrow you can talk to her. She ought to be coming around by then. And maybe someone will have found a Japanese to translate."

Marty shook her head. "Not tomorrow. Got something coming up; the surprise I mentioned to you. Remember?"

"You bet," said Matt, reaching for the third button. "Here or on the bed?"

Marty laughed. "*That*'s not the surprise, Matt. It's a story." She turned to him, eyes shining with excitement. "I've got a chance for an exclusive— something that'll be front-page news around the world, if I can pull it off." She got up, untangling herself from him, and began to button her jeans. "And I'll tell you all about it, soon's you've cooled off and I make us both some coffee."

She leaned down and gave him a soft kiss on the cheek. "You stay right there, babe. Won't be a minute." She stopped on her way to the stove and turned. "You should be proud of yourself, saving that lady's life like that." She grinned. "Kinda reminds me of when we first met, actually."

Matt settled back on the couch. "That time I saved your life you weren't particularly grateful, as I recall."

"Just my girlish modesty, babe."

He smiled, remembering. Out in the Iraqi desert during the eerie weeks leading up to the Gulf War, Matt's group of Coyotes had been dropped behind the lines for reconnaissance. Late in the afternoon of the fourth day, somewhere east of As-Salman in the desolate Al-Hijarah quarter, Matt had—quite literally—run into Marty.

Driving a stolen Soviet-made jeep, he'd been pushing hard, heading to his rendezvous point near Nisab on the Saudi border, counting on speed and luck to bring him to the pickup point before the authorities figured out that he wasn't the Iraqi soldier his "borrowed" uniform showed him to be. Roaring up over a small rise he'd found a broken-down Chrysler sedan directly in front of him. He'd jammed the brake pedal to the floor, but it was too late. The front of his jeep slammed into the Chrysler with a crash, pitching him forward onto the steering wheel. Dazed, he clambered down off his seat, unsnapping his stolen Makarov service pistol, to confront the other driver, now opening the door.

What greeted his eyes was not an Arab but a very attractive black woman, her hair done up in a scarf, dressed in a safari suit with a dozen pockets, and carrying two cameras around her neck. She was smoking a cigar and glaring at him.

Matt approached warily, his pistol at the ready. As he drew closer, he noticed that the woman wore a button on her lapel. It said NO WAR FOR OIL. Jesus Christ, he thought; she's an American.

"Who the *hell* taught you to drive?" Her dark eyes flashed as she spoke. "Not a damn thing for miles, and you score a fucking bull's-eye."

"What the hell are *you* doing here?" challenged Matt.

The woman fished in one of her many pockets and came up with a grimy card, thrusting it at Matt. It read, MARTHA LARSEN, and underneath, in smaller letters, FREE-LANCE PHOTOJOURNALIST.

She walked around and inspected the front of the Chrysler, kicking a tire, which Matt saw was flat. "Damn car's a piece of shit anyway," she muttered. "Two flat tires, one spare. It's those thorns—they're big as tenpenny nails." She looked over at him. "How far am I from Jammah, anyway?"

A ghost of a smile tickled the corners of Matt's mouth. "Jammah's a hundred klicks behind you. Back there." He pointed down along the sandy track to the northeast.

She followed his pointing finger. "Shit fire," she said softly. She peered at Matt then, her large brown eyes narrowing as she took in his uniform. "You mind telling me who you are? If you're an Iraqi, I'm Strom Thurmond."

Matt grinned in spite of himself. Despite the sand and sweat and dirty clothes she was certainly a knockout. "My name's Matt," he said. "And you don't look much like Strom Thurmond to me." He glanced at the sun. "Listen, Martha—"

"My name's Marty, okay? Marty Larsen. I know it says Martha on the card, but—"

"Okay, Marty. Look, we're in trouble."

"You mean like dying of thirst and all that stuff? Hey, no sweat. I've got water, candy bars, even some Fritos, would you believe—"

He shook his head. "That's the least of our worries. There's an Iraqi armored column headed this way, not fifty kilometers away."

She looked at him, interest sparkling in her eyes. "No shit? Well, hell, I came out here for a story. Here it is."

"Story?" Matt grabbed her arm. "Marty, listen to me. Watch my lips carefully. I work for the Defense Intelligence Agency. I'm a spy, and you're a woman. If the Iraqis find us, they'll shoot me first, and then they'll all take turns with you." He paused. "There's no story here except the one about the end of your life."

She looked at him for a long moment. Then she walked around his jeep and sat down hard in the passenger's seat. "You're a persuasive sonofabitch, I'll say that," she said at last. "How fast you think this mother will go?"

They were on the road again in minutes, the shadows racing out in front of them as they tore down the road toward safety. As he drove, they talked. Matt told her a highly sanitized version of both his career and his personal life. He didn't mention his ex-wife.

She nodded politely, her gaze steady on the horizon. When he'd finished, she said, "You ever do Vietnam?" She shot a sideways glance at him. "Or were you too young for that shit?"

"I'm forty-one," said Matt. "And, no, I wasn't involved in Vietnam."

"Involved." She grimaced. "Bullshit, baby, everybody was involved. At least if they were alive and conscious. My brother got killed in Vietnam just two weeks before he was due to ship on back. Nineteen seventy-fucking-two, do you believe that? I thought I'd die too."

Matt smiled. "But you didn't."

"No. I turned into an activist alcoholic instead." In short, quiet sentences she told him about her revolutionary days at Syracuse and Wisconsin, about her flirtation with the Weather Underground, and about her start in journalism with a local story about the Algiers Motel incident.

She fished in one of her pockets, took out a small cigar, and stuck it in her mouth. "You got a light?"

Matt found matches in the glove compartment and gave them to her. She lit up, dragged deeply, blew out smoke, and took a breath. "Those were good times for me—got some pieces in *Ramparts* and *Mother Jones*—but they were bad times too. I was stoned for most of it. Alcohol, mainly, a fifth or more a day, and some drugs." She shook her hair loose and looked directly at him. "Spent almost fifteen years that way; it nearly killed me. I got straight in ninety—

spent a month in detox, joined AA, and never looked back. I been clean and sober ever since.

"Took me all that time to figure out that I wasn't gonna ever get my Pulitzer, wasn't ever gonna get Connie Chung's job. The brothers and sisters'd tell me, 'Yeah, babe, that's tough, being black's sure a bitch, ain't it?' I'd just look at 'em. Where you been, folks? Black and a woman, gorgeous and smart as hell"—she flashed him a wicked grin—"why, Christ, I could be *pope*." She laughed then, a rich sound that came from deep within her throat. Matt laughed with her.

Before he'd dropped her off at the forward staging point, she'd given him her address and telephone number in D.C., asking him to call her "whenever." Then, with a smile and a wave, she was gone, the helicopter pulling up and back, raising clouds of gritty sand, making Matt turn away.

It had taken him over a year to call. After the time in Somalia, after Sally's death. After the drinking. They'd had dinner, discovered that despite their different temperaments, they actually liked each other.

She'd helped Matt after he made his decision to leave the Agency. She'd served as a sounding board for his ideas and was a quiet, supportive listener when his frustrations with his writing projects sometimes boiled over. In return he consoled her when sometimes her stories didn't sell, and he cooked for her when she came in from an assignment too bushed to do anything more than sprawl on the big leather couch. Through innumerable late-night conversations he told her all about his divorce and the death of his wife; she told him more about her recovery from alcoholism and drug abuse.

When they finally became lovers, it was almost as an afterthought.

He'd long since ceased trying to define the nature of his relationship with Marty. Yes, they were occasional lovers, and although the sex was electric and highly satisfying, it did not define their bond, and indeed, it probably wasn't even a major part of it.

In fact, Marty had recently begun to worry that sex might get in their way. Her theory was that sex between a man and a woman inevitably drove a relationship forward, changed it into something more than whatever it had been before the act of intimacy. And eventually, she said, choices would have to be made, terms and conditions offered and accepted.

That prospect made both of them a little uneasy, they'd decided.

Right now, they'd agreed, they liked things pretty much the way they were. It wasn't broke, so to speak, and so what was the point of fixing it?

"Coffee's on." Her voice broke into his thoughts. She stood over him, two cups of steaming Louisiana blend on a tray. She set them down and picked up the remote for the television. "You're missing the news, babe."

". . . *In other news today, the Pentagon refused to comment on reports that its supersecret Ragnarok missile system was due to undergo tests in the California desert.*

"Dubbed the 'invisible Norseman' by members of the Congressional Budget Committee, some of whom say there is no such weapon, the missile system is so hush-hush that it has never been seen. According to Washington insiders this may soon change. Persistent rumors point to an upcoming test of the Ragnarok system, perhaps in the next few days.

"Spokesmen for TransCentury Systems, the California-based contractor developing Ragnarok, are denying that such a test is planned, however, and have so far declined to release any information, including photographs, of the new weapon. When we come back—"

Marty muted the sound and turned to him. "Ragnarok. Jesus H. Christ, how politically correct. The Norse equivalent of Armageddon, doomsday, and the apocalypse all rolled into one. The end of one world, and the beginning of a new golden age." She looked at him. "How's your writing coming? Dug up any more information?"

Matt snorted. "About Ragnarok? It'd be easier to get information about God's shoe size than any solid data on the missile. 'Invisible Norseman' is right. I don't even know what it looks like, for Pete's sake. No pictures, no sketches, no dimensions, zip." He paused. "And my publishing deadline's coming up next month. The technical stuff is in great shape, but without pictures or even just a description, we're dead."

He indicated the silent television. "Everybody at work's heard the rumors about the test, of course.

But nobody's optimistic about getting any real information. If the test actually happens, they'll never allow live coverage." He shrugged. "I don't know how we'll be able to publish the book without more information."

Marty sat down next to him. She gave him her most radiant smile. "Well, that's what I wanted to talk to you about, actually. That's my surprise." She took out one of the thin cigars she favored and turned to him. "Got a light?"

"Sure." Two years ago she'd given him a classic Zippo for his birthday, explaining that while she knew he didn't smoke, she thought he ought to have something classy with which to light her cigars.

When she had it going, she leaned forward and held him with her eyes. "You ready for this?" He nodded. "Okay, how'd you like the first peek at pictures of Ragnarok? Before anybody else?"

He stared at her. "What are you talking about?"

"The test. I know when and I know where." Her eyes sparkled with excitement. "If everything goes okay, I've got a ringside seat for Ragnarok's debut. TransCentury's got a test site out in the high desert, near the Nevada border. I've got a friend who works for them. According to him they've scheduled the test for day after tomorrow. I'm flying out tomorrow morning to Los Angeles. Rent a car, be up there by afternoon."

Matt's eyes narrowed. "They're letting journalists observe the test? The area's restricted."

She grinned. "So I've heard," she said. "But I'm not going to be knocking at the front gate, if you see what I mean." She squeezed his thigh. "I'm gonna have an exclusive, babe, how about that?"

Matt sat up. "You're going to sneak into a top-secret research facility and spy on a weapons test? Marty, if they catch you—"

She shook her head. "Ain't gonna catch me, sugar." She pointed to the clutter in the corner. Matt turned, and saw her camera and video equipment, and beside it a pile of backpacking gear. "I can take care of myself, you know. I don't think I'll have too much trouble staying out of sight."

She caught his look of concern and put cool fingertips to his cheek. "Hey, babe, don't look so worried. This isn't just gonna be all right, it's gonna be *fun*." She winked. "Lighten up. When I get back, you'll have action pictures of Ragnarok before anyone else does. That oughta make you happy, right?"

He frowned. "I'd be happier if I felt more comfortable about you. Are you sure you want to do this?"

She laughed. "Hell, I want to do it. I'm gonna make prime-time news with this, you wait and see."

"You mean it, don't you? Dammit, Marty. It's not *safe*."

Her voice was soft. "A ship's safe in the harbor, Matt. But that's not what ships are for."

He scowled. "But, Jesus, nobody in their right mind would try and sneak into a top-secret test facility."

She smiled sweetly and took another drag on her cigar. "Yeah, but I'm not in my right mind, babe, that oughta be very evident to you by now."

He gathered her into his arms. "Marty, you be very careful out there."

"Trust me, babe," she murmured. "This is gonna be a piece of cake. And besides," she added, snuggling up to him, "Aren't you curious about Ragnarok?"

He began unbuttoning her blouse. "You know I am," he said, guiding her smooth brown arms out of the sleeves. "But right now I'm a little more interested in something else."

She laughed then, a deep purring noise deep in her throat. "Take your time, Matt," she whispered, reaching back to unhook her brassiere. "The plane doesn't leave until ten tomorrow morning."

3

At the airport Matt had gripped her shoulders hard. "Take care." He'd looked into her eyes. "I mean it. No unnecessary chances."

She'd kissed him lightly. "Don't be so uptight, babe. What're they gonna do if they catch me? Shoot me?" Then she'd turned, letting her fingertips brush his cheek. "See ya."

And then she was through the door and out of sight.

An hour later Matt stood in front of the reception desk of GW University Hospital.

"Matsushima," said the Hispanic duty nurse, whose name plate read ROSITA GONZALEZ, the face above it a dark-eyed dead ringer for the young Carmen Miranda. "Came in last night, right?"

"First name"—she peered at the computer screen—"wait a minute—Yuko—no, Yuki*ko,* that's it." She grinned broadly. "Yukiko Matsushima." Her smile changed to a frown. "Unless they do it last name first or something weird like that. You're a friend, right?"

"Well . . ." Matt said.

"I mean, you're not a *relative,* right?" She grinned, fingers flying over the keyboard. "Hey, just kidding, amigo. Room three eleven."

Matt entered the room cautiously. The Japanese woman in the bed lay still, and only when he drew within a few feet of her did he see that her puffed eyes were actually open, staring into space. He stopped at the end of the bed. "Hello," he said softly.

Her eyelids moved slightly, and her mouth shifted. Her face was badly bruised, the marks starting to turn color, her long hair disheveled and matted.

"Hello," he repeated. "I—I came to see how you're doing."

She murmured something then, the dry sounds barely slipping past her bruised mouth. *"Anata—anata wa dare desu ka?"*

"I'm sorry." He leaned forward. "I don't understand."

She blinked her eyes twice, focusing slowly on him. She moaned, fear twisting her face. "No." Her voice was a croak. She brought her hands up slowly, covering her face. "Please," she whispered. "Leave me alone. Go. Go away!" Her voice fell to a ragged sob.

A nurse appeared at Matt's side, her thin Asian face framed by a stylish punk cut. She beckoned Matt outside. "Sorry," she said. "Rosie should have told you, no visitors yet. She's not that tightly wrapped." She looked at him with curiosity. "You the guy who brought her in?"

Matt nodded. "Matt McAllister. I found her on the street in Georgetown."

"I'm Nancy Okamoto. They called me early this morning. Normally I'm only in on weekdays, but I'm the only one around here who speaks Japanese."

They walked together toward the lobby. "Don't worry too much about what she said," Nancy Okamoto said. "She's still pretty dopey. And scared." She paused. "Physically, she'll be okay. Slight concussion, two cracked ribs, a lot of bruising, and some cuts. She went into shock, apparently, but they took care of that. X rays seem okay." She glanced at Matt. "Can't tell you about her mental state yet. This is every Japanese tourist's nightmare, of course. If we could, we'd send her straight home. What happened to her, anyway? Mugging?"

"Attempted rape," Matt said. "Two guys had her in an alley, up by the Safeway in Georgetown." He paused. "I happened along, and they, ah, took off."

Nancy Okamoto regarded him thoughtfully, her dark eyes serious. "Just like that, huh?"

Matt returned her gaze. "Just like that."

"You saved her life, Mr. McAllister. That must have been quite some dustup."

"Dustup? What are you talking about? I found her on the street."

She grinned. "Yeah, you already said that. But two cops showed up here about an hour ago with a different story. Seems they found two guys last night, right about where you said you'd found the woman. Turns out both guys had been missing from the penitentiary since last weekend." She paused. "They were pretty messed up, the cops said. So much so, they figured somebody else must be messed up too. They were sort of checking around."

As she watched Matt's expression her smile widened. "Course, I know you don't know anything about that at all, but I gotta tell you: you're either very lucky or very, very good with your fists."

Matt decided to change the subject. "Any idea who the woman is?"

"Some; not much. She's a Japanese national named Yukiko Matsushima, and she teaches mathematics at a university outside Tokyo. That much we learned from her ID. She had a flier in English from some sort of writer's conference here in Washington, and two Grateful Dead CDs with a receipt from Olsson's. I also found a health insurance card, which made a lot of people here very happy."

She frowned. "As for what she's doing in Washington, I have no idea. We've called the Japanese embassy, of course. She won't remain a mystery for much longer." She looked at Matt. "If you want to see her again, I'd recommend trying tomorrow. She'll probably be in better shape then."

"Suppose she doesn't want to speak to me?"

Nancy Okamoto smiled. "Bring her something. Patients love presents. Flowers, whatever."

Matt nodded. "It's a deal."

Outside the hospital Matt checked his watch. Not yet one o'clock. Plenty of time for what he had originally planned for the day.

Twenty minutes later Matt exited the Beltway and started up Route 270 toward Gaithersburg, pushing his aging Miata as fast as he dared. Traffic was light, most people already having arrived at their weekend destinations. In the back of the tiny convertible he had a package of frozen steaks, a six-pack of Molson, and three thick red files on his current book project, the Ragnarok missile system.

It felt good, doing over eighty along the interstate, the top down and the wind whipping his hair. Matt pushed the Miata hard, whistling tunelessly through his teeth as he kept a sharp eye out through his aviator sunglasses for cops.

The Miata was a rarity, and still provoked stares —some of them angry—from other motorists. In the past five years it had become first fashionable, then politically correct, and finally manifestly patriotic to buy American-made automobiles. Matt had kept his cherry-red Miata partly out of a sense of stubbornness, and also, dammit, because it had been a well-made, reliable car. Now, approaching its tenth birthday, it had lost a lot of its zip while picking up the dents and wrinkles of old age. Matt had decided long ago that he would keep it for as long as it would keep him.

Half an hour to the exit, he thought, checking his watch. Another ten minutes from there to the dirt road, and then five more to the turnoff. He'd arrive before three.

He was headed for Toad Hall, his ramshackle mountain hideaway that no one but his wife, Sally, and he had ever visited. When Sally had been alive and with him, they had spent the odd weekend there during summers, more to escape the Washington heat and humidity than for relaxation, since, as Sally had been fond of pointing out, actually living there would have required the skills of an eighteenth-century pioneer.

Toad Hall was his special hideaway, his bolt-hole. A place, since Sally's death, that only he knew about. Not even Marty had been introduced to Toad Hall, for Toad Hall had been special. It had been their place—his and Sally's—back in the days before the marriage went bad.

Since her death Matt had taken to spending most Sundays there, sometimes even sleeping over in good weather. A day or so at Toad Hall, he'd found, was good preparation for the week's work in Washington. It focused his mind and relaxed his body, and if he had brainwork to do, Toad Hall had no distractions at all, unless you counted the insects.

He checked the road again for cops and, finding none, pressed the pedal to the floor.

Three quarters of an hour later he approached Toad Hall on a narrow dirt road, winding through the trees. Sally and he had bought it together, in the first year of their marriage. Ten secluded acres of forest, high up on the side of the Monocacy River Valley, with a spectacular view toward the west. The area was historic as well as beautiful; during the Civil War, General Lew Wallace and the Union army had fought Jubal Early's Confederate troops here, delaying their progress toward Washington.

They'd made plans to clear the land and build a dream home here, a country mansion, but somehow they'd never gotten around to it. Matt had spent one summer constructing a two-room cabin on the premises, and they'd paid a local dowser to find and open a spring on the hillside. But the mansion had never materialized, and even today Toad Hall had neither electricity nor plumbing. And Matt had finally decided that this was pretty much the way he wanted it.

In fact, he thought, as he braked for a pothole, anything more elaborate than the two-room shack would only have reminded him constantly of Sally, and of the failure of the marriage.

As with many things that deteriorate, the marriage had died slowly, almost imperceptibly. And by the time Matt had noticed, it had been far too late. He'd read somewhere that if you throw a frog into a pot of boiling water, it will instantly leap out. But if you put the same frog in a pot of water at room temperature and then heat it up, a degree at a time, the frog will quite cheerfully allow itself to be boiled to death.

I boiled to death by slow degrees, Matt thought.

Shortly after joining the Defense Intelligence Agency, straight from the master's program at Johns

Hopkins, Matt had met and married Sally Devereaux, a long-haired brunette beauty from Bolinas. At first, the work with the Defense Intelligence Agency had seemed exciting, interesting, and, best of all, important, in the national interest. The first few years of the marriage were fine, almost blissful, as the young couple settled into life in suburban Washington and tried—unsuccessfully—to start a family. But slowly, cracks developed in the happy façade they showed the world.

Matt was the best Coyote the agency had and, in consequence, got most of the rough assignments. He was so successful that he got nicknamed the "Handyman." Have a troublesome problem you need fixed in a hurry, without fuss or bother? Call the Handyman. Quick work, satisfaction guaranteed, total discretion assured. On call anytime, day or night. So they called him often, all through the eighties: Ethiopia, the Baltic States, Lebanon, Somalia. With each assignment Matt died a little more inside.

Back in Washington, Sally got worried. As Matt began spending more and more time away from home, Sally grew increasingly unhappy, until eventually their marriage was little more than a hollow shell. Children might have helped, Matt often thought, but Sally had proved to be barren, and although they sought medical advice several times, nothing had worked.

After the embassy bombing in Lebanon, in which he'd lost two close friends, Matt began to come apart, a seam at a time.

"Give it up, Matt," Sally had pleaded with him.

"You're killing yourself, for God's sake. Every time you come back from one of these trips you're a little less human. At night you moan in your sleep and grind your teeth. What the hell do you *do* over there to give you the creeps like that?"

Matt couldn't tell her. Security reasons aside, the horror and brutality of the things he'd witnessed surpassed any outsider's comprehension. He tried drinking, purging the demons raging inside his head by putting them to sleep. When that failed, he turned to pills for a while, with no greater success.

Finally he simply withdrew into himself, stopped going to parties, stopped reading the papers. Stopped talking to Sally very much.

"You're turning into a goddamned zombie, Matt!" she screamed at him one day in a frightened rage. "Don't you *care* about anything anymore?"

That had been precisely the trouble, he thought; he cared too much. In a business where one of the basic rules was not to get personally involved in the work, he'd made the mistake of allowing himself to care. And now the violence and suffering had overwhelmed him. Too many fires, he thought; not enough water.

Finally, Sally announced that she wanted a divorce. When Matt returned from work the next day, he found an empty house and a one-paragraph note taped to the fridge. She was, she wrote, tired of living with a chimera, with someone who was always somewhere else. She had gone back to California, packed up and walked out of the old town house they had fixed up together on the edge of Georgetown, leaving nothing but dust and memories.

The next day the Agency called and said there was an urgent assignment in the Gulf, and could he please come in for a top-secret briefing? Three days later Matt parachuted behind the lines in Iraq.

Iraq had been the beginning of the end. And a little later Somalia had provided the final grim chapter to the breakup of the marriage.

As bad as Kolwezi had been, Somalia had been worse.

Much worse.

Refugees were fleeing west out of Belet Ouen ahead of the advancing guerrillas, trying desperately to reach safety across the Kenyan border. They trudged single file down a dusty road on the edge of the Ogaden, the sun bright and hot in the limitless pale sky, their rubber-tire sandals raising dust that could be seen for miles. Matt had been sent in with a scout helicopter and long-range radio equipment to monitor the situation and to give American relief units waiting at desert airstrips in northern Kenya precise coordinates for their daily airdrops of food.

During the day Matt and his guide, Hasan, would quarter the desert, making slow passes in the helicopter across the red sand. The land was so flat in places that you could actually see the curve of the earth. Flat, and empty. No camel herds survived, and few warthogs; almost everything had been eaten long ago. As each day wore on, the fierce sun turned the landscape into a washed-out color photograph, the smell of dry grass rising off the land in waves.

Somalia was a surreal dreamscape of death, dust, and heat.

In the evening they sat on the sand beside the helicopter, eating *anjero,* the flat Ethiopian bread, and drinking tea flavored with ginger and cardamom. Matt watched the Southern Cross in the night sky and thought of Sally. Beside him Hasan chewed khat and crooned softly to the wailing Somali music coming from his small cassette player.

For ten days Matt searched for guerrillas, returning every day or so to check on the refugees, watching their columns raise an unending plume of dust as they trekked toward the distant border and safety. And as he watched, he thought. On the tenth day he came to a decision: this would be the last assignment. As soon as he returned to Washington, he would resign. And perhaps then he could start again with Sally.

The next day he told Hasan to stay in camp. Then he drove a borrowed Land-Rover back a hundred kilometers to the Red Cross camp, where he sent a telegram to Sally in California. *I'm coming home,* it said. *Can we start again?*

On his way back the next afternoon he saw the thick coiling smoke long before he could hear the shooting. From the cover of a nearby ridge he watched helplessly through field glasses as the rebel soldiers attacked the refugee column, their machine guns stitching death's design among the fleeing women and children. Finally, their ammunition spent and the relief food loaded on board, their jeeps turned eastward, seeking other prey. Near his camp by the river he found Hasan's body, next to the burned-out hulk of the helicopter.

The Pakistani U.N. colonel who found him the next day regarded him gravely, eyes rimmed with fatigue. "We have been looking for you, Mr. McAllister. We had reports of an attack. . . ."

Matt nodded, his eyes fixed on Hasan's crude grave.

The Pakistani colonel licked his lips with a nervous gesture. "There is nothing you could have done. Nothing anyone could have done." He fumbled in his blouse pocket, extracting a telegram. "This arrived at headquarters yesterday." He averted his eyes, holding the folded message out. "Sir, I'm sorry."

Matt unfolded the paper and read the printed words, his lips moving in disbelief. There'd been a car crash. Sally was dead.

From Nairobi he telephoned the States and got the rest of the story. She'd been killed instantly in a freak automobile accident with two friends. A drunk on the Bay Bridge on-ramp had been going the wrong way: three people had died in the head-on collision, one of them his wife. And with her a part of Matt's own life disappeared.

He resigned from the Agency, and went through more than a year when all the songs were sad and all the movies made him cry. Little by little he poured his grief out into an indifferent world. And then slowly, with Marty's help, he began to come back. The pain and sadness over Sally had almost disappeared these days, he thought. And although he could never entirely forget her, he could recover.

* * *

Matt braked, turned, and gentled the Miata in through the trees, following a driveway that was little more than a track. Fifty yards later he drew up before Toad Hall and killed the engine.

It was quiet under the trees, as usual. Matt got out, pulling his one suitcase from the back of the car, picking up the red folders on Ragnarok, and walked around to the front of the cabin. Toad Hall itself might be a bit of a dump, but the view was first class.

The view had attracted Matt and Sally to the property in the first place, he remembered. His first move, after buying the acreage, had been to rent a chain saw. He'd spent three days felling pines, and another three months of backbreaking toil hauling cut logs up the hillside. When he was through, he reckoned he had enough low-quality firewood to last them for ten years. And a vista that was second to none.

The next summer he'd put up the two-room shack. A living-room–kitchen and a bedroom, everything absolutely bare bones and crude as could be. The wind whistled through cracks in the siding, and the roof leaked the first time it rained. But eventually the place became habitable and, after a time, actually took on a certain primitive charm of its own.

Little by little Matt furnished the cabin, scrounging items from garage sales and junk stores—a pot-bellied woodstove, a swaybacked sofa, several over-stuffed chairs. He invested in a decent double bed and four hurricane lamps with tall glass chimneys, and installed tight screens on the windows to keep the bugs out. A shelf of paperbacks, a cupboard stocked with canned goods, and a butane-powered fridge that could run for months on its own completed the picture.

Matt used Toad Hall as a refuge, a place to recharge himself. And although there was no doubt that his job as a researcher for the Jefferson Institute was a hell of a lot less demanding than being a Coyote, he still felt a frequent need to get out of Washington and spend a day or two sitting on the front porch at Toad Hall, watching the river valley below, and the play of sunlight on the hills beyond.

Matt unlocked the door, threw his gear inside, took a bottle of Molson's from the six-pack, and stowed the rest in the fridge. Then he picked up the red files on Ragnarok and walked back out to the porch, settling slowly into the Adirondack chair he kept there for serious reading. He turned the pages in the first file, scanning his notes.

There were three of them working on the Ragnarok project, with Matt as coordinator, hammering the technical chapters into shape, translating the jargon into readable prose, hurrying to have something ready to auction to the publishers who had been calling the institute daily for the past several months.

The Jefferson Institute's reports were highly regarded by the international security establishment, because they provided objective and detailed assessments of weapons capabilities and performance under real-world conditions. Officials around the world would base their decisions on what technology to buy on reports such as the one Matt was racing to finish.

The manuscript was in good shape, he thought, except for one small detail—no one outside the TransCentury Corporation had ever seen the Ragnarok missile, and as far as anyone knew, it had never performed.

Well, Matt thought with satisfaction, all that was about to change. Marty's eyewitness report from the scene of the test would give her—and Matt— exclusive information and incalculable amounts of credibility.

He smiled to himself as he turned the pages. From Coyote to weapons analyst wasn't as much of a jump as some people supposed, he thought. After all, he'd spent years dealing with weapons systems at close range. Too close, at times. In that sense he was already an expert.

In the months following Sally's death Matt had sometimes wondered—when he'd chanced to be sober—what he'd find to do now that he was no longer with the Agency. In between bouts of self-pity he'd hit the streets, looking for work. Given that he was thirty-eight years old, his master's degree in political science was hardly worth the paper it was printed on.

Geoffrey Ellsworth—"Buttons" to his cronies— had given him his chance. Buttons had been with Matt in graduate school, and when he learned Matt's story, he offered him a job at the Jefferson Institute. The institute was Buttons's own private think tank, operating out of a sedate brownstone in northwest Washington.

Matt's salary wouldn't make him rich, but the work was exciting. He got a six-month contract—a straightforward ghost-writing job—to produce an analysis of the history of modern tech-war and its impact on strategic policy. All he had to do was read a four-foot-high stack of reports and boil them down to two hundred pages. He'd surprised everyone—including himself—by sobering up, getting down to work, and proving to be as good at research and writing as he'd been at intelligence work.

He'd produced an excellent, original analysis two months early. Buttons read it, smiled, and sent it immediately to the Brookings Institution, where it was reprinted as a research monograph. The Pentagon ordered five hundred copies, it was reviewed favorably in *Foreign Policy,* and for a few brief moments Matt was that most envied of Washington creatures, an overnight expert.

Fame didn't last, but it was enough to land him a permanent job with the institute and generate his present project: to find out all he could about Ragnarok and write it up. And interest in the "invisible Norseman" was definitely building again, inside and outside the Beltway. *Jane's* had been calling weekly; three publishers had offered fat contracts on the strength of the outline alone, but people in the institute were holding back, waiting to see how high the bidding might go. The report, as Buttons rightly pointed out, would be worth a lot of money to a lot of people.

Provided, that is, that it came out *before* Ragnarok went on sale to the world's armies. By that time whatever Matt had found out would be old news. He smiled to himself, turning the pages of his notes. New job, same old game: information's only valuable as long as it's secret. Once everybody knows it, where's the fun?

Marty would be back from the desert in a day or two, Matt reflected. And if she was successful, both she and Matt would have the scoop of the year. All he had to do was keep his mouth shut and his hopes up, until she returned.

Matt got up, heading for the fridge and another Molson's.

4

Matt McAllister sat in the clearing as the daylight waned, scanning the files, skimming over his background chapters. A complex, extremely versatile defensive missile system, Ragnarok—sole survivor of the ill-fated "Star Wars" concept—had been designed to meet the challenges of the post-Soviet world.

And challenges there had certainly been, in abundance. From the wreckage of the former Soviet Union had come a broken-backed Commonwealth of Independent States, which, as Buttons was fond of saying, was inaccurate in every aspect of its title, being neither wealthy, independent, nor particularly statesmanlike in character. He preferred another name for the group: ACNE, or Association of Countries with No Economies.

The Soviet breakup had spawned a host of smaller countries, each with nuclear capabilities far beyond the nightmares of the Pentagon analysts of the eighties. Proliferation had never been a priority for U.S. policymakers, and so suddenly at the end of the nineties—as so often in the past—the U.S. found itself playing catch-up, as countries like Ukraine and Kazakhstan suddenly became world-class nuclear powers.

Other countries were keeping pace. Iraq turned out to have quite a bit more nuclear capability than anybody realized. The Pakistanis achieved their long-awaited breakthrough, and produced the Islamic Bomb. And both the Turkic Bloc and Trans-Caucasia emerged as regional powers. Places no one had ever really heard of before were suddenly in the news. Checheno-Ingushetia; Kabardino-Balkaria. The People's Republic of Tannu-Tuva.

"Like something out of a Tintin comic," Buttons had said dismissively. "The lot of them together don't add up to one decent, competent nation."

"Decency and competence have little to do with it," Matt had replied. "Membership in the Nuclear Club is the issue. And I don't think many of the newcomers are going to play by the rules."

By the early 1990s over twenty countries had missiles capable of delivering a nuclear warhead. The Soviets had passed out FROGS, SCUDS, and various models in the SS series to a number of their clients before taking a bow and walking off the stage. Other countries had developed their own: the Argentineans had the Condor and Alacran, the Brazilians had the

Avibras series, Israel the Jericho, and India the Prithvi and Agni. Taiwan had the Ching Feng. All of them accidents waiting to happen.

And by the time the analysts had realized this, an even worse thing had happened. Dozens of weapons specialists, latter-day Werner von Brauns, had slipped out of former Soviet research and military establishments to offer themselves to the highest bidder, and in the backwaters of the Third World the competition for their services had been intense.

With them had come ample supplies of fissionable material, obtained from lightly guarded stockpiles in remote and badly managed installations such as Chelyabinsk-40 in the Urals. In other cases the nuclear cores had been extracted from the missiles themselves. The international drug trade had known for years of ways to get things from one place to another discreetly; this knowledge was now put to good use by other countries. The deadly cargo proved easy to move, slipping through airport customs under diplomatic seal, coming ashore at night from nondescript freighters, airdropped into remote areas by private planes.

Entire delivery systems were now available to the highest bidder. The first of these deadly auctions —the sale to Iran of three complete tactical nuclear missiles by a former Soviet republic—was reported in detail by Cairo's *Al-Watan al-Arabi,* thus providing everyone with a blueprint for other transactions. Soon thereafter the bidding began in earnest. For hard currency nearly anything could be bought, and a brisk trade blossomed, centering on the last of the Soviet series, the so-called "smart SCUD."

The smart SCUD particularly worried the Pentagon. Until the mid-nineties, SCUDs—unreliable and inaccurate—had proved little better than Hitler's old V-2 rockets. As an instrument of terror they had worked well enough against civilian populations during the Gulf War, but their awkwardness and high failure rate hardly qualified them as serious military weapons. Ground troops dragged them into the desert, aimed them as best they could, lit the fuse, and said a prayer. But as primitive as they were, the Gulf War had shown that many of them managed to penetrate the Patriot defense system.

And now things had gone from bad to worse. Soviet scientists in Iraq, delighted to be supplied for once with decent working conditions and high rates of pay, proved extremely adept at turning out vastly improved versions of the old standby. Faster burn rates had been achieved, throw weights had been considerably increased, and new, sophisticated guidance systems made it possible for the smart SCUD to not only evade an oncoming Patriot bent on its destruction, but to actually seek and home in on a specific target—be it a densely populated area of Tel Aviv, or an air base in India.

The geopolitical equivalent of the Saturday Night Special was born.

As the nineties drew to a close, military analysts realized that their worst case scenario had now come true: the Third World—much of which had always had the motivation for nuclear assault—now had both means and opportunity. The Trans-Caucasian Federation, fueled by Turkic political ambition and Wahhabi religious fervor, created a major destabilizing element in the region. Farther to the east and south the Pathan peoples, hell bent on building up their own nuclear delivery systems, posed even more problems.

Armageddon had come a giant step closer.

The United States now faced a painful dilemma. Years of deep recession had made it both politically suicidal and economically impossible for the government to engage in any sustained military buildup even remotely comparable to that which had been undertaken during the Carter and Reagan years. The taxpayers, exhausted by crime, domestic problems, and falling real incomes, refused even to discuss letting the Pentagon spend more tax dollars.

At the same time another trend had also become much clearer. This was known euphemistically—and somewhat incorrectly—as the "Japanese problem," and it had been evident since the late seventies. Although the American industrial machine rolled on, some observers thought they could detect a certain slackening of momentum, low-pitched grinding noises from the machinery, a slight wobble in the ride. And shadows cast by Japan's rising sun were deepening, as America's former enemy and chief competitor loomed ever larger on the horizon.

Televisions, stereos, video cameras: Americans had accepted the loss of these manufactures to Japan without so much as a second thought. Home entertainment, the thinking went, hardly qualified as a heavy industry. But automobiles, then robotics, and finally aircraft also fell to Japanese producers. And in other areas too—telecommunications, laser technology, and medical research—America had lost its edge. As the national economy limped toward the twenty-first century, its people viewed Japan with increasing apprehension and hostility.

True, the Japanese, too, had been hard hit by the economic recession, but as their recovery got under way, American economic interests suffered even more, and in the halls of Congress there were renewed cries for protectionism. There were even those who advocated an all-out trade war, while the U.S. was still strong enough to wage one.

Confronted with new military enemies on the one hand and a powerful economic threat on the other, American policy makers worried. The 1996 elections proved to be the turning point: the victorious party had somehow come up with a proposal that captured the imagination of enough of the voters to permit them to squeak into the White House.

In essence the idea was simple. America needed to do three things, simultaneously and quickly, to ensure its national superiority well into the coming century.

First, it needed to counter the military threat to world order posed by the increasing numbers of Third World nations with atomic weapons and missile systems capable of delivering them over short to medium distances.

Second, the country needed to regain the innovative edge over Japan, through the development of highly advanced technology.

And finally, America needed markets—arenas in which it could outsell the Japanese.

If the nation could achieve these three things, the reasoning went, a stable and secure world would emerge, one in which American technology and its consumer spin-offs could find their way into the vast markets of Asia, Africa, and the lands of the former Soviet Union. America would regain its former advantage, rebuild itself economically, and once again be number one.

Within a year the special presidential task force had drafted a comprehensive plan. Its centerpiece was a major initiative, a latter-day Manhattan Project, designed to give the U.S. a commanding technological lead that would result in both export sales and increased global security. Although its detractors called it "voodoo electronics," even they could see the attractions. Ragnarok was born, based on the belief that the most effective way for the U.S. to control the future was to invent it.

There was a clear need, the experts argued, for an effective antimissile—something fast, maneuverable, and one hundred percent accurate. The first country to produce one could sell it around the world, in vast quantities. The Pentagon and the defense contractors dusted off their plans, sharpened their pencils, and got busy again.

If successful, Ragnarok would provide a truly effective defense against medium-range nuclear missiles, both of the ballistic variety and the slower but often more deadly cruise type.

The strategy adopted used America's traditional comparative advantage in computers—a lead the country still held, although by an increasingly slim margin—to achieve a breakthrough that would ensure that the U.S. dominated the field for years to come. Ragnarok would use a true artificial-intelligence brain as the basis for its guidance system, enabling each missile, in effect, to function as its own battlefield commander.

Over the inevitable protests the Ragnarok system went ahead. ARPA—the Pentagon's Advanced Research Projects Agency—awarded the contract to TransCentury Systems, a small, relatively obscure software firm based in Los Angeles. After nearly three years of top-secret work Ragnarok's guidance system, dubbed "Odin" by the Pentagon publicists, was ready. All that remained was to test it.

Since then, hard information on Ragnarok and Odin had been almost impossible to obtain. Matt had grown increasingly frustrated at his inability to penetrate the wall of silence that descended between him and even his closest contacts the moment the names of Ragnarok and Odin were mentioned.

There was good reason for the secrecy. The development of a workable artificial-intelligence guidance system held out enormous promise, and the first nation to achieve a breakthrough would gain an enormous advantage. An impenetrable security cloak soon surrounded the project. By presidential order an embargo had been placed on the exchange of any information regarding Ragnarok, its software or hardware systems, with groups inside or outside the country.

And particularly with Japan.

The Japanese had always been good at copying American computer technology, and in the nineties they had achieved considerable skill with software innovations. But in cutting-edge computer technology America still held the lead. The Odin guidance system for Ragnarok was intended to maintain and considerably widen that lead.

And make America hundreds of billions of dollars at the same time.

The sheer volume of money that could be expected to flow into the United States from the sale of such technology was staggering, limited only by what the market would bear. Domestic industries would flourish, the massive and swelling budget deficit would shrink, and our lopsided trade imbalances would disappear.

And success had even broader implications as well, for a true artificial-intelligence system had thousands of other powerful—and practical—uses. And finally, there was the prestige factor. Ragnarok would be "Made in the USA." And sought after by countries around the world.

That, at least, was the theory.

At first Odin and Ragnarok had created a media sensation. *Time* and *Newsweek* both devoted cover stories to the new generation of "genius" weapons, asking whether this meant that battlefield soldiers would now become obsolete. Eventually, as no further news from the Pentagon was forthcoming, attention gradually subsided. But within the Beltway establishment, and especially at the Jefferson Institute, interest sharpened. For Matt and his colleagues knew full well that when there was silence from the military, one of two things must surely be happening: Either significant progress was being made or the program was in great difficulty. Buttons had once suggested during a staff meeting that perhaps with Ragnarok, the situation was both at the same time.

And so the idea for a technical book on the missile was born. And as the chapters began to take shape, the publishing industry's interest sharpened. Substantial advances had already been offered, but the institute was holding out for an auction, once the manuscript was ready.

But despite a promising start Matt's attempts to research Ragnarok had been only partially successful. It was, as he discovered, possible to describe Ragnarok and its Odin guidance system in general, yet fairly accurate, terms, and after several months of hard work Matt now had six detailed chapters on the technical aspects alone.

Although incomplete, the description that Matt had pieced together from data fragments was tantalizing. Odin was less of a computer than a personality —a fully independent artificial-intelligence system combining the brains and shrewdness of General Schwarzkopf with virtually none of the bulk. Odin didn't have to be fed, or paid, or promoted, yet he— or it—was capable of acting like a fully fledged battlefield commander.

The research that created Odin came, fittingly enough, from two Rust Belt cities. Joint experiments between Carnegie Mellon University in Pittsburgh and Syracuse's big Northeast Parallel Architecture Center suddenly produced a breakthrough—a workable, tiny, self-contained artificial intelligence package.

And what a breakthrough it was. For years software designers had faced the problem of giving their computers an accurate enough model of the outside world to enable them to take all relevant factors into account in making their decisions. It had, ultimately, proved to be a hopeless task. Even the simplest real-time tasks—ordering a meal in a restaurant, for example, or buttering a piece of toast—proved beyond the reach of all but the most sophisticated machines, and only then if they were linked to enormous mainframe systems containing millions of lines of programming.

Throughout the eighties researchers in Pittsburgh and elsewhere had been working on the problem from a different angle. Rather than attempting to describe in advance all the possible characteristics of the world outside, they reasoned, why not build a system that learned exactly as a human being did—through experience?

The result, after years of experimentation, was Odin. Weighing less than fifty pounds, it learned more quickly and accurately than any human could. Odin's architecture contained two built-in features crucial to its operation. One gave Odin a logical and coherent set of *beliefs* about the world it operated in.

The second provided, in a similar way, a set of *motivations*—reasons, so to speak, for wanting to operate in the world at all.

In these respects Odin operated like a real human intelligence: Odin believed certain basic things to be true of the world it lived in, and it dealt with that world in terms of a few very simple but very powerful motivations. For Odin the world was essentially divided into three basic categories: friends, enemies, and neutrals. Odin's motivational system, while equally simple, was also extremely powerful, and organized around one simple mission—to detect, locate, and destroy the enemy. Odin's belief system told him who was an enemy; his motivational pattern drove him to destroy that enemy, as quickly, efficiently, and thoroughly as possible.

Great, thought Matt. We've created the electronic equivalent of Frankenstein's monster. But what the hell does it look like? When do the wraps come off?

The night crept up on Matt slowly and quietly, pressing softly on the glow from the hurricane lamp by his elbow. He yawned and closed the file. He could go no further without more information. If Marty succeeded in bringing back pictures, the book could be ready in a matter of days.

But for now he was stalled. He'd pieced together the available facts on Ragnarok as best he could, and made intelligent guesses about the rest. If TransCentury Systems had succeeded, then they had created an artificial genius, one that would transform international security and might well reinvigorate the American economy.

Only one intangible question remained. No one knew—or cared to tell—what kind of a temperament the genius had. And that, Matt decided, was what he really wanted to know.

Below him he could see points of light in the valley. Fog drifted up from the valley bottom, sending exploratory tendrils like ghostly scouts up into the forest slopes. Above, the high, cold stars filled the heavens. The darkness was immense and absolutely still, as if the world were holding its breath.

Matt yawned again. Toad Hall qualified as one of the best places in all the world to sleep, he had decided long ago. And now it was time to do just that.

He stood, picked up his folders and the hurricane lamp, and walked inside. His last thoughts, as he blew out the lamp and wrapped the blankets around himself, were of Marty.

5

Pulling up early the next morning in front of the three-story brownstone on Jefferson Place, Matt saw Teddy waiting for him at the curb.

"Hey, kid," Matt said, smiling. Theodore Edwards—Teddy to one and all—was the newest member of the Jefferson Institute. Fresh out of Georgetown he still worked on his doctoral dissertation in his spare time. Tall and gawky, Teddy had a pleasant, open face and a lank mop of disobedient black hair. He favored casual clothing and a relaxed, almost flippant attitude toward the world, under which lay, as Matt had learned in the past six months, a first-class mind.

Teddy had done more than his share on the Ragnarok project, and Matt intended to see to it that he got full credit for his efforts. For his part Teddy clearly regarded Matt as a big brother.

"Hey yourself," Teddy replied with a grin. "How was the weekend? You and Marty go somewhere?"

Matt grimaced. "She went to California," he said. "I stayed home."

"Tough." He sobered. "Big meeting this morning. You get those last chapters done?"

Matt shook his head. "Not yet. We've had no luck getting specifications out of either the Pentagon or the contractor."

"Nigel's gonna shit," Teddy observed solemnly. "He just called. He's on his way in from the airport now."

"Let him," said Matt. "You can't make something out of nothing, and that's exactly what we've got right now. Nothing." He put the Miata in gear. "See you in a couple of minutes. Got to park."

Teddy put out his hand. "Hey, I'll do that for you. Might even see to it that the car gets washed and waxed."

Matt grinned, wondering what it would cost him, as he tossed him the keys, and watched as Teddy levered himself into the tiny sports-car and happily gunned the engine.

"I'll bite. What's this going to cost me?"

"You think I could maybe borrow the car for Friday night? Just the one night. I got tickets to the Wagner concert at the Kennedy Center. You know that girl from Sweetbriar I was telling you about? She's gonna be in town this weekend."

Matt grinned. "Deal." He gave him a playful tap on the shoulder. "But take it easy," he reminded him. "Don't get any ideas."

Teddy rolled his eyes. *"Moi?* Surely you jest." With a screech of tires and a cloud of blue smoke he shot off down the narrow street, his lank hair flying in the wind.

Matt smiled, picked up his files, and entered the building.

The Jefferson Institute took its name from Jefferson Place, the quiet Washington side street on which it was located. A three-story brownstone, it had been converted from an elegant, if somewhat shabby, residence in which had lived Buttons's maiden aunt, a woman of considerable means.

In 1968 she died, suddenly and without warning, of a massive stroke, leaving the building—and a large trust fund—to her favorite nephew. Buttons had used rather a lot of her money to gut the inside of the building and completely remodel it. And the rest to start the institute.

As Matt mounted the narrow staircase to his second-floor office, he could hear the throaty pipes of the Miata roaring into the parking lot at the rear of the building. On the landing he met Buttons, clumping down from his third-floor aerie, big brogans clattering on the wooden risers.

Buttons grinned as he spotted Matt. His round, pleasant face was slightly sunburned, leading Matt to think that he'd either spent the weekend playing golf, or else he'd had another stab at sailing, his latest passion. Buttons, like many bachelors with time on their hands, collected hobbies, with sailing as the current passion. Boats having already absorbed a great deal of Buttons's spare time and cash the summer before, Matt's prediction that the luster would soon wear off might, he thought, have been premature. He hadn't endeared himself to his friend when, after having spent a weekend on Buttons's yawl helping Marty throw up and bailing seawater out of the bilge, he'd remarked that Buttons could achieve the same general effect by standing under a freezing shower in a raincoat and ripping fifty-dollar bills into confetti.

Buttons raised his coffee mug in greeting. "Matt. Ready for the meeting? Nigel's on his way."

"Ready as I'll ever be."

"Um. Bring any doughnuts?"

Matt shook his head.

"Useless bugger," Buttons mumbled. "I'll send Teddy, then." He waved and wandered off down the hall.

Matt entered his tiny office, dumped the files on his desk, and flipped on the voice-mail system, listening to the hiss of the empty tape which told him that no one had called over the weekend.

Three months ago Nigel Hastings—a transplanted Briton and de facto director of the institute these days—had installed the automatic system, over protests by Buttons. Since then everyone's telephone messages were electronically recorded, stored, and played back at the touch of a button. Matt detested the system but said nothing. Marty took every possible occasion to leave strange and sometimes X-rated messages on the machine, despite Matt's warnings that the system was hardly secure. He'd half expected to find something from her now.

Plopping into his chair he poured himself coffee from the machine that he bribed Teddy to turn on for him first thing in the morning. As he took his first life-giving sip, he glanced over at the framed photo beside his computer—a group shot of the Annual Jefferson Memorial Picnic and Skunk Summit, held last summer at Cabin John Park.

There they all were—Matt and Marty (an honorary skunk, Buttons had said), Buttons and a CIA secretary he'd run into somewhere, Teddy with some underage mall rat he'd found in lower Georgetown, and Nigel, as usual without his wife—she seemed to spend most of her time in London—but looking relaxed and happy in his baggy Empire shorts and faded polo shirt. Buttons had set his ancient Pentax on a tripod, pushed the timer, and hurried back to join the group just before the flash went off. They stared into the camera with slightly squint eyes, clutching their beer cans (in Marty's case, a diet Pepsi), broad smiles on their faces.

That had been the day, Matt remembered, when they had first talked about the Ragnarok system, and about doing a monograph on it. Easy days, optimistic times.

A good group, Matt thought; easy and smooth with each other, yet intellectually high powered. Nigel and Buttons presented almost polar opposites —Buttons with his old southern money, manners, and morality, alongside Nigel's sharp-pressed no-nonsense Oxbridge mind. Strange bedfellows indeed, he thought, together more out of necessity than choice, but somehow, it worked.

Close friends as graduate students at Johns Hopkins, Matt and Buttons had gone separate ways after graduation. Matt had become a Coyote, and Buttons had gone abroad to England, to the University of Sussex, where he'd acquired Nigel Hastings as his tutor, and eventually, a Ph.D. in politics.

Nigel, a gifted if erratic lecturer, specialized in East-West relations. Sussex at the time had a well-deserved reputation as the "reddest" of the redbrick universities, a veritable nest—according to the Tories —of Trotskyites, Marxist-Leninists, Revolutionary Socialists, and proponents of anarcho-syndicalism.

Nigel, an unreconstructed Cold Warrior of the purest stripe, stood well apart from the herd, an enigma to his colleagues, most of whom assumed that only Americans could identify with the Children's Crusade against Godless Communism. Given the prominence of Americans among the hard core of the Sussex left wing, it was a curious—and to Nigel, amusing—reversal of traditional roles.

Despite their vastly different personalities—Buttons a slightly overweight version of Jimmy Stewart, easygoing and open, and Nigel the well-tailored, Waspish intellectual—the two men got on well, their differing views of politics no barrier to their friendship and mutual respect. At Sussex, Nigel served as advisor to the Monday Club, a group characterized by Buttons as a collection of antediluvian throwbacks. For his part Buttons's enthusiasm for rallies involving shouted slogans—"disembowel Enoch

Powell" was one of his favorites—drew little more than raised eyebrows from Nigel.

Buttons lived briefly in his aunt's house after the old lady died, but his liberal compulsion to do good, as Nigel put it, eventually got the better of him. Seriously alarmed by Nixon's election, he created the Jefferson Institute at the time of Watergate as a candle against the gathering darkness.

Nonpolitical but vaguely left of center, the institute ran largely on Buttons's inheritance money, and on his faith that one could do good in the world by doing research. Beginning in the mid-seventies the Jefferson Institute began to make a name for itself, its high-quality research publications attracting the attention of policy analysts, planners, and governments.

But respect didn't translate into financial success, and one day the accountants brought Buttons the bad news: he was broke. Never a particularly good businessman, he'd overextended himself badly. Just as he was about to give his staff their notice, the cavalry arrived, in the form of a telephone call from his old tutor, who'd just landed a substantial research grant and was looking for somewhere to park it.

By the time spring came, Nigel Hastings had effectively gained control of the institute, by virtue of his superior management skills and—more importantly perhaps—the funding he brought with him from Hong Kong.

Nigel had proved to be the salvation of the institute, even though, as Buttons sometimes confided, he'd also changed its character. Seeing Mrs.

Thatcher's handwriting on the wall, Nigel had fled the incipient wreckage of the British university system in the 1980s and lit out for the territories. He'd landed on his feet in the Crown Colony of Hong Kong and, by his own account at least, done quite well for five years and a bit. It was, according to Nigel, a place where there was money to be gathered by those who had the right connections, and Nigel had wasted no time establishing his network.

The British treaty with the People's Republic—a giveaway, in Nigel's terms, even greater than that of the Panama Canal under Jimmy Carter—signaled the beginning of the end. It was time to move on, and the call to Buttons had done the trick. Three months later Nigel was comfortably installed on Jefferson Place, and about to close on a three-bedroom suburban house in Bethesda, the keys to a new Infiniti making a slight bulge in the vest pocket of his Bond Street suit.

He hadn't come empty-handed. He brought to the Jefferson Institute his own large two-million-dollar research grant on Southeast Asian trade, and in the five years since, he had personally garnered another twenty million dollars in related support, all of it, apparently, through his far-flung network.

Nigel had quickly become the head of the family, replacing Buttons, who had a good heart but no real head for figures. Although Buttons's name still headed the institute's letterhead, Nigel was now the driving force, the conceptualizer, the action man. Indeed, it was Nigel who had blessed Matt's own induction into the group, and who had crafted his first assignment. As Matt had groped his way through the research and the writing, Nigel was there, offering helpful comments, shrewd advice, and once in a while some whiplash criticism in case things, as he put it, began to go wonky.

Teddy poked his head around the corner, breaking Matt's daydream. "Himself just walked in," he announced. "Wants us all in the conference room, pronto. Here's your keys, thanks." He tossed the Miata's keys to Matt, who fielded them automatically.

Matt took one last look at the photograph. There wouldn't be another Skunk Summit for many months, not with spring just arrived in the city and the cherry trees yet to blossom. Reaching into his drawer, he pulled out a slightly soiled necktie and put it on, using his computer screen as a dim mirror. Time to make the doughnuts, he thought, checking his watch.

He picked up the Ragnarok files with one hand, his coffee cup with the other. Unless they made real progress on Ragnarok in the next few weeks, he thought, the next Skunk Summit wouldn't be nearly as convivial.

The long conference room was dominated by an enormous scarred teak table, a prize Buttons had hauled back from a hotel auction in Saratoga Springs many years ago.

Buttons was already in place. "Ready?"

"As I'll ever be," Matt replied.

Just then Nigel appeared in the doorway. How he managed to appear so fresh, Matt thought, after eighteen hours spent on a plane from Hong Kong, Tokyo, or wherever his last stop had been, was a mystery. Whippet thin, Nigel Hastings wore his well-tailored pinstripe suit with ease. He set his leather briefcase down on the table and nodded to Matt and Buttons, smiling affably, his sharp blue eyes bright and alert. "Morning, chaps. Nice to see you both again. Tokyo was hell, I don't mind telling you. Where's the damned boy?"

"Right here, sir." Teddy spoke from the corridor behind him, entering with a large tray of Danish rolls and doughnuts from the corner shop, the traditional fare for institute conferences. "Anyone want coffee?"

Nigel and Buttons each helped themselves. Matt declined, indicating his own nearly full cup.

Nigel came, as was his wont, straight to the point. "Right," he said, rubbing his hands together as if to warm them. "We're up against it, I don't need to tell you that. Ragnarok is quite possibly being tested even as we speak, although that may all be media rubbish, as usual." He paused, fixing Matt with a beady eye. "But we've a chance here for a *major* coup, and unless we can come up with something, we're going to miss it. People are beating on our door. So, Matt, what have we got for them?"

Matt shifted on his seat. "Frankly, we're not much farther along than we were last week. We've filled in some of the missing technical pieces, written up what we've done so far. The background's done, but what we need now is the performance data in order to do the analysis."

"Which is going to be damned near impossible,"

Buttons said sourly, "unless a miracle occurs. We don't even have a picture of the stupid thing."

"A bit frustrating," Nigel agreed. "When do you think we'll have something?"

Matt hesitated, wondering how much to tell them about Marty's trip to the desert. Hold on to it, he told himself; wait until she gets back. "End of the week," he said finally. "I'm, ah, working on something right now."

Nigel's head came up. "Need help?"

Matt shook his head. "Not necessary."

Nigel harrumphed, adjusting his tie. "Very well, then. Why don't we at least run over the high points of what we've got so far, just to make sure we're not missing anything."

"Sure." Matt leaned forward and put his elbows on the table. "Buttons, why don't you go first?"

Buttons cleared his throat, and adopted what Matt liked to call his listen-my-children-and-you-shall-hear posture. "The first section contains chapters on the political and economic background," he began, "Star Wars and all that. Ancient history, practically."

Matt smiled. Ancient history was right, he thought. Teddy probably didn't remember Star Wars at all; or if he did, he probably thought it was the old movie.

"Billions spent," Buttons continued, "but no real results, although some subcomponents were successfully tested under limited-reality conditions."

He looked around the room. "Don't you just love military jargon? *Limited-reality testing* means it's rigged; like a quiz show where you feed contestants the answers in advance. I call it 'retrospective archery.' You shoot an arrow at random into the forest, find the tree it hits, and paint a big bull's-eye around the point of impact."

Nigel chuckled dryly. "I like that. Plan to use it in the book?"

Buttons shrugged. "Maybe. Anyway, Ragnarok was a fresh start. They needed to develop two new technologies—one in propulsion, the other in computer programming. Let's take the propulsion system first—it's simpler." He turned to Teddy, raising his eyebrows expectantly.

Teddy cleared his throat and squared his pages neatly. "I wouldn't call it 'simpler,' necessarily," he said. "But it's the area we know the most about. We've got two chapters ready on the development of the solid fuel for the rocket motors, and another chapter nearly done on the environmental and legal aspects of using endoatmospheric weapons."

He glanced down at his notes. "Basically, Ragnarok's propulsion system is a very advanced version of earlier work by Lockheed under a program called THAAD—Theater High-Altitude Area Defense. It produced some interesting work on a long-lasting, high-thrust rocket engine that uses solid fuel. They'd been trying this kind of thing for years, starting back in the fifties, but it went nowhere. Originally, they wanted a heavy-duty booster, something that would loft big payloads into space. The military developed some incredibly powerful fuels under THAAD, but didn't have the metals technology to contain the heat they generated. We're talking about temperatures in excess of twenty-five hundred degrees—"

"Fahrenheit?"

Teddy shook his head. "Centigrade. That's *hot*. To contain temperature like that you need special metals and ceramics. Which only became available about a year ago." He closed his file. "So we think they've got it. We know about some of the static tests that were run up at the military's High Peaks test facility, and if the data are correct, they were successful at producing specific impulse readings of between seven hundred and eight hundred seconds."

"And what, pray, does all of this mean in practical terms?"

"It means," said Teddy, "that they've now got a very powerful rocket. It's endoatmospheric, which means it's not headed for outer space or anything, and using the new propellants means they can reduce the size and weight of the missile. The solid fuel is much more stable and less complicated than liquid fuel would have been. That means the rocket is transportable, storable, and less complicated to use and maintain. But that's not the main advantage. Staying power is."

Nigel's eyebrows rose. "Staying power?"

"Ragnarok will stay in the air far longer than previous designs—you can use it on multiple incoming missiles if necessary. Engineers talk of the efficiency of rocket engines in terms of something they call 'specific impulse,' or how much thrust a given quantity of propellant will generate. A standard chemical rocket motor will give you, say, around three hundred seconds of specific impulse. With Ragnarok's system you can probably get three to four times that."

Nigel leaned forward. "So what does this mean, in real-world terms?"

"Since it has a longer burn time, you've now got options. Ragnarok can go higher, go faster, or go longer—whatever you want. Going longer was what they were after, obviously—the SS-type missiles that Ragnarok is designed to hunt and kill aren't terribly high fliers, relatively speaking.

"So it's now possible, once you've got a high specific impulse, to keep the rocket up for a long time, hunting for enemies." He leaned forward, excitement sparkling in his eyes. "See, in the old days, back when you guys were all my age, they used these things like arrows. I mean, that's all they really were, you know—supercomplex, very expensive arrows. You aimed one, lit it off, and hoped it would hit its target. But with a long-lasting missile, something that can just keep on trucking, you've got a *real* guided missile, something that you can maneuver around the sky. With the earlier SDI systems it was one missile, one kill, at best. If you missed, too bad—the two projectiles went shooting past each other, and you didn't get a second chance, not unless you fired a second interceptor.

"But with Ragnarok you can actually turn the thing around and have another try. Or, if you prefer, you can kill one of the incoming missiles with a laser beam, and then go off in search of a second. For as long as the fuel lasts." He smiled happily. "It's actually a wonderful system, when you think about it."

Nigel cleared his throat. "So you think they've solved the technical problems?"

Teddy shrugged. "Only a live test will tell us that. I'll tell you what the biggest problem is, though —the speed of the thing. The missile is too darn fast for ordinary guidance systems. So control of it is an issue. Which is where Odin comes in."

"Odin," murmured Nigel. "The master brain. Norse god of battle, death, and inspiration; wise and omnicompetent." He smiled. "But subject, as all gods are, to fate's caprices. And, if I recall my classics, not entirely to be trusted."

He waved a hand languidly in the air, dismissing his own objections. "But enough. It's time for a break. I suggest we take an early lunch—go down to Ali's for a bite, perhaps. I'll treat."

He looked at Matt. "And when we reconvene, we'll hear about Odin, shall we?"

Matt got up. "Fine. Teddy can brief us. See you back here in an hour. I've got to run out."

"Not coming with us, Matt?" said Buttons. "You shouldn't miss an opportunity to make Nigel buy lunch, you know. What's so important?"

Matt grinned. "Believe it or not, I'm visiting a sick friend. See you in a bit."

6

Nancy Okamoto stood in the corridor, a clipboard in her hand. She smiled when she caught sight of Matt. "Hi. Here to see Yuki?"

Matt nodded. "How is she?"

"Much better than last time, Mr. McAllister." She glanced at the Styrofoam cartons he was carrying. "What are those?"

He grinned. "A get-well present. I took your advice."

"Go on in, then. She's awake and doing great." She smiled. "Got rounds to make. See you." She walked off down the corridor.

Cautiously, Matt edged into the room. The woman in the bed was awake, watching Matt approach with silent, careful eyes. He looked at her with interest. Even with her bruises and cuts she was very attractive, Matt thought. Her eyes, large and very dark, held his without wavering. Her hair, long and thick, was carefully brushed, and gathered with a ribbon. Even without makeup her skin was clear and virtually flawless, almost ivory in color.

He stopped at the foot of the bed. "Hi."

"Hi." Her voice was low and soft. "I remember you. You came yesterday. You're the one who—who stopped them." She spoke English clearly, almost without accent. She paused, emotions fleeting across her face like clouds in the wind. "The nurse told me about you. I—I wasn't very polite to you yesterday, I'm afraid." Her eyes dropped. "I'm sorry. You—you were very brave."

Matt came a step closer. "No apologies necessary. You've had a pretty rough time. Those two guys were probably going to kill you when they'd finished." He didn't add, *raping you.* Her eyes met his, and he could see the gratitude for his omission. "I'm glad you're alive." He paused. "I'm Matt. Matt McAllister." He held out the cartons. "And this is for you."

She opened one and gave a little gasp of pleasure. "Japanese food," she whispered. "Rice. Noodles. Fish. I don't believe it."

Matt grinned. "Food's that bad here, huh?"

She nodded. "Oh, yes indeed. This hospital is costing many hundreds of dollars a day, but the food is terrible. No Japanese could survive here for very long. I will surely starve to death if I eat only what they give me. Oh, thank you so much."

Her hand reached out and took his. Her fingers were long, her hand cool and dry in his. "Matt. That's Matthew, I think. From your Bible."

He nodded. "But I prefer Matt."

She unwrapped her wooden chopsticks, broke them apart, and began to eat, taking small tentative bites, smiling with pleasure. "Oh, this is wonderful, Matt," she breathed.

She set her chopsticks down. "I am impolite once again. My name is Yukiko," she said, putting the accent on the first syllable. "It means 'snow child' in Japanese. You can say Yuki." She picked up her chopsticks and resumed eating.

"Yuki," Matt repeated. "So, Yuki, how are you doing?"

"Okay, I guess." She gave a small smile, making her nose wrinkle. Her teeth were even and very white as they bit into the raw fish. "But I bet I look like hell, huh?"

The colloquialism made Matt grin. Her English was nearly perfect, he thought. "You look just fine." She really was very good looking, he decided.

She blushed. "They say I have to stay some more days. Until the ribs are better and they have taken more tests."

"And then?"

She looked at him. "Then I go home, of course."

"To Japan?"

She nodded. "Tokyo. I'm a professor—a mathematician—at Saitama University. You have been to Japan?"

"Never."

She finished her fish and put her chopsticks down neatly. "Well, I promise that when you come to Japan I will cook a wonderful big meal for you."

He laughed. "You've got a deal," he said. "But I doubt I'll get to Japan anytime soon. Where did you learn to speak such good English?"

She smiled. "Here, of course. Most Japanese are terrible at English, I know. But I went to school in the U.S. I came first as an exchange student, in high school. Later I went to Cornell. And Stanford for my Ph.D."

"I'm impressed," Matt said. "So what are you doing here? On vacation?"

She shook her head. "Conferences. One in New York, then here. Yesterday was the last day. I was staying at the Holiday Inn in Georgetown. I—I was on my way down to one of the restaurants on Wisconsin Avenue, when those two men approached me. They—" She stopped, her face flooding with pain and anxiety.

Matt put his hand on her shoulder. "Take it easy," he said. "You don't need to talk about it." Searching for a way to change the subject, he said, "What was your conference about? Mathematics?"

She smiled. "That was the one in New York. The one here—well, not exactly." She looked sheepish. "Can you keep a secret?"

Matt looked around. "Who am I going to tell?"

She took his hand and pulled him closer. "I was at a writer's conference. At George Washington University."

"You're a writer?"

She blushed. "No. Well, not yet, that is. What I mean is, I'm trying to be. I write things in my spare time, you see." She shook her head. "They're not very good, I'm afraid. I have a draft of a novel, actually. I was hoping—well, to get advice on what I should do to revise it."

"And did you?"

Yuki shook her head. "No, unfortunately not. Everyone was very nice, but they all said the same thing: 'Write from your experience.'" She gave a sad smile. "So perhaps my novel will never be published."

Matt smiled. "I have a friend who's a journalist," he said. "She'll be back in town in a day or so. You could talk to her, show her some of your writing."

Yuki nodded. "I would like to. But my writing is in Japanese. Is your friend someone you work with?"

Matt smiled. "No. A friend."

"A girlfriend?"

"Not exactly."

"Ah. You are married, then?"

"No."

She sighed. "I don't think I'll ever understand relationships in your country."

Matt laughed. "I'm not sure I do either." he said. "But I'm sure you'll be able to finish your novel if you try."

Yuki frowned. "I am not so sure," she said at last. "They told me writers should write from experience. But I'm trying to write a romantic adventure story. One with a beautiful woman and a brave, strong hero, what we call a *tateyaku*." She paused. "I am thirty-five years old, Matt. I have done nothing adventurous; nothing romantic. I do not know any *tateyaku*. My work is very time consuming, you see. It leaves little time for other things."

"No husband? No boyfriends?"

She looked at him, a trace of defiance in her eyes. "I have had boyfriends, Matt. I'm not exactly what you would call a wallblossom."

"Flower."

"What?"

"The word is *wallflower*."

She nodded. "Ah. Thank you. But you see, to write romantic novels, one must live a romantic life, and I don't." She grinned ruefully. "I am nothing but a mathematician. And mathematicians are among the most boring and conventional people in the world, if you want to know the truth." She looked at him earnestly. "And that's my problem, I think. My life is ordinary—*too* ordinary. Every day the same. In Japanese we say '*meshi —furo—neru*'; eat, take a bath, go to sleep. If writers are supposed to use their experience, what experience does a mathematician have?"

She shook her head sadly. "No, I think perhaps I have nothing to write about."

"Well," said Matt, "if it's adventures you're after, you just had one. Not a very nice one," he added, "but getting mugged in an alley doesn't happen to everyone, you know."

She gave him a small smile. "Not exactly what I had in mind, Matt. But thank you for saving me." She squeezed his hand. "You saved my life, truly."

She paused, thinking. "By the way, what happened to them?"

"Who?"

"The two men who attacked me."

Matt shrugged. "I left them there. It was more important to get you to the hospital. I think the police found them, later."

"But you hurt them, didn't you? I remember something—you broke his arm, the big one." She looked at him. "How did you do that? Are you a policeman? A soldier?"

Matt shook his head. "I do research. Boring stuff, really; I practically live in the library."

She studied him. "Well," she said after a moment, "perhaps so. But you have not always lived in the library, I think. You're different, somehow. I have a feeling you might be several different people, in fact."

"You might be right about that." He stood up. "Listen, I've got to get back to work. Big meeting today, all afternoon. When are they going to let you out of here?"

She shook her head. "No idea. The doctor says maybe two days, three." She picked up her handbag from the bedside table and rummaged through it, pulling things out. "I am forgetting my manners again," she muttered. "Where are they . . . ?" The Grateful Dead CDs slipped out. She held one up, showing it to Matt. "Do you like this group? I do. When I was at Stanford, they played in Berkeley on the weekends, free concerts. I thought they were wonderful. So, well, so *American*."

"That's an accurate description, I guess," Matt said.

"Here it is," she said, extracting a card from the clutter at the bottom of her bag. Taking a pencil she printed an address and telephone number on the back, and then handed it to him.

"There. Very Japanese, to give business cards. This is my address and telephone number." She pointed to her neat script. "I work at Saitama University outside of Tokyo, but I live in the city, in a place called Shinjuku; sort of like a neighborhood or a section of the city. Our addresses are very confusing for foreigners, so I have written the name of a large store very near my house. It's called Yodobashi Camera, and anyone in Tokyo can take you there. I live five doors away, at this number." She smiled. "I meant what I said about cooking you a Japanese meal."

Matt took the card and put it in his wallet. "I'll bring you one of my cards when I come back," he promised. "Along with some more decent food. Meantime, you take it easy."

She smiled, her face beautiful under the bruises. "Come here, Matt. Come closer." She tugged on his hand until he came close. He could feel her breath on his cheek, smell her faint perfume.

She reached up and kissed him lightly on the forehead. "Thank you, Matt McAllister. Thank you for saving my life. You are a very good person, I think."

Matt squeezed her hands. "See you soon," he said.

On the way out he met Nancy Okamoto in the hall. "How'd it go?" she said.

"Fine," said Matt. "She seems to be recovering fast."

She looked at him. "Sure looks that way," she said, grinning. "You've got lipstick on your forehead, right over your eye." She winked at Matt then, and continued down the hall.

7

Everyone had reassembled in the conference room. Teddy sat in the hot seat, shuffling his papers nervously and making small notes in the margins with his pencil. Buttons, looking slightly flushed, adjusted his belt and sighed. "Missed a damn good lunch, Matt."

Nigel swept into the room, carrying his ever-present cup of coffee. "We ready to continue?" He fixed Teddy with his eyes. "You were going to summarize what we know about Odin. Odin the all wise." Nigel's voice was edged with sarcasm. "All right, let's hear it. Just how smart *is* our Norse friend?"

Teddy swallowed and nodded, his Adam's apple bobbing. "That's, ah, not an easy question to answer, put that way. Let me start instead with what the Pentagon sees the problem to be, and that will make it easier to understand whether or not Odin is a solution to that problem." He cleared his throat. "Odin is basically a battle-management computer with what the Pentagon calls enhanced C-three capability—command, control, and communications. The original system specifications were very comprehensive."

He glanced down at his notes. "The system had to be able to track incoming missiles, often several at a time. It had to be able to receive, hand off, and use data from other friendly sensing systems, while at the same time fending off attempts at electronic interference from unfriendly systems. To do this effectively it needs to code and decode messages very, very quickly. And finally, of course, it needs to be able to choose targets and destroy them. Again, very quickly. This is what's known as a STAKA system—Surveillance, Tracking, Acquisition, and Kill Assessment. The system specifications were for a computer system that could take over all the battle-management functions, operate independently of human oversight, and work one hundred percent of the time."

"And can Odin actually do this?" Nigel's voice was soft.

Teddy blinked and adjusted his glasses. "Well, that's what they claim, sir. But I'll reserve my own judgment, if you don't mind, until we see some actual test data."

He shuffled his papers. "See, there have been lots of problems with earlier battle-management systems. They're just computers, after all, and so they're fundamentally stupid. They really only do what they're told."

"Garbage In, Garbage Out," murmured Buttons. "GIGO. One of the fundamental maxims of our age."

"That's right," agreed Teddy. "Battle-management specialists generally divide GIGO errors into several different types. Level One errors, for example, are where the human operator makes a programming error of commission."

"An error of commission?" Nigel shook his head. "Who on earth dreams up these terms? The Jesuits?"

"I don't know, sir. But Level One occurs when you feed wrong data into the system. There was a well-known case where some of the Navy systems were programmed in statute miles instead of in nautical miles. That's a typical Level One error, and it happens all the time."

"And Level Two?"

"Those are errors of omission—you don't input faulty data, you just leave out stuff altogether. Computers don't even notice, most of the time. So, for example, the Gemini V space shot came down a hundred miles from where it was supposed to, because of a Level Two error. Somebody had forgotten to input the motion of the earth around the sun into the reentry program."

"Jesus." Buttons coughed. "Well, doesn't surprise me, frankly. I don't know how they remember all that stuff, anyway."

"This is fascinating," said Nigel. He leaned forward. "Tell me more."

"Level Three errors are actually the most interesting," Teddy said. His voice was growing stronger, gaining in confidence now, as he worked his way through his material. "Level Three is where you input a bunch of parameters about the real world in which the program has to operate, and where, after you input them, these parameters change. It's also called the *Sheffield* Effect."

"The *Sheffield* Effect? Whatever for?"

"Well, during the Falklands war there was a British warship, the *Sheffield,* that was blown up by an Exocet missile."

"The *Sheffield* was a Royal Navy destroyer," Nigel said. "One of my younger cousins was serving on board at the time." He paused. "Fortunately, he survived. Unlike most of his companions." He frowned. "What's the sinking of the *Sheffield* got to do with Level Three errors?"

"Well, sir, the *Sheffield*'s defense systems were pretty good—state of the art, actually. But their battle-management programs had the Exocet listed as a *friendly* missile, because it was used by the British forces. So the system worked, in a sense. The *Sheffield*'s programs picked up the Exocet, identified it, and once they'd concluded that it was friendly, that it was on their list, they just forgot about it." He paused. "But in the meantime the parameters had changed. The Argentineans had the missile now, and nobody'd updated the battle-management program."

Nigel made a little steeple of his hands. "Yes, I

see," he said after a moment. "So it's quite important to have it clearly in mind as to who's the real enemy, isn't it?"

"Absolutely," Teddy agreed. "One of the biggest problems in building an effective battle-management system is the uncertainty about the exact nature of the enemy threat. The enemy is going to *try* to conceal himself, to camouflage his real intentions, to divert attention to false threats. So a system designed to identify that enemy has to process a stream of images, some only slightly different one from the other, which change rapidly. The essential task is to decide whether what's coming at you is something that must be dealt with or not, and if so, how."

"And if you conclude that the incoming Exocet is friendly," Nigel said, "you file that interesting fact, and forget it."

"Exactly. The whole problem is so complicated, in fact, that it makes the design of the Apollo moon shot look like a trip to the corner store. Ragnarok's battle-management system has to continuously modify actions and responses based on feedback from the outside. But as the computer scientists were quick to point out in the eighties, you can't possibly know or calculate all the variables in advance. So they needed a way to combine algorithmic programming with neural networking."

"Algorithmic programming?" Buttons asked.

"Algorithms are the formulas that give the program architecture its structure. The facts, basically. One plus one equals two, the area of a circle is the diameter times pi, stuff like that. But the algorithms are only the base; the system has to be able to actually *learn*, very quickly, from events in the real-time real-world. The 'arena,' as the guys in the Pentagon call it."

"So we're not just talking here about a so-called 'smart' computer, are we? How did they do it?" Nigel asked, regaining Teddy's attention.

"The first attempts, in the seventies and eighties, didn't work. They tried to beef up the computing power, develop bigger and better hardware, and write more complicated algorithmic programs. Millions of lines of software, running at high speed through very complex machines." He paused. "All they got was gridlock. Nobody could build anything able to survive in the real world for more than a few hours. Sometimes the system just stopped running. Sometimes the machine would reason itself into a corner, get totally confused, and become inoperative." He smiled. "Most of what was developed didn't have the basic intelligence of a gnat; the systems would freeze or jam after only a few hours, because they generated too many rules. If you learn too much, you can create logical paradoxes that shut down the system."

"Like some people we know," said Buttons.

"Then they tried something else. Subsumption architecture; a fancy term for breaking big problems down into little ones. See, originally, the programmers thought they had to have a map of the entire world, as it were, a definitive guide to how everything in the area worked and what it would do, *all the time and under all circumstances*. It drove them crazy, trying to pack it all in. To get an idea of the magnitude of the problem, consider this: the AT&T program to control the U.S. phone system has fifty million lines of software code. They figured that unless they found a way to let Ragnarok learn on its own, they might need at least this many lines.

"Size wasn't really the binding constraint, though. By the late eighties you could fit the computing power of a Cray-1 machine into a hundred-gram package, and thanks to guys like Eigler at IBM and his single-atom switches, even smaller subminiatures were on the way. They'd achieved teraflop performance—a trillion calculations per second—by 1995. But even the enhanced computing power couldn't handle more than a few real-world scenarios. So at Carnegie Mellon they took another way in, working on a different set of assumptions about what a truly 'intelligent' system would look like. They figured it would look a lot like our own learning systems, which use neural networks to both group data into meaningful subsets and also generate a set of flexible rules that change as new data come in. The machine actually learns as it goes along. You don't need an 'everything map' to get started."

"But don't you have to have *some* rules to get started, as it were?" Nigel said. "Otherwise, how would you even know how to group data into categories at all?"

Teddy nodded. "Good point. Well, you still have two kinds of rules, built into the program architecture. One of them deals with beliefs; the other with motivations. These say in effect to the system: Here's what a friend looks like, and here's what an enemy looks like."

"Sounds a bit simpleminded to me."

"Not really. The routines are pretty sophisticated, as far as we can tell. We know that they were designed into the architecture of the chips themselves, and that they use the Chambers Principles as their base."

"Chambers Principles?"

"It's an industry term. Osborne Chambers is the twenty-three-year-old prodigy at Carnegie Mellon who engineered the breakthrough. He incorporated two principles into the architecture: Optimal Ignorance and Appropriate Imprecision. They keep the machine from trying to figure everything out."

"Optimal Ignorance? What the hell does that mean?"

"Optimal Ignorance means deciding what's *not* worth knowing, which keeps one hell of a lot of data out of the system; saves space and running time."

"And Appropriate Imprecision?"

"That tells you how much you need to know about something new before you draw a conclusion about it. When you're getting dressed, for example, you want to know what the weather's like outside. 'Hot' or 'cold' will generally do it; you don't need more precise information. On the other hand, if you think you're getting a fever, you're going to want to know your temperature very precisely, to within tenths of a degree. So Odin is set up to pay very careful attention to some of the attributes of the world outside, and very little attention to others."

"And this works?"

"It's supposed to. I mean, you can see how it would radically improve the system. Suppose you wanted a robot not to run into walls. There are a couple of ways to set this up. The old way would be to equip the robot's memory banks with a complete map of all the buildings that it was ever likely to be in, with all the walls marked prominently. Then you identify all those walls by their individual characteristics, and write program lines telling the robot to avoid them. That way you could be pretty sure that once the robot had identified its own location, it could keep away from the walls."

"Pretty impractical, isn't it?" said Nigel.

Teddy nodded. "The other way—the way they used with Odin—is to make up a kind of generic description of what a wall looks like. That's the 'belief' part of the program. Then you give Odin a very specific instruction—stay away from anything that looks like this. That's the 'motivation' part. And then you let the machine loose in the environment and, using the Chambers Principles and a bunch of other preprogrammed stuff, let it figure out for itself whether the area in front of it is a wall, a window, or whatever." Teddy paused. "If we go back to the *Sheffield* for a moment, Odin would have a general description of what a missile looked like, and it would have certain beliefs about what enemies did. And it would decide that if the Exocet was a missile and it was coming toward the ship, it was probably unfriendly."

"If it walks like a duck," Buttons murmured, "and talks like a duck . . ."

"Exactly. You embed algorithms, beliefs, and motivations, and let them work together. The hard facts relate to the overall arena in which it has to operate; things that are static and always true. What time it is, the motion of the earth around the sun, stuff like that. Then there are things that Odin is programmed to believe about some of the things in the arena. Who's a friend and who's not, for example. How missiles in flight behave. This helps Odin tell the difference between a bunch of incoming Super Scuds and a flight of waterbirds. Then you've got a third level of embedded programming, which are the motivational sets: what Odin sees as its mission in life, what it needs, or wants, to do." He paused. "So Odin, for example, is programmed to want to shoot down incoming missiles. You might say that it *likes* to do this; it gets a charge out of it."

Nigel leaned forward. "All right, lad. But the question I keep coming back to is this: How smart *is* Odin, actually?"

Teddy grinned. "That depends," he said, "on what you mean by 'smart.' In some ways Odin is a genius. In other ways the system is probably no more intelligent than our voice-mail system here in the office. It's basically a dedicated missile-eater—sort of like an incredibly competent bloodhound. That's all it knows how to do, and that's all it cares about doing. It's absolutely state of the art, and uses parallel, neural, and optical-recognition systems that all work together. It can learn, and learn fast, but its learning is deliberately channeled and limited, so that it doesn't tie itself up in knots. So the machine that results from this is very, very smart at some things, and incredibly stupid at others."

"And is it going to work?"

Teddy shrugged. "We'll know soon enough," he said. "The test is supposed to be any day now, right, Matt?"

Matt held back a smile. "Far as we know."

Nigel leaned forward. "So if I can summarize," he said, "what they've created here is a machine that actually *thinks*—"

"No," interjected Teddy. "It doesn't think. Not in any meaningful sense. What it *does* do, however, is learn. And fast."

Nigel waved his hand impatiently. "All right, all right. But it operates independently, am I correct there?"

Teddy nodded. "Absolutely."

"Once you fire this thing, it's on its own."

"Yep."

"My God." Nigel was silent for a moment. "Do any of you realize what we've got here? An idiot savant in charge of a military weapon."

Matt dumped his groceries on the kitchen table and opened the fridge. Taking out a beer, he popped the top and got a glass from the cabinet. He glanced at the wall clock; he was just in time for the news. He poured the beer into the glass with one hand, while with the other he reached over and turned on the tiny TV set on the counter.

"More rumors today about the elusive Ragnarok supermissile, which insiders say is about to be tested somewhere in the California desert. As before, both Pentagon spokesmen and representatives of Trans-Century Systems, the main defense contractor, have refused to comment on speculation that the test is imminent. A press conference is scheduled for later this evening. In the meantime aerospace stocks showed a slight jump in value, indicating that the market is watching events closely. In other news, meanwhile . . ."

The telephone rang. Matt took a long swallow of beer, snapped off the TV, and crossed the room. "Hello."

"Hey, babe." Even across the miles Marty's voice sounded tired.

"Hey, yourself. Where are you?"

"God, who knows? Some desert ghost town with one motel, a post office, and a 7-Eleven that doesn't even have Dr Pepper. Listen, babe, have I got a story for you!"

"Did you see the test? What—"

"No problem. But it's the car. Right now I'm waiting for the only shade-tree mechanic in this place to finish fixing it. Damn fan belt broke about fifty miles back up the road."

"Jesus, how'd you get the car back to town?"

She sighed. "Never heard of using pantyhose instead of a fan belt? I used up two pairs getting here. Anyway, I dunno if I'm gonna be able to get out of here tonight, so I thought I'd call you."

"So the test went off okay?"

"The test went off, all right. And it's gonna be the story of the year, believe me." She paused. Her voice sounded very tired, and, Matt realized, something more. Scared?

Silence on the line. Then, "I'm booked back tomorrow afternoon out of LAX, United three fifty to National. Meet me?"

"Sure thing. How'm I gonna recognize you, though?"

Her chuckle was music to his ears. "I'll be the gal with a videocam on her shoulder and a shit-eating grin from ear to ear." There was a pause, and he could hear the electronic long-distance hum echoing in his ears. "But, hey, not a word about this to anybody, okay? Not even to your buddies at the institute. I wanna come in and show you the tape first and have you all tell me what you think. Until then not a word to anybody, understand?"

"Sure, sure."

"Babe, I mean it. You gotta promise. Promise?"

"What? Yeah, I promise. I promise, all right?" Matt frowned. "Marty, are you okay?"

"Finer'n frog hair. This desert's just a funny place, babe. Too many shadows or something. Don't pay any attention to me; place just got on my nerves, that's all. I want to get the damn car fixed and back on the road."

"Want me to wire you some money?"

She laughed. "I'd like to see Western Union try to get cash into a place like this. No, babe, I got plenty of money. I just wanna get out of here. I—I got a little nervous today, something that happened. I'll—"

A computerized voice broke in. *"Please deposit another three dollars and fifty-five cents to continue talking."*

"Shit, no more change. Look, babe, gotta go. See you tomorrow. Believe me, you're not gonna—" Her words were cut off by the buzz of the dial tone as the line automatically disconnected.

Matt went to bed early that night after an uninspiring dinner of leftover spaghetti followed by salad. He forced himself to spend half an hour reviewing the Ragnarok files and going over his meeting notes, and then treated himself to a third and final beer as he got ready for bed. Just before he dozed off, he caught the tail end of the late-night news.

". . . as we reported earlier, TransCentury Systems this evening announced the successful test of the supersecret Ragnarok missile. Although no pictures are available, Roland Chalmers, a TransCentury executive, said that the missile had performed exactly as expected."

The camera showed a plump man, face drawn and sweating under the camera lights, reading from a press release. The voice-over continued.

"Pentagon officials commented that the first public test of Ragnarok will probably take place sometime next month, and that the Secretary of Defense is ex-

pected to invite a group of overseas officials and military experts to join him at the test site. The upcoming test, unlike the one just concluded, will be open to the press."

Well, that's that, Matt thought as he turned off the set and settled himself in bed. Marty will be back tomorrow with the film, and we can put some flesh and bones on Ragnarok.

Hot damn.

The morning dawned warm and bright, rising thermals making the wings of the United jumbo shimmer as it drifted down to kiss the runway, a dainty puff of smoke rising from the tires. Matt stood patiently at the gate, watching the passengers disembark, peering up the corridor, looking for Marty's characteristic long-legged lope.

Half an hour later he finally admitted to himself that she wasn't going to show. The gate was closed, and the lounge crew was already sliding a placard for the next flight up on the board, while the cleaning crew filed in. He found an airline agent and, after a few minutes of persuasion, managed to learn from her computer that Marty had indeed been booked on the flight, but hadn't shown up at the airport in Los Angeles.

Matt stood for a moment, confused. "Shit," he muttered, turning away and heading for the parking lot.

Heavy traffic on the parkway stretched his return time to over an hour. Going straight to the fridge, he yanked out a jug of orange juice and poured a glassful, gulping half of it down at once. Where the hell _was_ she? he thought. Marty didn't miss flights, not without a good reason. Her car still wasn't fixed, that was probably it.

But why hadn't she called, in that case?

Maybe she had. Matt got up from the kitchen table and went upstairs to his study. It was the second bedroom in the small town house, and books were jammed into every possible inch of space. A door laid flat across two metal sawhorses comprised his desk. On his desk were an ancient IBM PC, an even older black-and-white portable TV, and more books.

The answering machine lay on the floor beside the desk, in its usual place, the message light blinking. He pressed the button, expecting to hear Marty cursing a missed flight or an incompetent mechanic, but instead an unknown male voice came on.

"This is a message for Mr. Matthew McAllister. My name's Dan Simmons, Mr. McAllister; I want you to call me as soon as you hear this. Area code 714, the number's 555-7888. Soon as you can, please."

A beep, then the buzz of a dial tone, then silence. No more messages.

Matt finished the rest of his orange juice and stood in front of the answering machine, looking down at it thoughtfully. "What the hell," he said quietly, to no one in particular. His words seemed to echo in the empty house. He reached for the telephone.

Where was area code 714? Out West somewhere, wasn't it? He felt a chill start to spread up his back as he punched in the numbers.

Five rings, six, seven. "Yeah?" The voice was sleepy, gruff, and male.

"Dan Simmons, please. This is Matt McAllister."

"McAllister." Pause. "Yeah. Well, Mr. McAllister, my name's Dan Simmons, and I'm with the sheriff's office out here in San Bernardino County. You know someone named Martha Larsen?"

"Yes, I do." Matt's voice suddenly seemed very loud in his own ears. "What's—"

"There's no good way to tell you this, so let me just get it out. Ms. Larsen is dead. She—"

"Wait." Matt's voice was caught in his throat. "Hold on a second." His words seemed strangled somehow, bottled up under pressure in a very small space. He reached behind him, grabbed the back of a chair, dragged it over, and sat down.

He took a deep breath and held it, clutching the telephone hard, staring at it, feeling the hard thumping of his heart kick in as the adrenaline took over. After a moment he found his voice. "Dead? Marty's dead? That's impossible, I spoke to her just last night. She—"

"She's dead, Mr. McAllister. Now, look, I know this isn't easy, but just listen to me, okay? I don't like tellin' you this any more than you like hearin' it. So just listen a second, if you don't mind." He paused. "You a relative? Brother or something?"

"No," Matt whispered. He seemed somehow outside his body, receding rapidly in time and space from the room, listening with increasing difficulty to the sounds coming from the tiny telephone receiver. "Just—a friend. Go ahead, I'm listening."

"Okay, here it is, McAllister. Ms. Larsen was in an automobile accident. Happened last night, about twenty miles out of town. Way we put it together, she must have lost control of her car. It went over the guardrail and down into the arroyo, straight down." He paused. "The coroner says she probably died right away. Broken neck."

"Lost control?" Matt's voice sounded very small and distant.

"Probably going too fast," Simmons said. "The back roads around here are dirt and gravel, mostly. Folks from out of town sometimes aren't used to desert conditions. Also—" He stopped.

"Also what?"

Silence. Then Simmons said, "She was drunk, Mr. McAllister. Sorry, but that's the story."

"Drunk? I don't believe it."

"Not asking you to believe it, sir. Just telling you what the coroner found. She was stinking of it, if you'll excuse the expression." Another pause. "Anyway, sir, your name was in her wallet, written in on that medical form people sometimes carry. I'm sorry, I really am."

Matt held the telephone receiver tightly, his mind racing. Finally he said, "What happens now?"

"Well, Mr. McAllister, that sort of depends on

you, I guess. What were Ms. Larsen's wishes with respect to burial, would you know that?"

Matt cast his mind back to a conversation long ago, the two of them sitting on the bank of the Potomac up by the Palisades, passing a lazy summer day with books and talk and drowsy contemplation. "When I die," she'd said, "I hope it's in a place like this."

He had laughed. "You're not going to die for a long time, Marty. And this'll probably be a parking lot by that time."

She shook her head. "Even so. Look at it this way: I've had a pretty full life, if you think about it. Been a lot of places, done a lot of things. Haven't got my Pulitzer yet, and Connie Chung's still got her job, but aside from a few details like that, I can't complain. So if I were to die, I'd die happy, y'know?" She turned to face him. "And to hell with that burial shit; where I drop, that's where they bury me. It's in my will that way, in fact."

"You're serious? You don't care?"

"Why should I care?" She gave him her brilliant, heart-stopping smile. "I'll be *dead*, remember?"

"Mr. McAllister?" Simmons's voice brought him back to the present.

"I'm here," he said after a long moment. "She'd want to be buried out there. If that's possible, that is."

"Here? Well, I guess we could fix that up. There's a funeral parlor in town. I could get them working on it if you wanted. You, ah, gonna take care of the expenses and all?"

Matt took a deep breath and stood up. "I'll take care of them," he said. "And I'll be there by noon tomorrow. Just don't put her in the ground before I get there, okay?"

8

Matt stood at the graveside, bleary-eyed, unshaven, and mortally tired. The flight from Washington to LAX had been nothing short of brutal, the California heat oppressive and cloying as he climbed into his rented car and braced for the long drive up into the high desert on the Nevada border.

He had driven up through San Bernardino to Barstow, stopping there to call Buttons at the Jefferson Institute. Sweating inside the filthy phone booth, he was relieved for once to reach the answering machine. In short flat sentences, he told what he knew of Marty's death, and promised to check in in a day or so. Then he headed out along Route 15, driving northeast for what seemed like endless hours, until he reached the tiny junction town. Following Sheriff

Simmons's instructions he found the funeral home without difficulty. Not too hard in a one-horse town, he thought, surveying the bleak and windswept main drag of the desert settlement.

He'd parked his rented Chevy, got out, and entered the modest one-story building. In the parlor Marty's coffin was set out on display. There were exactly three people in the room: a short, almost dwarflike man in a dark suit; a portly uniformed trooper with a San Bernardino County shoulder patch; and a tall, slim black man, dressed in pressed Levi's and a raw silk jacket.

The short guy in the suit is the undertaker, Matt thought. The cop is Simmons. Who's the black guy?

That question was answered a few seconds later. The black man stepped forward and extended his hand. "You're McAllister, right?"

Matt nodded.

"I'm Arthur Emerson. They call me Ace. I'm—I was a friend of Marty's." He shot a glance at the cop. "Simmons said you'd be here."

Matt looked from Ace Emerson to the coffin, and back again.

Emerson nodded. "Yeah, it's really her, and she's really dead." He took Matt gently by the elbow. "C'mon, man. It'll make you feel better."

The two men stood silently beside the coffin, staring down at the face of Martha Larsen, peaceful in death in a way she had never been in life. The undertaker had done a good job; Marty looked almost alive, the ghost of a smile on her full lips, her eyelashes long and full. Matt felt his breath catch, and he gripped the side of the coffin hard.

"Listen up, McAllister." The voice beside him was so faint as to be almost inaudible. "Keep your head down, don't turn this way." Matt opened his eyes and flicked them sideways, meeting Ace Emerson's hard stare. "Stay cool, don't react." The man was speaking like a ventriloquist, hardly moving his lips.

"There's a diner on the way out of town back toward L.A., 'bout a mile from here. You meet me there tonight at eight o'clock, just you alone, you got that?"

Matt gave a barely perceptible nod.

"Good," said Ace Emerson. "And now," he added between clenched teeth, "I'm getting the hell out of here. Bury her good, man, and say good-bye for me. She was one hell of a lady, but I guess you knew that. See you later."

And with that he left, striding out the door into the sunlight, never looking back.

Matt, Sheriff Simmons, and the undertaker watched Marty Larsen's coffin disappear into the ground. Silently, the undertaker handed Matt the shovel. He threw one shovelful onto the top of the coffin and then turned away.

Simmons appeared beside him as he walked away from the graveside. "You're a good man to come out here all this way," he said quietly. "Didn't she have any family?"

Matt shook his head. "None that I ever heard of, at any rate."

"You, ah, knew her pretty well?"

He swung around. "About as well as anybody." He swallowed, gaining control of his emotions. "You want to tell me about the accident?"

Sheriff Simmons looked up at Matt, squinting his eyes against the raw desert wind. "Yeah, I can do that, I guess." He opened the door to his patrol car. "Let's get inside here. Gettin' cold now."

Matt nodded. It was late afternoon, and already the sunlight had a cold underbite. By nightfall it would be colder still. Matt thought of Marty's body lying trapped in the wrecked car, in the cold, in the night. He got in.

Simmons shook a Pall Mall from a crumpled pack and shot a glance at Matt. "You got a problem with this?" Matt shook his head. "Good. It's about got to where you can't fart in this state without some sonofabitch citing you for air pollution." He lit up and sucked a life-giving cloud of smoke into his lungs, grimacing.

"Found her last night, 'bout two hours before I called you," Simmons said, letting the smoke spill from his mouth. "We were lucky in a way—not a hell of a lot of people go up that arroyo road. Fact is"— he glanced over at Matt—"we kinda wondered what the hell *she* was doing up there. You got any ideas about that?"

Matt looked at him. He would play this straight down the middle, he decided. "No, Sheriff, I don't." A beat. "She told me she was going to L.A. on vacation. Mentioned she might take a trip to Las Vegas if she had time."

Simmons nodded. "That fits—the car was rented from the airport in L.A. She sure traveled light, though. We didn't find a damn thing in the car 'cept her overnight bag, her purse, and a couple bottles of whiskey. One full, the other mostly not." He heaved himself around and reached into the backseat, pulling up a plastic evidence bag. "Here they all are, Mr. McAllister. Guess they're yours if you want 'em."

"There was nothing else?" Matt kept his voice carefully neutral.

"Nope. I checked with the rental company in L.A., see if I could find out more about her, but all they said was that she rented the car for a week and told 'em she was gonna do some sightseeing." He shook his head. "Well, some folks like the high desert, that's true. But they don't usually drive through it at night when they're drunk. Man, if she'd put away nearly a fifth of Corby's up there somewhere on that road, it's no wonder she lost control of the car. That's one hell of a drive, even in the daytime."

"You do a blood test?" Matt asked.

"For the alcohol?" Simmons snorted. "Hell, no, son; no need to. Car was stunk up with booze, she had it on her breath, bottle down under the seat— shit, the coroner's got better things to do than restate the obvious. Why?" His eyes darted to Matt's.

Back off, Matt told himself. "Don't get me wrong," he said after a moment. "I was just asking a question. It wasn't a challenge."

Simmons nodded. "Sorry, son. I guess I'm a little

touchy today. We don't get many deaths around here, tell you the truth."

Matt nodded, looking at the old sheriff, trying to read his eyes. He could see nothing there but concern. Whatever's going on around here, he thought, this guy's not a part of it.

Simmons stubbed out his Pall Mall, mashing the butt to shreds, and immediately lit another. "Well," he said finally, "guess you'll be heading back East pretty soon."

"Tomorrow morning," Matt said. "I'd drive back to L.A. tonight, but I'm too bushed."

Simmons gave him a smile then. "I'll bet you are." He sighed, his belly pushing up against the steering wheel of the patrol car, and opened the door. "Okay, Mr. McAllister, I guess we're done here. You got a card or something where I can get your address and phone number? Just in case anything else comes up."

Both men got out. Matt took out one of his cards and gave it to the sheriff. Simmons squinted as he read it, his lips moving silently. "Jefferson Institute? What the hell's that, some kind of fancy college or something?"

Matt shook his head. "It's a research firm. I'm a writer for them."

Simmons looked up. "No shit, a writer? I always wanted to be a writer, to tell you the truth. Don't really look that complicated." He fixed Matt with a beady eye. "My wife, now, she likes those romance books—you know, the ones they call bodice rippers?"

He took a long drag on his cigarette. "Damn things're all exactly the same. Girl leaves home, meets a good guy and a bad guy. The good guy fights the bad guy and wins. Then the *real* bad guy comes along, and they spend the rest of the book fighting him before they ride off into the sunset."

He frowned. "Hell, damn near anybody'd be able to write that, don't you think?" He looked at Matt. "So what kinds of books you write?"

"Technical ones, Sheriff. Not like those at all."

Simmons shook his hand. "Well, you keep on writin'. Thanks for coming out, Mr. McAllister. You were a good friend to this poor woman here, and if there's a God in heaven, she'll know that and be comforted. You take care now."

And with that he climbed into his patrol car, started the engine, and drove off down the windswept highway, leaving Matt staring after him, out across the scrub.

Matt watched him go until his car was out of sight. Then he turned his gaze to the north, toward the border. Somewhere out there, Matt thought, is the launch site. Where Marty saw the test of Ragnarok.

Where someone killed her for what she saw.

Because, Matt thought, there's no way she would have been drunk on that back road. No way in hell.

So someone saw her at the test site. Followed her. And killed her, making her death look like a drunk-driving accident.

But it wasn't an accident, Matt thought. It was murder.

Why? What had she seen that was important enough to kill her for?

He didn't know, he thought as he climbed into his own car and started the engine. But he would sure as hell find out.

9

At twenty past eight Ace Emerson slid into the booth across from Matt McAllister, glanced at his half-eaten plate of burger and fries, and winced. "Shoulda told you not to eat the food," he said. "This place is good for coffee only, and even that only in an emergency."

They sat in the back, away from the windows. From his vantage point against the wall Matt could watch the entrance to the diner. Only one other booth was occupied, by a half-drunk couple too intent on each other to notice anyone else around them. Five or six grizzled truckers sat on revolving stools at the counter and picked at their food, reluctant to leave the company of other human beings for the impersonal loneliness of the night highway.

Matt finished chewing his mouthful and looked across the table at the black man. "If the food's so bad," he said evenly, "—and it is—then why'd you ask me to meet you here?"

Ace Emerson returned his stare. " 'Cause this is a safe place to talk," he said. "The food keeps most everybody from the site outa here, see. I needed to talk to you."

"So talk."

Ace leaned forward. "Look, you gotta understand one thing. I don't *know* you. Now, I don't much like that. I don't much like what I'm doing right now, and to tell you the truth, it's a little scary. But I gotta trust somebody, and you're the only one around. So if you're gonna shit me—if you're gonna play it cool with me, fuck around with my head— then I'm outa here, you comprehend that?" His eyes darted from place to place as he talked.

"I could say the same about you," Matt said quietly. "Who the hell are you? What do you want? And why should I trust you?"

Ace looked him full in the face. "Because you and I, McAllister, are apparently the only two people in the whole state of California who know that Marty didn't have an accident." His voice was low and intense. "That she was killed."

"Wrong."

"Say what?"

"There's three of us. You, me, and whoever killed her."

Ace let his breath out. "Yeah, right. Forgot

about that." He looked up at Matt. "She *was* killed, wasn't she?"

He nodded slowly. "She wasn't drunk when that 'accident' happened, that's for sure."

"Right. You know Marty, so do I. She's been clean and sober for years. No way that woman's gonna go on a toot up in the hills at night, alone in a rental car." He grabbed Matt's arm tightly. "So you tell me this, McAllister—what the fuck is going on here?"

"I wish to hell I knew." He pushed his plate away. "Let's go back to the beginning. When she said she was coming out here, she told me she had a friend who was going to help her get into the test site. Was that you?"

Ace Emerson sighed. "Yeah, I guess it was. You want the whole story?"

Matt nodded. "I think I do."

Ace nodded, getting up from the booth. He went to the counter, ordered coffee, brought it back, and sat down. He sipped once, twice, made a face, and took a deep breath. "Okay. I'm a programmer. I work for TransCentury, live in L.A. Been going back and forth to the site here for about six months, doing some of the infill work on the guidance system for Ragnarok." He looked up at Matt. "You know much about what they got out there in the desert?"

"A little. I've been trying to find out more, as a matter of fact." Matt quickly filled Ace in on his work with the institute.

When he had finished, Ace shook his head. "Well, you're shit outa luck, McAllister. I worked on

Odin's system architecture all last year, but once that was done, I kinda lost touch with things. These days all I am's a data mechanic out there—they don't let me anywhere near the bird itself. Never even seen it, in fact. All I do is, I sit in an air-conditioned trailer out there on the perimeter and run debugging programs through the guidance codes. The whole thing's automated—I just start 'er up and shut down at the end of the day."

"So you didn't see the test the other day?" Matt watched the man's face carefully as he spoke.

"You kidding? *Nobody* saw that test. Nobody but a couple of company guys and a skeleton firing crew. Maybe four, five people in all. Shit, you gotta have a number-one security clearance to even get into that site, let alone stick around for a test. Place was closed up tighter'n a nun's asshole." He shook his head. "Naw, they gave everybody the day off with pay. I saw on the news it went okay, so that's good—means we've all got a job next month." He gave a quick grin. "Times are tough, babe. Bird don't fly, we're all looking for work."

He pulled a copy of *USA Today* from his jacket.

"TransCentury stock's way up today, so the wolf ain't at the door yet. They were behind on the schedule, see, and everybody got worried the feds would yank the funding, but it's all right now. If we'd lost the Ragnarok contract, the whole company'd go tits-up, believe me. There was just a whole *buncha* guys waiting it out." He shook his head. "It musta been something to see." He glanced behind Matt, and lowered his voice. "Think Marty got all the way inside?"

He doesn't know what she saw, either, Matt thought. "No idea," he said. "But I know that's where she wanted to go."

Ace nodded. "Yeah, I gave her some help there, she probably told you." He paused. "She and I go back a ways; we knew each other back in Wisconsin, at school. Seems like a long time ago now, man, but we were part of the same political group." He laughed lightly then. "By the way, I'd appreciate it if you didn't mention that little fact to anyone, okay? I mean, everybody was into those kinda groups back then, y'know, didn't mean shit, but these days, you gotta watch what you say, specially if you work for a defense contractor."

Matt looked at him with curiosity. "So what's a former radical doing working for a defense contractor?"

Ace smiled. "It's a job, right? And a damn good one." He leaned across the counter. "You know all that shit about black males being an endangered species and all? Take a good look at me, McAllister: I'm unmarried, forty-five years old. No kids, no ex-wives, nothin'. I got a nice, sweet girlfriend who I see a couple times a week, maybe we'll get married one of these days, but neither of us are in a hurry. I don't do drugs, not even weed. I drink beer, mostly, and once in a while I'll have a glass of wine. I got all my teeth."

He raised a finger. "I got a few more things too. I got a master's degree in engineering and a Ph.D. in computer science. I graduated top of my class. I've done original research on automatic programming, I've published papers in the professional journals, and I've spoken at the conferences."

He sipped his coffee, his eyes watching Matt over the rim of the cup. "You know how many black Ph.D.s in computer science were graduated last year? You got any fucking idea?"

Matt shook his head.

"*Five*. That's all. *Five* black men walked out of the four thousand–odd institutions of higher learning in this country with their little scrap of goatskin or whatever the hell it is."

He leaned back. "Endangered species? Hell, man, I'm not an endangered species. I'm *buried fucking treasure*, is what I am. I am the hottest of the hot shits. A smart, tame, clean-living, user-friendly black man who wants to *get on* in life." He smiled, showing all his teeth. "But why am I telling you this, you ask? I'll tell you why. As hot a shit as I am, I looked for a job for *ten months*. Ten terrible, dreadful, long months. And believe me, *that* had an effect on the old self-esteem, let me tell you."

He picked up his coffee and sipped. "Understand what I'm telling you, McAllister. This wasn't about prejudice and discrimination. It was about the lousy fucking economy. Hell, I was gonna be pushed up to the head of the line for any available job, however remotely connected with my field. I knew it, and so did every single personnel officer who ever laid eyes on me." He leaned forward. "But the goddamn jobs *weren't out there*. You know where they were?" He swept his hand west. "Asia. The jobs all went to Asia.

And there wasn't jack-squat for a high-level programmer to do over here on this side of the Pacific, no matter what color you were."

Ace's face was drawn and serious in the fluorescent light of the diner. "So when TransCentury opened up, when they got the contract to do Ragnarok, you can believe that this young country boy was a very, very happy man." He paused. "Shit, anybody'd told me I'd be working for a defense contractor, I'da said the man was loopy. But here I am, and I'm glad to have this job."

He looked at Matt. "And not just because it's a steady paycheck. It actually means something to me." Excitement crept into his voice. "See, what we're doing at TransCentury is the breakthrough of the century. Ragnarok is just the beginning—if we can really produce a compact AI package that operates on its own, why, hell, we can sell the technology to everybody in the world. The way we did Model T's and Boeings."

Ace leaned back in his seat. "If we can get Ragnarok going, think what it'll mean to the economy. We'll be selling the things as fast as we can make 'em. And there's not gonna be any discount sales either; if they work, every damn country in the world will want hundreds of 'em. And along with the missile we get to sell 'em the support systems, the radar arrays, the backups, hell, everything right down to the spare tires on the flatbed haulers. This is gonna be bigger than Boeing ever was.

"And that's only the beginning," he continued. "Because Ragnarok isn't just a damned fine machine

—it's an idea—a symbol. A symbol of what this country can do." He broke off and chuckled, shaking his head. "Shit, listen to me—talking like I was some kinda goddamned patriot or something. It's money and power, sure, but it's something more, man."

"What?"

Ace's expression was almost luminous. "It's *discovery,* man. Almost like the time they went to the moon."

Matt was quiet for a moment. "Okay," he said at last. "Now I know why a former radical does defense work. Tell me about Marty; about how you helped her."

"Marty." Ace sighed. "Well, after college we kinda lost track for a while, but there's a bunch of us who kinda keep up, cards at Christmas, that sort of shit. We had a college reunion couple of months ago, back on campus. I didn't go, but somebody told Marty I was working down here, and a couple of weeks ago she got in touch. Once she found out where I worked, she started asking a lot of questions about the test." He paused. "So I sorta helped her out."

"Helped her out how?"

Ace Emerson raised his hands, almost a defensive maneuver. "Hey, don't get the wrong idea, okay? I feel bad enough about what happened; I mean, if I hadn't told her where to get into the test range, she'd —well, she'd probably still be alive." His eyes looked at Matt, imploring. "I mean, wouldn't she?"

Matt laid his hand on the man's forearm. "Stop blaming yourself. You and I both know, Marty was the kind of woman who could take care of herself. What happened to her wasn't your fault—she's dead because somebody murdered her."

Ace's eyes narrowed. "Yeah, but who? That's what's so weird about all this shit. Anyway, I told her a little bit about where the test-site border comes close to one of the old prospecting roads. She and I talked about it, she figured that with a backpack and enough water, she could get in there and hide during the day. Hard to imagine they got any real surveillance out there; they probably figure people aren't gonna walk the ten miles in, and anyway, even if they do, they won't necessarily know where the test site is. The desert's a hell of a big place, and it's not that friendly." He shrugged. "So I gave her the map location of the site, and one more thing."

"What was that?"

"The date of the test."

Matt nodded. "Did you see her the other day, before she went in?"

"Not for long. She was in a hurry, so I met her for lunch and we talked. I sketched out the road on the back of a napkin, told her a little about the lay of the land, and that was it." He sighed. "Jesus, if I'd known I'd never see her again . . ." He shook his head. "I was expecting her to call, y'know, but I never heard a goddamn thing. I only heard about the funeral 'cause I got a police scanner in the car." He looked at Matt. "And now she's dead. Why?"

"She saw something," Matt said slowly. "Something up in the desert." He lowered his voice. "She took a videocam in with her. She called me last night, said she'd got the test on tape."

Ace's eyebrows went up. "Where's the tape, then?"

"Good question. Simmons gave me her bag, but there was no camera in it. No tapes, nothing. She had a sleeping bag and a backpack, too, but they weren't in the car with her, either, according to the sheriff."

"So what are you going to do now?"

Matt finished his coffee. "Go back to Washington in the morning. Think a little bit, try and piece things together."

"You let me know when you come to some conclusions, you hear?"

Matt nodded. "Give me a number where I can get you."

Ace wrote on the back of a napkin. "Here's my number at home." He wrote a second number. "Also got a phone in the car." He grinned. "Don't call me there unless you really have to. The fuckers charge for incoming calls."

Matt stood up. "I'll get in touch if I come up with anything. In the meantime," he added, "I wouldn't talk about this with anyone else."

"No fear, man. But, McAllister—"

"What?"

"What the *hell* is going on with this?"

"It's a bodywash," Matt said quietly.

"A what?"

"A bodywash. When somebody turns up where they're not supposed to be, doing what they're not supposed to be doing, they sometimes get killed. But then you have to take the body away from the site of death and fix up an accident of some kind, to make it all seem normal."

Ace watched him carefully. "Bodywash, huh? That's an interesting term. Wonder where you picked that one up."

Matt moved toward the door. "Just be careful, that's all. Somebody killed Marty, and they could kill you too. Or me." He gave a thin smile. "So let's all be on our best behavior."

Together they walked out to Ace's car. The desert night had turned chilly and bleak. Ace put a hand on Matt's arm. "Listen, man . . ."

Matt turned. "What is it?"

"You be careful too. I got a bad feeling about this whole thing, you know? So you be sure to give me a ring when you find something out, hear?"

Matt nodded. "I'll let you know. But when I call, I won't give you my name. I'll just say I'm the Handyman." He caught Ace staring at him. "It used to be my nickname," Matt explained. "A long time ago."

Ace frowned. " 'Handyman'? Don't make sense. Why'd they call you the Handyman, anyway?"

"No reason," said Matt. "It was just a name. No reason at all."

10

The Miata's tires squealed as Matt spun the tiny car into the parking lot behind the Jefferson Institute, braking hard to avoid slamming into the brick wall of the rear of the building. He'd spent an uncomfortable, sleepless night in a third-rate motel outside of San Bernardino, listening to semis roaring by along Route 15 on their way down through the pass from Victorville to Cajon. In the morning he'd overslept, and pushed the speed limit all the way to LAX airport, only to find that a wildcat strike by baggage handlers had grounded most flights.

Including his own. He joined the throng of angry travelers as they milled around the airline desks, waving their tickets in the air, desperate to get out of Los Angeles to almost anywhere. In midafternoon he managed to squeeze aboard a flight to Las Vegas, and from there, hours later, he slowly made his way via several connecting flights back to Washington, only to join the rush-hour traffic around the beltway.

He was almost home before he remembered that he'd left his files at work. Tired and angry, he'd cursed under his breath, and swung right off the Key Bridge onto M Street, heading for Dupont Circle.

A single light burned on the first floor, and as Matt emerged from his office, his arms full of files, he met Teddy Edwards in the hallway.

"Matt, I heard about it last night," Teddy told him. "God, I'm sorry. She was a wonderful person."

"Thanks," he said simply. "What are you doing here at this hour?"

Teddy looked almost guilty. "Working on some of the Ragnarok stuff," he said. "Nigel's as nervous as a pregnant fox in a forest fire. Wants us to try and finish everything by next week at the latest." He paused. "Are you . . ."

"Okay?" Matt tried a smile, found it didn't work, and nodded instead. "More or less. I was planning to work at home for a few days."

"Good idea," said Teddy. "Anything you want me to do for you? Any chapters you want looked at?"

Matt managed a smile this time. The kid was as enthusiastic and eager as a puppy. "Thanks for the offer," he said. "I just need some time on my own." Something occurred to him then. "Didn't you want to borrow the Miata this weekend?"

Teddy looked stricken. "Golly, no, I mean, yeah, I thought—but no, Matt, you've got—"

Matt fished the keys out of his pocket and tossed them to Teddy. "Run me home and she's yours until Monday," he said. He held up his hand to quell further protest. "I'll be at home anyway, so this works out perfectly."

Teddy stared at the keys in his hand. "Gee, you mean it? You sure?"

Matt gave him a full grin this time. "I mean it. Now how about getting me out of here?"

Matt said good-bye to Teddy, reminded him to check the Miata's oil daily, and took the back stairs to his town house two at a time. A quick shower to wash away the long day's accumulations, and then it would be time to think about dinner. Peanut butter sandwiches would do for tonight, he decided. He intended to do nothing more demanding than watch television and think about the events of the past two days.

Yanking open the screen door he heard a muffled thump, and looked down to see the familiar red, white, and blue of a priority-mail envelope. Someone had delivered it while he'd been away. He turned it over, peering at his name, scrawled in a looping, familiar hand.

He opened the package. It was a videotape, with a taped note in Marty's untidy scrawl. _The local 7-Eleven had a video business on the side, so I got a dupe made and paid the mechanic at the garage twenty bucks to send it priority mail. Just to be on the safe side._

Marty's tape. The one she'd shot at the test site.

She'd mailed it before she died. "Jesus," he whispered, turning the tape cassette over in his hands, weighing it carefully, as if some of her own spirit might still be alive inside.

He unlocked the door and slipped inside. He grabbed a can of Heineken from the fridge, popped the top, and carried it and the tape into the living room. He snapped on his VCR, pushed the tape into the machine, and hit the play button.

The screen showed nothing but white static for almost a minute, then blackness. "Hey, babe, let's see if this mother works, okay?" Marty's disembodied voice boomed out eerily from the speakers, startling him, and Matt shot forward to turn down the volume. Now he could hear her humming tunelessly, random bumps and scrapes as she did something to the microphone.

Blank again, and then, suddenly, there she was, smiling into the camera. She nodded, and gave him a wink. "Think we got it set up now. That goddamn tripod was a pain in the ass to haul all the way out here, but I wanted to make sure y'all saw *me* as well as the rocket."

Matt sat stock-still, watching her image on the small screen. Suddenly he felt wetness on his hand, and looked down to find that he had crushed the can of beer, sending the foaming liquid dripping onto the carpet. He threw the beer aside and hitched his chair closer to the television.

She paused, transforming herself into a reporter. "This is Martha Larsen, reporting from somewhere north of Barstow, California." Her voice had changed completely now, modulated into the clipped, professional accents of television journalism. "I'm standing here on a hill overlooking the place where, later today, the first test of TransCentury System's supersecret missile, Ragnarok, will be conducted. What you are about to see are the very first pictures—ever—of one of the most sophisticated weapons in military history."

She stopped, and then raised the mike again. "There. That oughta get 'em up off their asses, don't you think?" Her old, bantering voice was back now. "We're gonna do a voice-over when this airs, so I'm just gonna run my mouth a little now. Wish you were here, Matt; this desert's a real trip. Hot as hell, but interesting too. I got into L.A. yesterday morning, rented a car, and was up into the high country by the time the sun went down last night. Spent most of the night hiking in here—full moon helped a lot—and it's about nine in the morning right now. Hot as buggery out here, babe; I feel like I'm a clay pot in a big kiln."

A second of darkness, and now the picture came back again, Marty nowhere in sight. Instead, the camera surveyed a desert landscape of earth hues and harsh, glaring reflections, the lens moving slowly over gullies and washes, flat areas of salt glittering in the sunlight. Distant mountains loomed purple-black against the horizon, dwarfing the low building huddled on the flats below.

"This is the desert test site, so secret that it has no name." Marty's voice was that of the professional anchorwoman once again, smooth and authoritative. "What you are seeing here is a temporary installation, which has no other purpose than to conduct a real-world test of Ragnarok. According to sources at TransCentury, Ragnarok will be fired at a cluster of target balloons towed behind a drone aircraft. Its task is to destroy them all, one after the other."

The camera panned back across the barren land. "Nothin' out here but a whole lotta nothin', more of it than I've ever seen before." Sotto voce now. "Even Iraq had more character than this place. It's enough to give you the creeps, almost." She paused, and the camera stopped its pan and held steady. "Okay, that's enough until later. We'll get some more footage once people start showing up. Stay tuned, babe."

The screen went blank for a few seconds, and then blossomed with light once again. This time several hours had obviously passed; the shadows looked different now, the light more intense.

"Show time, babe." Marty's voice was tinged with excitement. "Just about noon, and here comes the main attraction." The camera, steady on its tripod, zoomed in slowly on two vehicles approaching the site from the south. First came a jeep with two men inside, followed by a long and ungainly-looking flatbed trailer, carrying two more men in the high cab. Canvas tarpaulins covered the trailer's load.

As Matt watched, the men hopped out of the jeep and began to pull the tarps from the trailer. Marty's low whistle came through the speakers as the gleaming needle-nose of the rocket was exposed. Matt edged forward on his seat.

The camera tilted back, framing Ragnarok in the center of a wide-angle shot. Now the tarps came fully off as the launching ramp inched upward, thrusting the missile toward the sun. "When this baby takes off, I'm gonna have trouble tracking it, so here's a slow zoom in"—the missile got slowly larger on the screen as the videocam's lens shifted—"and then y'all can see what this thing looks like. Nasty sucker, don't you think?"

Thin, long, and deadly, Ragnarok looked brutally efficient, matte black except for its nose cone, gleaming bright silver in the harsh desert light. The camera tracked slowly up and down the pencil-thin fuselage, as if probing for weaknesses.

Instinctively, Matt found himself mentally measuring the weapon, calculating dimensions and weights. Ragnarok, he estimated, measured about ten meters long and a meter wide, with short, thick fins, sharply tapered back for minimum wind resistance. No numbers, insignia, or other markings appeared anywhere on the missile.

Well, he thought, we wanted a photo, and now we've got one. An hour or so with the computer and a shelf of reference books, and we ought to be able to work out some rough figures on payload, boost, and burn time.

"Here we go, folks." Marty's voice came again, low and full of suppressed excitement. The camera pulled back wide, showing the vehicles moving away behind the blast deflector. Matt's heart began to pick up the beat as the ground crew headed for the low cinder-block building.

"I think they're gonna light it off pretty soon now. Oh, yeah, there go the flares—see 'em?" The camera tilted upward, revealing three flares in the high distance, red, white, and blue against the pale desert sky.

"That means the drone is on its way." A loud siren split the air, and the camera angle suddenly jumped back to full wide.

"Here we go," said Marty's voice. "I think something's gonna—" Her words vanished in a massive roar and a flash of light as Ragnarok streaked from its launch pad and hurled itself into the sky.

"Goddamn," he heard her muttering as the camera tried to keep the streaking missile in sight. "Look at that mother."

Although caught unawares, she was doing a good job of keeping up, Matt thought. The missile, shrunk to the size of a ballpoint pen now, still headed nearly straight up. Now, as Matt watched, it began to turn, flattening out slowly.

"It's tracking," Marty said on the soundtrack. "Looking for the drone." A bright orange flash seared on the screen, throwing the automatic exposure off. "There—can you see that? It got one."

A pause. "Now—it looks as if it's coming back, damn, will you look at that, the thing *is* smart, it's actually hunting the drone. Here we go"—another flash—"look at that sucker go!" The camera followed the arcing course of the missile as it dived toward the ground, pulled up, and went into a high, wide loop, before finally heading back toward the third and final target balloon.

Another flash, and then the sky was clear. "That took less than a minute," said Marty's voice on the tape. "Don't know how long the fuel lasts, but it's still going strong. In fact—it's—shit, it's coming back this way. Jesus, what's happening now?"

Matt leaned forward. The missile, now flying almost parallel with the ground, had turned 180 degrees, heading back toward the test site. The camera tracked it all the way.

"I don't know—holy shit, it's gonna hit, it's gonna—" Her words were engulfed by the roar of a rocket motor. As Matt watched, Ragnarok, moving terrifyingly fast, plowed into the bunker, *straight through the observation window*, and exploded with a roar.

Matt shot from his seat. Hands shaking, he stopped the tape. He pushed the button for rewind, and then ran it again in slow motion, frame by frame.

It was all there on the screen. The missile entering the hardened-glass viewing window, shards of glass flying back from the impact. Then it was all the way in, out of sight, a split second before the flash and boom, a wave of light and dust wiping out everything on the screen for a moment, and then, when the noise stopped, the dust and sand settling back to reveal—

Nothing. A few scraps of masonry and wire, a small cloud of shrapnel and debris settling slowly back to earth now, but no trace of the building or its occupants.

The camera continued to film, soaking up the silence. Below, nothing moved. Matt sat rooted to his chair, his pulse pounding in his ears. Finally, Marty's voice. "Ah—I, ah, hope the camera caught all that,"

Marty said at last. "I—Jesus *Christ*!" Her voice broke. "Dead! They must all be dead! Never had a chance. Never had time to react, nothing! Oh, my God, what happened? Oh, sweet Jesus, I don't believe this."

There was the sound of scratching and shuffling, and then Marty's face appeared in the lens, her eyes puffed and red, her cheeks streaked with tears. "This is, ah, Martha Larsen, reporting from somewhere in the desert north of Barstow, California. What you just, ah, witnessed, is—well, I don't know *what* it is. A disaster and a tragedy. The film speaks for itself. This was supposed to be a test of the new secret Ragnarok missile system, designed to provide, ah, a foolproof and, ah, highly sophisticated defense against medium-range ballistic missiles. But—oh, my God"—she wiped at her eyes, trying to pull herself together—"as you just saw, something—God alone knows what—something just went terribly wrong, and now—those—people"—she broke off again, fighting to keep control—"those people down there are dead."

Matt saw her straighten, purse her lips, and take a breath, fighting to get herself under control. "The question now is *why*? Ragnarok was supposed to be the most sophisticated weapon in the world, practically able to think for itself. It's taken five years and many billions of dollars to develop, and this was its first big test."

She paused. "The result is a total failure of the system, loss of life, and a major setback for Trans-Century Systems, the prime contractor for Ragnarok's guidance system, the superbrain that the Pentagon has nicknamed Odin. Below me in the desert just now, Ragnarok literally ran amok, plowing into its own control center with almost uncanny accuracy."

Another pause. "Lots of questions are going to be asked in the weeks to come. Unfortunately"—a beat here—"some of the people best equipped, perhaps, to answer them have just had their lives snuffed out by the very intelligence that they themselves created. A hideous modern version of the Frankenstein story? Maybe. All that is certain at this point is that Ragnarok, far from being an effective defense weapon, has proved a disaster."

A pause, and then her chin came up, her eyes flashing with the old spirit. "This is Martha Larsen, reporting from California."

He stopped the tape then, freezing her image on the screen, staring at her face. Marty, his late-night companion, the warm, sexy woman he'd known for nearly eight years, through good times and bad. Marty, his best friend. Marty, his lover.

Marty, dead and buried now in a dusty desert town in California.

He hit the button, and her face came alive again. "Well, I guess I got a story, all right. Shit, babe, what the hell just happened here, do you know? I'm sure gonna be glad to get back to you."

She smiled then, the wry Marty smile that had always tugged at his heart, and which he now found almost unbearable. She blew him a kiss. "See you soon, lover."

The screen went light with snow and static. Matt

McAllister sat still as the tape wound on blindly, tears filling his eyes and spilling over, running down his cheeks.

After a while he got up, snapped off the VCR, and popped the tape out of the machine. Almost dark now, in the street outside the lamps had just come on, casting soft cones of light. In the gloom of his study he held the small videocassette, tapping it reflectively against his chin as he thought.

This is what she saw that got her killed, he thought. No wonder she sounded strange on the telephone. The Ragnarok test ended in flames and death, and no one knows about it. But she taped it, and somehow they found out about it. And murdered her.

Who, he thought, are "they"? People connected with TransCentury Systems? The Pentagon? Or some other group, driven by motives he couldn't even guess at?

Time to find out. He picked up the telephone, dialed Buttons's number, let it ring ten times, and finally hung up. He's out on his bloody boat again, he thought.

He dialed the number of the Jefferson Institute and got the precise, sugary accents of the voice-mail system. *Damn.* He waited patiently until the beep sounded, and then he punched in Buttons's office. "This is Matt, Buttons. I just got back from Marty's funeral, and I've got a videotape she made just before she died. I'm going to be, ah, out of the office for a couple of days. I'll call you when I get back; I really think you ought to look at this tape."

He cut the connection and stood in the near darkness for several minutes, thinking. Then he took the folded paper napkin from his pocket, looked at it, and dialed again.

"Ace? This is the Handyman."

11

"**G**oddamn." Ace Emerson's voice was low and hoarse. "I mean, *goddamn*." He turned away from the screen, his eyes bright with tears.

Matt leaned forward and snapped off the VCR. His watch read midnight, but he felt like he'd been awake for a week. Coast-to-coast twice in twenty-four hours was pushing it a little bit too much, he decided. His stomach was sour from too much bad airline coffee, and his nerves were like exposed wires.

He moved to the window and looked out. Cars purred quietly down the street of the Los Angeles suburb, the hissing of their tires drifting in through the screen. Ace Emerson sat very still on the sofa, staring at the blank TV screen where just seconds before, Marty Larsen's image had reported the Ragnarok disaster.

Matt said, "There it is. That's why she was killed. She saw what really happened."

"Yeah." Ace kicked at a pile of newspapers on the floor beside the sofa. His voice was heavy with sarcasm.

"TransCentury's stock is *still* goin' up. Shit."

Ace looked up. "What are you going to do with the tape?"

Matt popped it out of the machine and stuck it in the pocket of his windbreaker. "I don't know yet," he said. "But until I know, I'm not letting it out of my sight." He stretched. "I could use a drink. You know any places?"

Twenty minutes later they pulled up in front of Ace's local. The sign displayed a crude drawing of a pink flamingo and the words BEER-POOL-MUSIC. "Not much to look at," Ace said, "but they got their priorities set out right up there on the sign. Food's good and the regulars are relatively normal. Not like some of the ravers and night creatures you get other places around here."

Matt paused in the doorway, glancing around at the late-night crowd, looking for anything different, anything out of place. Am I being paranoid? he asked himself as he walked slowly toward the bar. He shook his head in the dim light, keeping his eyes moving across the barroom. Remember the spy's motto, he reminded himself: Just because you're paranoid doesn't mean they're not out to get you anyway. It was a long shot to think that whoever'd killed Marty might have also put a tap on Ace's phone, but it was possible.

And since whoever had killed Marty would be very interested in what Matt knew, it paid to be alert.

They reached the bar and rested their elbows on the polished countertop. The barmaid, her back to them, was busy with a knot of customers at the far end.

"Man, I don't *believe* this shit," Ace said quietly, staring straight ahead of him into the smoky mirror.

Matt glanced over at him. "What don't you believe?" he asked. "You saw it, just like I did. Ragnarok launched successfully, and then it turned around and blew up its own control bunker." He paused. "Along with everybody inside it."

"Jesus. But nobody *knows* about this?"

"Marty knew," Matt said quietly. "And I know. And now you know."

Ace nodded. "Uh-huh. Marty knew, and she got killed."

"You catch on quick."

Ace's face was somber in the half-light. "You know, it all starts to make sense now. Yeah, that could be it."

"What are you talking about?"

Ace shot him a glance. "What happened at work, man. I remember it real well, 'cause they gave everybody the day off after they announced that the test firing had been successful. We were all down in the Pit—that's where we do the programming—and it came on over the intercom. Somebody let out one of those rebel yells—" He broke off. "Did you know that California's got more rednecks than Alabama, in terms of sheer numbers?" He nodded. "It's a fact. After Nashville and Memphis, Bakersfield's the biggest country-and-western center in the country. Parking lot at TransCentury's full of those fuckin' pickups with stars 'n' bars on 'em. Goddamn, but those guys irritate me."

He grimaced. "Lot of 'em don't like folks like me much, either, so I guess we're about even. Where the hell was I? Oh, yeah. They announced about the test, and then they said that we could all go home, come on back on Thursday." He looked at Matt. "Shit, man, nobody thought twice about it—I mean, everybody was heading for the beach or the bar."

"Did you know any of the guys that were in the crew?"

"You mean the guys who carried out the test?" He shook his head. "Naw; just to look at. You gotta have top-secret clearance to do that shit, and anyway, it's not my line of work. Those guys are more like aerospace engineers, stuff like that." He paused, glancing down the bar. "There is one guy, though, come to think of it—"

"What?"

"Uh-oh. Here she comes now." Ace raised his head, indicating an attractive brunette behind the bar who was heading toward them.

"Ace."

"Jeanette, how you doing?"

"I've been better. I'm looking for Stoner. You seen that cocksucker"—she glanced at Matt—"sorry, mister. I got to watch my language sometimes, I guess." She turned back to Ace. "So. You seen that fuckwit around?"

Ace shook his head. "Not since last week, Jeanette. Sorry."

"Yeah, well, you see him, you can tell him to sit on it for me." She looked up and down the bar, her pretty features distorted with anger. "Jesus, men are shitbirds," she muttered, turning and heading back down the bar.

Matt watched her go, her buttocks twitching angrily under her tight slacks. "What was that all about?"

Ace sighed. "Stoner's one of the crew out at the site. *Was* one of the crew. He drinks in here a lot. We don't really know each other, just to say hi. Don't ever get together or anything like that. Reason I mention it, Stoner's humping Jeanette, the barmaid you just got a blast of. He's in here most every night after work, suckin' up the drafts, working on her."

He shook his head. "She's a real fox too—don't blame the man one bit. So last night I expected to see him in here; shit, I was all set to buy the guy a drink, y'know? Figured he'd want to tell Jeanette all about it. I got in here about nine, ordered a draft, looked around. No Stoner. Jeanette's all dolled up, hair done, nice dress on, makeup I ain't seen before, and she's sittin' there like somebody just pissed all over her picnic. So I go over. 'Where's Stoner?' I ask. She gives me a look coulda driven nails. 'Ain't comin' in,' she says. Oho, I think, the bastard stood her up. 'What'd he do, call and cancel?' I ask. '*He* didn't call at all,' she tells me. 'The goddamn company called. Stoner's gonna be out in the desert awhile longer, they say. Special fucking assignment.' That's the way she says it too—special *fucking* assignment, like he had another kind of fucking assignment back at home that he forgot about."

"She said Stoner didn't call? Just somebody from TransCentury?"

"That's right. And nobody's seen Stoner since." He raised his shoulders in a shrug. "Jeanette and Stoner had a date, see, to go out and celebrate after the test. So she's still waiting. Probably figures he went on up to Vegas with some other woman."

"She'll wait a long time," Matt said dryly. "If Stoner was in that bunker, he's dead. Along with everybody else in there with him."

"Sounds like it." He turned to face Matt. "This makes Watergate or Iran-Contra look like little white lies, doesn't it? Marty got proof that a multibillion-dollar weapons system wasn't worth shit, and once somebody found out what she knew, they killed her. Have I got it right so far?"

Matt nodded. "All her camera equipment, film, everything—all gone. They cleaned her out, and when they were through, they killed her. Or they killed her first, and then went through the car. I hope it was the second."

"The second? Why?"

"Two reasons," said Matt. "First, if they ran her off the road first, then she probably died pretty quickly. And they probably didn't torture her."

"And the second reason?"

"If they didn't torture her," Matt said, "then they might not suspect that there's a duplicate tape."

Ace's eyes went wide. "Oh, shit, I see what you mean."

"But if they dig a little," Matt continued, "they'll find out about the duplicate. She told me she had it done at some desert 7-Eleven where they rent videotapes. Think about it. There's a lot of desert out there, but not many places selling tapes. If they start asking, someone's sure as hell going to remember a good-looking black woman who wanted a tape copied. And somebody in the post office is going to remember sending a priority packet. And they'll have the address it went to."

Ace nodded. "Yeah. But just one question."

"What is it?"

"You keep talkin' about 'them.' Who's 'them'?"

"That's what I hope you're going to be able to tell me." He looked at Ace. "I want you to tell me all about TransCentury. Who runs it, what they do, how they do it."

Ace sighed. "Let's sit down, man." He signaled the barmaid, peeled off a bill, and pushed it across the bar. "Jeanette, gimme a pitcher of Bud down here, willya?"

They moved to a corner table out of earshot of the other customers. "What can I tell you?" said Ace as he poured the beer. "The corporate image is great: fast-moving up-and-comer, aggressive, innovative, high-risk/high-gain, all that bullshit you read about in *Forbes* and *Business Week*. But the reality's a little different nowadays."

He sipped beer and swilled it around in his mouth before continuing. "See, before all this Ragnarok business started, TC—that's what we call TransCentury—was basically a software firm. They didn't do a whole lot of defense work. But back in the eighties they started to get involved in the Star Wars game. They did some of the subsystems for SDI under contract to Martin Marietta, General Dynamics, couple others. They got hungry then; decided to play with the big kids. So they went out and got hold of some movers and shakers—not technicians, but money boys. Rollie Chalmers was one of 'em. He joined the team, and that's when I guess you could say the corporate culture changed. Up till then we'd been a pretty small outfit—everybody knew each other, we all more or less agreed on what we were doing. Now we were three times as big all of a sudden, and the whole thrust of things seemed different. Basically, TC said to hell with the private market—they were going for the really big stuff, for the government contracts, where you could skim off the top and spend it on whatever."

He shook his head. "I ain't gonna bother telling you how that goddamn company's been managed lately, but it's a miracle that we got Odin put together on time. Too many parties, too many perks, too many salary raises for the big guys, not enough money for mainframe time and new equipment, that kinda thing."

He took a long drink of beer. "Software development is high risk, high gain; a great business for people who're smart. Gates made Microsoft into one of the most successful companies in the world, and three quarters of all the computers in the world still use his programs. Steve Chen worked on his own and developed the next generation of supercomputers. And TC moved from a basement mail-order firm to one of the best R-and-D outfits in the business." He paused. "So Chalmers got us the Ragnarok contract and a year or so later, using the research data out of Carnegie Mellon, we had Odin's system architecture all worked out. And then things got all fucked up."

"How?"

Ace looked over the top of his beer glass. "We ran out of money. It's an old story, I guess. There'd been rumors for about a year that TC's credit was going bad, way overextended, all that shit. We got the Ragnarok contract, all right, but we fell behind on the deliverables. I mean, *way* behind. The Pentagon let TC run out the string for a while, but eventually they wanted results."

He poured more beer. "Bad management. You get a whole team of guys on a project like this, *nobody* understands the whole thing. Anyway, we had what was politely referred to as a 'fiscal readjustment' about a year ago, when they got everybody together down in the gym and told 'em nobody'd be gettin' paid that week. That went on for about a month, and then in comes Rollie Chalmers, grinning like a possum eating shit out of a wire brush, and announces that the money's started flowing again. Since then things have been okay. Real good, in fact."

"And Chalmers turned it around?"

"Far as I can tell, yeah."

"Tell me about him."

"Chalmers? He's okay, I guess. Bit of an asshole at times, but I never saw a boss that wasn't. He's not a computer engineer, he's a 'packager'—that's what he calls himself, at any rate. He's really just a kind of lobbyist—spends a lot of time in Washington, sucking around the Pentagon and Congress and all that shit. He's overseas a lot too—travels around trying to market TC in other countries."

"The money Chalmers brought in—where'd it come from?"

Ace shrugged. "Who knows? It's there, and that's about all anybody cares about in this business. The defense industry lives from one contract to the next, you know that. Kinda like street whores—nobody looks too hard at who's coming down the sidewalk." He paused. "Right after he bailed us out, Chalmers started making staff changes. Transferred some people off the project and brought in the two new guys, part of some bullshit exchange program we got into with the Japanese. Kanji Nakamura came on board as a visiting researcher, but he's hardly ever there as far as I can see. Comes in a lot in the evening, according to one of the security guys I know. Him and the Dragon, that goddam goon of his."

"The Dragon?"

"That's what I call him. I don't know his real name. He's supposed to be Kanji's research assistant, but all he does is just hang around, never more than ten feet away from Kanji. Almost like a bodyguard." He paused. "If he's a research assistant, I'm the fuckin' pope."

"Why do you call him the Dragon?"

"The man wears thin black leather gloves, all the time. One day I came into to the washroom, saw him at the basin with his gloves off. On the back of his left hand he's got this really strange tattoo, kind of like a Chinese or Japanese character." He dropped his voice. "He caught me looking at it, gave me a smile that practically turned me white. Man, I got the fuck out of there as fast as I could."

Ace took another sip of his beer. "Couple days later I'm sitting in the bar talking to Jeanette, and Steve Hattori comes in. He's a programmer works for the city, we went to school together, have a few beers from time to time. I never thought about whether he knew Japanese or not, so that night I asked him. 'Sure,' he says. 'I'm a nisei; I was born here, but Mom and Dad made sure we all spoke Japanese. Read and write it too. Why?' So I told him about what I'd seen. He made me draw the tattoo. And then he told me what it meant."

"And?"

"It's the character for *dragon*."

"But why would he have it tattooed on his hand?"

Ace shook his head. "Beats the shit outa me," he said. "But there's one more thing. When he had his gloves off, I saw something else too. The fucker's got both his little fingers chopped off. Right at the second knuckle, both of 'em." He looked at Matt. "And I know what *that* means, because Steve told me. The guy's a *yakuza*—a gangster. That's what they do to 'em if they mess something up. Fingers, ears, shit like that."

"Chalmers has got a *yakuza* working for him? That doesn't make sense."

"None of it makes sense to me, man. The Dragon's one scary motherfucker, I can tell you. He speaks English pretty well, but most of the time he doesn't say a damned thing—just stands there with those goddamned dark glasses on and that fuck-you smile on his face."

Matt thought for a moment. "You know where this guy lives?"

Ace shook his head. "Got no idea. But if you're planning on paying the Dragon a visit, I'd think twice if I were you. You mess with him, McAllister, you'll be needing a new asshole in a hurry."

"It can wait. What about Rollie Chalmers?"

Ace shook his head. "Chalmers won't tell you shit, man. Why should he?"

"Because I've got something he wants; Marty's videotape. If that doesn't open his mouth, nothing will."

"You be careful. Remember what happened to Marty."

"Just give me Chalmers's address and phone number."

Ace scrawled on a scrap of paper. "Chalmers lives up off Topanga Canyon, up in one of those high-rent ravines. Don't know his home number; ne er had call to talk to the man. But this is the main r ber at TC—you call there after about ten, h there."

Matt folded the paper and put it in his pocket. He stood up. "Thanks for the beer and the company," he said. "Almost midnight—time I was in bed."

Ace fixed him with a suspicious eye. "What are you planning to do?"

Matt flashed him a quick smile. "Not sure yet. But I'd suggest you forget you ever saw me tonight."

"You think this is gonna go bad?"

Matt shrugged. "If a tree falls in the forest and nobody hears it, does it make a noise?"

"Say again?"

"That test out in the desert—how many people know it was a failure?"

Ace nodded slowly. "Yeah, I see what you mean. Marty knew, and *she*'s dead. You know and I know, and—" he stopped.

"—we're still alive," Matt finished for him. "So far. I don't know about you, but I intend to stay that way."

12

Matt toweled himself off in the tiny motel bathroom, thinking about his next move. He looked at himself in the mirror, recognizing something in his expression that he hadn't seen in quite some time. Hello, Handyman, he thought. How's it feel to be back at work after so long?

He combed his wet hair back, remembering how it had been in the old days. You want something fixed, call the Handyman. Odd jobs, the odder the better. He'd spent years, he thought, rummaging through the back alleys of the Third World, turning over rocks and poking into holes, to see what might turn up. Sometimes he got results, sometimes he suffered the consequences. Now he was about to do a little more poking and prodding, just to see what happened. First Rollie Chalmers. Then the Dragon.

He picked up the bottle of after-shave and splashed some on, wincing at the sting of the volatile liquid against his fresh-shaven skin. Damned stuff must be almost pure alcohol, he thought.

He slipped into his clothes and checked his watch. Almost noon. Time to go to work.

His first call was to the Jefferson Institute.

Teddy answered the phone. "Hi, Matt. Where are you? Nigel's been having a cow, man. He thought you'd be at the meeting this morning. Had me call your house, but you weren't in."

"Something's come up," said Matt. "Put him on, and I'll explain it all to him."

"Sorry. He's out of the office now. He'll be back this afternoon, but I don't know when. Want to talk to Buttons?"

"Sure. Can you transfer me?"

"I'll try." There was ringing on the line, and then Teddy was back. "He's not in his office either," he said. "Want me to give him a message?"

"Just let him know where I am, okay?" Matt told him the telephone number and address of the motel.

"Wow," said Teddy. "What are you doing in L.A.?"

"Tell you later," said Matt. "Just make sure he gets the message, okay? I'll be back in a day or so. There's no need for him to call unless he wants to."

His second call was to Yuki. After a few minutes

of switchboard-hopping Matt heard her voice. "Hello?"

"Yuki, it's Matt."

"Matt! I was hoping to see you. Where are you?"

"California. Some business that came up. I ah, may not be back in Washington right away. How are you?"

"Better. The doctors say I can go home soon."

"Go home?"

"To Japan, of course. My university is arranging a ticket now. Will I see you before I go?"

Matt hesitated. "I'm not sure," he said at last. "I'll have to call you again as soon as I know what my plans are."

"Of course." He could hear the disappointment in her voice.

"Maybe we can go out for a *real* Japanese meal," he added.

"Yes, Matt. I'd like that." Her voice softened. "Call me. Please."

When he had hung up, Matt took out the scrap of paper Ace had given him the night before and dialed Chalmers's number. As it rang, he rubbed the last vestiges of sleep from his eyes with his free hand.

"TransCentury Systems, how can I help you?" The woman's voice sounded professionally groomed, a hint of promise under layers of hand-rubbed competence.

"Roland Chalmers, please," Matt said.

"Mr. Chalmers is in conference right now, I'm

afraid." The voice sounded *very* sympathetic. "May I take a message?"

"Yes," Matt said. "And give it to him right away, even if you have to interrupt him. It's important to him."

"And what exactly is the message?" The voice sounded doubtful.

"Tell him it's Martha Larsen's lawyer, and I've got a videotape I'd like to show him."

"Excuse me?" A tinge of alarm.

"Martha Larsen's lawyer wants to talk to him. About a videotape. Got that?"

"And will he know what this is in relation to, Mr., ah—"

"He'll know exactly what it's about," Matt said. "Tell him I'll call him back in exactly twenty minutes." He hung up. Time to test the water, he thought.

He lay back on the bed, thinking of Marty, remembering how her skin felt, how her hair smelled. Outside, traffic roared by on the freeway, barely audible. He closed his eyes.

TransCentury's line rang twice. "This is Roland Chalmers. With whom am I speaking, please?"

"Wanted to have a talk." Matt kept his voice light and pleasant.

"Who is this?" Chalmers's voice was sharp, that of a no-nonsense businessman whose time was measured in hundred-dollar bills.

"A friend of Marty Larsen, Mr. Chalmers. Remember her?"

"Who?"

"Martha Larsen. The woman who was killed in a car crash a few days ago. Out by your test site. Remember that?"

"I heard about it," Chalmers said crisply. "Could we get to the point, please? I'm in a meeting."

"Here it is, Mr. Chalmers," he said. "Marty Larsen had a videotape with her when she died. It didn't seem to be among her effects when the sheriff's office found her. You know anything about that?"

The silence at the other end of the line was almost palpable. After a long moment Chalmers said, "I don't know what the hell you're talking about." His voice had dropped a register.

Matt smiled to himself. Bull's-eye. You're lying, you sonofabitch. "I think you do, Mr. Chalmers. And I'll bet you're curious about what was on the tape. You wonder about that at all? Well, I've got some great news for you. There's a copy, and I've got it." He paused. "You ought to see it, Mr. Chalmers. What's on that tape will really open your eyes."

This time the silence lasted even longer. Finally, Chalmers said, "I think you're crazy. I don't know what the hell you're trying to do, but I've wasted enough time." There was a loud click as he hung up.

Matt let his breath out and stretched back out on the bed. The trap was baited. Now came the waiting.

Matt ate a bacon cheeseburger at a fast-food joint several miles down the freeway. From his seat he had an uninterrupted view of the highway. He spent almost half an hour lazily watching an endless ribbon of vehicles, their outlines wavering in the exhaust fumes, crawl toward the horizon and disappear over the edge of the world. It was almost mesmerizing, he decided, like watching endless tons of water cascading slowly over the edge of a falls.

He finished his shake, belched quietly, and considered what to do next. He'd thrown out the bait, and now the man would make a move, something that would bring him into the open. Chalmers would think about things for a while, maybe make a few phone calls. Matt would call back in a couple of hours. The most obvious move for Chalmers would be to try to buy him off. He'd call at four, he decided; stir things up a little more.

And until then? Too soon for an afternoon nap, he thought. Then he remembered the pool out behind the motel. That was it, he thought: an hour or so of laps, to take the edge off lunch and get his system moving again. Matt picked up his keys and headed for his car, pausing to buy a local paper from the machine. Might as well see what's on the tube while I'm at it, he thought.

Matt caught the smell as soon as he swung the motel door open. A rank, animal-like stench, as if someone had brought a caged panther into the room. An odor compounded of sweat, unwashed clothes, and tobacco, it filled the tiny room.

Someone's in here. No sooner had the thought flashed across his mind than he caught movement out of the corner of his eye, a flicker at the very edge of his vision, moving fast.

Matt reacted instantly. Throwing himself forward and down he felt a breeze across the back of his neck as the man standing behind the door brought a length of iron pipe slicing down into the space he had just occupied. He heard a curse and the splintering of wood as the pipe shattered the doorjamb.

Rolling away from the noise Matt scrabbled backward into the room, trying to put as much distance as possible between him and his attacker. He turned over and bounced to his feet, keeping low, his arms out in front of him, as he looked the intruder over.

Male, white, dirty. Well over six feet tall with shoulder-length hair that shone with grease. The man wore a biker's uniform of filthy denims, studded engineer boots, and forearm tattoos. He held a length of lead pipe in one hand, a switchblade knife in the other. Two gold teeth gleamed briefly in a wide mouth opened and spewing curses.

Matt backed away slowly, keeping his breathing steady, scanning the room for possibilities. "Who the hell are you?" he said softly.

"Shut the fuck up, asshole." The man's voice was a rasp over jagged tin. He took a step forward, raised his knife, and pressed the stud. An eight-inch stiletto shot forward with a dry, sharp click. "Where's the fuckin' tape?"

The man's eyes were wild, his muscles tense as steel wire. He's high on something, Matt thought. High and angry.

"Wait a minute, man—"

The biker gave him a maniac's grin, showing his

gold teeth again. "I just told you to shut up, remember? Or do I have to shut you up myself?" He lunged with the knife, missing Matt's arm by a fraction of an inch.

This guy is going to kill me, Matt thought. He backed up another foot, hitting the wall of the bedroom. Solid wall to his right, curtains to his left. Lunging to the side he grabbed the curtains and ripped them from their fixtures, wrapping the heavy fabric around his left arm. With his right hand he picked up a heavy ashtray.

"Gimme the tape, asshole. I ain't gonna ask you again."

Matt kept moving, circling the room, moving foot by foot toward the bathroom. "There's no tape," he said evenly.

"Then it's time to die, fucker." The biker charged like a maddened buffalo, pipe swinging, knife held down low for the kill.

Matt took a heavy blow on the arm, turned to avoid the upward arc of the stiletto, and threw the ashtray with all his might. It caught the biker on the side of the neck, pushing him off balance and causing him to howl with pain.

Before the man could recover, Matt was behind him, searching the room frantically with his eyes, desperate for a weapon, for anything that would even the contest. His eyes passed across the bed, containing nothing more deadly than a book and several magazines, down to the floor and his extra pair of shoes. Nothing heavy, nothing sharp. Jesus.

The big man hit the wall, rebounded like a wrestler off the ring ropes, and came at Matt with surprising speed, his boot-shod foot catching him in the ribs.

Matt bent double, his breath whistling out of him. He hit the floor and rolled sideways just as the pipe crashed down onto the place his head had been. "Where is it, fucker?" the man screamed.

The pipe swung around again, catching Matt a glancing blow on the neck. His arm went limp, pain shooting down into his fingers. His eyes swept the room. Forget a weapon, he told himself. Just get out.

There was only one way to go. Matt chopped blindly with his good arm at the biker's throat, missed, and scuttled backward, into the bathroom. He slammed the door shut and locked it. Then he turned, his heart sinking as he realized that there was no window, no means of escape.

The biker's heavy shoulder slammed against the door frame, splintering the cheap composition board. In another ten seconds he'd be inside the room.

There was nothing sharp in the tiny room, nothing that would serve as a weapon. The biker's boot crashed into the door once, twice, splitting it in half. A hairy hand came through the opening, groping for the door handle.

Matt picked up his bottle of after-shave. Smashing the neck of the glass bottle against the sink, he held the jagged edge out in front of him with one hand, groping with the other hand in his trousers for his Zippo lighter.

The biker stepped into the bathroom, eyes bright with madness, a smile spreading across his face as he caught sight of the glass bottle in Matt's hand. "Cut your fuckin' heart out," he hissed, and started forward.

With a flick of his wrist Matt tossed after-shave in the man's face, causing him to roar with pain as the liquid stung his eyes, momentarily blinding him.

Matt waited for several beats. Then he took two steps forward, extended his arm until it was almost touching the man's chin, and lit his Zippo.

With a roar the volatile vapor ignited, forming a huge fireball. The man staggered backward, a hoarse shout erupting from his lungs. The flames billowed outward, wreathing his face in flame. He dropped his weapons and began to beat the air, screaming, as his hair began to catch fire.

Matt aimed a kick at his hip, spinning him around. Grabbing him by his wide leather belt Matt dragged him backward. He flung open the door and threw the man out onto the parking lot. Outside the motel office an elderly couple stopped and stared at the spectacle of a flaming man spinning like a top among the parked cars, beating at his face and his clothing.

Matt stood in the doorway, breathing hard. The biker was down on his knees now, screaming incoherently, hands swatting at the flames that enveloped his head like a bright halo.

From the end of the parking lot a motor roared into life. Matt looked over to see a late-model limousine with smoked windows heading toward them. As it drew closer, the car slowed to a crawl, the driver's side window purring down. Matt caught a glimpse of a thin, angular face, vaguely Asiatic behind dark glasses, watching the burning man intently.

People were pouring out of the motel office now, shouting and pointing at the man on fire, but Matt kept his eyes on the impassive Asian face as the limo drew up opposite the burning man.

Matt glimpsed the cylindrical shape of an Ingram MAC-10 coming up over the edge of the window, a black-gloved finger tightening on the trigger. The shout building in his throat died stillborn as flame spat from the Ingram. The biker's head exploded like a bloody melon, sending blood and brains across the parking lot.

The killer turned then, his gaze finding Matt and holding him in its sights. Behind the dark glasses he seemed to be thinking. Matt dived behind a parked car, flattening himself. A moment later he heard the limo accelerate out of the lot and into the traffic, its tires squealing as it made the sharp turn.

Matt stared after it, his breath coming in fast, shallow gulps. Gloves, he thought. Black leather gloves and dark glasses.

The Dragon.

Chalmers had reacted faster than he'd anticipated. And much more unpredictably. He'd sent the biker to get the tape, and the Dragon to back him up. And when the biker had failed, he'd been eliminated.

From somewhere far away sirens moved toward him.

"Asian? Asian how? Shit, *I'm* Asian." The CHP investigator was a curly-haired Samoan, broad as a locomotive in his perfectly tailored uniform. Behind his aviator sunglasses he watched Matt closely. "Japanese? Chinese? What?"

Matt shrugged. "I can't really say. He was Asian, and he wore a hat and dark glasses. That's all I saw." Matt paused, looking out the window of the motel office to the parking lot, where other cops were photographing and measuring. The Samoan's partner, a tall Anglo with straw-colored hair and a sunburned face like leather, sat in the patrol car, punching numbers into the computer and watching the screen closely.

"What else can you tell us about the killing? You think he was after you?"

Matt shook his head. "I can't imagine why," he lied. "I never saw either of them before in my life. The Asian guy had a clear shot at me, just after he took the biker down." He paused. "I saw him hesitate, and then he took off."

The cop tapped his pencil against his large white teeth. "So what was going on?"

It's obvious, Matt thought. An execution. That had definitely been the Dragon out there. He killed the biker after he failed to get the tape from me. He couldn't take a chance on letting the man talk. He didn't kill me because I've still got the tape, and that's what they really want. *But how did he know where I was?*

The Samoan's partner came through the door, a two-page printout in his hand. "Take a look at this shit."

The Samoan scanned the sheet slowly. "Well,

things make a little more sense now," he said. He looked up. "The biker's name was Farron Lascelles, from up around San Bernardino. He's a known user who'll do damn near anything for a hit of freebase. Farron's got a nice long sheet, mostly for B and E to support his several bad habits. Was he high when he confronted you?"

Matt nodded. "I think so. He was wound up, that's for sure. And strong as an ox."

The cop nodded. "Probably wired up on dust. He'd have killed you if you hadn't pulled that after-shave move. Nice thinking, by the way." He tapped his pencil on the printout. "It's the other guy I can't figure. Sounds like a gang thing."

"Gang?"

"Yeah. We got gangs of all colors and stripes out here, including some pretty rough Vietnamese and Cambodian organizations that keep their turf very well protected. Your Asian friend might have been in a drug deal with Lascelles that went bad." He shrugged. "A guy like Farron's gonna piss somebody off sooner or later. I'm just surprised it took as long as it did."

The Samoan's partner cleared his throat. "They found the limo two miles down the road, abandoned. Keys still inside, no prints, no shell casings, no ciga-rette butts, zilch."

"So our mysterious Asian is still as mysterious as ever," said the Samoan. He turned to Matt. "Okay, Mr. McAllister, what are your plans now?"

"I should be getting back to Washington," Matt said.

The Samoan nodded. "No problem. We know who you are, where you work. If we need you, we'll be in touch." He uncoiled himself from the motel manager's desk chair. "When were you thinking of heading back East?"

Matt shrugged. "I've got an open ticket. Anytime, really. Tonight, I guess."

The cop nodded. "That's maybe wise. Okay, we'll see to it that you get put on the plane. How's that?"

"I appreciate it," said Matt, trying to inject enthusiasm into his voice. Another damned complication, he thought. But nothing he couldn't handle.

The cop's broad strong hand came out. "You take care, now, Mr. McAllister." They stood at the departure gate, dusk settling down around the airport as passengers got ready to board the red-eye special. Although the big Samoan had reluctantly concluded that whatever had happened in the motel room had nothing to do with Matt McAllister, he'd insisted on driving him to the airport.

Matt smiled, shook hands, and picked up his single bag. "Thanks for bringing me out to the airport."

"Hey, no problem. Better to be safe than sorry, right?"

"Right." Matt kept his voice light and pleasant. He checked his watch. "It's just about that time, I guess."

Matt picked up his small bag and joined the queue for the jetway. A moment later he was inside the ramp, heading down toward the door of the plane. There was a minor logjam at the door of the aircraft, where passengers were being welcomed inside by several of the flight crew.

He slowed and stopped, pretending to search inside his flight bag for something. Behind him another group of passengers approached, clustered around an elderly woman in a wheelchair. The two flight attendants moved forward to help, and as they passed Matt, he moved back against the side of the movable ramp, feeling behind him with his hand for the door handle that led to the outside staircase to the ground.

It opened easily. He held his breath for a moment, expecting an alarm to sound, but nothing happened. In front of him everyone was occupied with the complex task of getting the old lady and her wheelchair on board. Matt glanced around once, picked up a maintenance worker's hard hat from the control panel beside him, and faded back through the door.

Thirty seconds later he was on the ground, jacket off to change the recognition pattern, and moving fast into the shadow of the airport baggage area. He walked quickly and purposefully along, glancing from left to right as he worked his way in the general direction of the parking lot.

First a car, he thought. Then a late-night sporting goods store.

And then, Mr. Chalmers, it's my turn.

13

Nighttime now, quiet up on the back canyon road near Calabasas, a mile or two off the Ventura Freeway. The roads up here wound steeply, pushing up into the Santa Monica Mountains, their slopes bearing signs of old mud slides and avalanches. The houses lay far apart, perched precariously on the steep ridges, with nothing but scrub trees and cyclone fences in between.

Matt shared the night with a few others. From somewhere behind him came the soft hooting of an owl, and a moment later ghostly wings beat past him as the bird took off on a night patrol in search of food. The moon, fully risen, hung high up over the canyon wall, turning the scene below into a ghostly negative. Across the canyon a coyote's howl wavered and then died. The area's cats and dogs probably provided a steady diet for the handsome silver coyotes, Matt thought. He wished them well.

Shifting slightly, he pulled his 7×50 night binoculars from the bag beside him and scanned the area once again, careful to keep the glasses down and out of sight below the upper edge of the grass, to avoid a telltale glint of reflected moonlight.

He had been watching Rollie Chalmers's house from the ridgeline for two hours now, changing position from time to time, probing with the binoculars through the lighted windows, watching Chalmers and the Asian as they moved from room to room.

The two men kept drifting back and forth across the lighted windows, never giving Matt more than a few seconds' glimpse, but he would have bet money that the Asian was the man in the limousine who'd executed the biker. Kanji's "research assistant"—aka the Dragon. He was looking forward to meeting him again, face to face.

But not tonight. Tonight he wanted Chalmers.

Earlier he'd searched the parking lots at LAX until he found an open car. Five minutes later he was heading north on the San Diego Freeway. He exited in Culver City, searching until he found an army surplus store, where he bought a flashlight, thin gloves, and a large hunting knife. The man who took his cash barely saw him, eyes glued to a TV game show as he chewed steadily on a large slice of pizza. Back on the freeway Matt headed north, whistling softly through his teeth.

Now he scratched at an insect bite and shifted on

the cold ground, wishing he had brought food. Chalmers and his visitor were still in there, and the way things were looking, they might be there all night. He didn't want to wait that long.

Chalmers had come roaring up the narrow road just after nine o'clock, the noise of his turbocharged BMW racketing off the sides of the canyon. Matt had been in place for more than an hour, and as he watched, Chalmers drove the car into the open carport under the house. A moment later a black Toyota came into sight, parking behind the BMW. The two men nodded at each other, exchanged a few words, and walked up the wooden stairs to the rear deck of the house.

They'd stayed out on the deck for over an hour, drinking two beers each and talking. Chalmers seemed nervous, excited, and fearful at the same time, with body language that betrayed his agitation. In contrast the Asian's movements appeared slow and deliberate, his speech careful and succinct. He nodded often and spoke little, listening intently to Chalmers as he blustered and expounded. I'd give a lot to know what they're talking about, Matt thought.

Finally, the two men moved inside. Matt watched carefully through the glasses as they moved from room to room, settling down at last across the kitchen table. Their talk grew animated, then angry. The Asian rose, spat out a long sentence, and made a chopping gesture with the edge of his hand. Chalmers sat still, a stunned look on his face. Without waiting for a reply the Asian drew himself up, gave a low bow, turned, and walked out the door.

A moment later Matt heard the roar of a motor, and the man's car emerged from around the side of the house, heading down the canyon road.

What the hell was *that* all about? he wondered. He put the glasses to his eyes again. Chalmers still sat at the kitchen table, staring morosely at his glass.

Matt checked his watch. Nearly eleven o'clock and growing cold on the hillside. Although he could last the night out here if necessary, he wanted to make his move soon. He needed information, and Chalmers was the person who could give it to him.

Matt slipped the binoculars around his neck, straightened up, and began to work his way carefully down the slope toward the house.

He stood quietly, hidden in the shadows on the deck at the side of the house, waiting for Chalmers to come outside again. He heard footsteps approaching and flattened himself against the wall. The sliding glass door opened, and Chalmers appeared, glass in hand.

Approaching from behind Matt tapped him lightly on the right shoulder. Chalmers gasped in surprise and turned. Matt moved quickly to the left, grasped his left hand, and forced it back up into the small of his back, keeping the wrist bent back at a painful angle. The glass fell, shattering on the deck.

"Don't do anything stupid," he whispered in Chalmers's ear. "Don't yell, don't try to get away. Otherwise I break your wrist." He applied pressure for emphasis, feeling the man wince in pain as he did so. "You understand me?"

Chalmers nodded. Matt could see sweat on his forehead. "Good," said Matt. "Now walk with me, that's right, forward, over toward the railing."

"What—what the hell do you want? Money? Shit, take it. Wallet's in my side pocket, there's more cash in the bedroom. Jesus, don't—"

"I'm not after your money," said Matt calmly. "Or your life. If I'd wanted to kill you, you'd be dead already." They reached the edge of the deck, and he pushed Chalmers up against the low wooden railing. Twenty feet below, rocks and scrub marked the edge of the canyon wall.

"What, then? Jesus, what? Who *are* you?" Matt could smell fear on Chalmers, feel his body trembling.

"I called you this morning, Mr. Chalmers. About Martha Larsen's videotape. You remember that?"

"Videotape?" Chalmers's head twisted back, and Matt could see his eyes, large and frightened, staring at him. "Oh, Christ. Hey, listen, mister, hold on just a second, don't get your balls in an uproar, look, I can—"

"Wait," said Matt, increasing the pressure slightly. "Before we get started, Mr. Chalmers, I want to go over the situation here. We have to be careful not to create any misunderstandings."

Matt's voice was soft in the evening air, his mouth close to Chalmers's ear. He spoke almost as a lover would.

It was scarier that way, he'd found.

Sweat beaded Chalmers's forehead. "You—you're the boss."

"I'm glad to hear you say that," said Matt. He moved in closer, feeling heat radiating off the man's body, smelling his panic. "You tried to have me killed earlier today, Mr. Chalmers. You went after my life, and for that you forfeited any claim to my consideration." He paused. "You stepped outside the rules, and now there are no rules left anymore. I can do anything I want with you."

Chalmers squirmed. "Are you going to kill me, then?"

"That depends on what happens in the next few minutes." With his free hand Matt took the hunting knife from its sheath. "Look to your right," he instructed.

Chalmers stared at the shiny knife. "I can kill you with this, anytime I want to." Matt spoke gently, as if to a child. "I'm going to let go of you in a minute, because I need to see your face while I talk to you, but before I do, I just want to ask you a question. Do you believe that I can kill you? That I *will* kill you if I have to?"

He applied pressure to the wrist. "This is probably the most important executive decision you'll ever make, Mr. Chalmers. It's about whether you live or die. I need information from you, and if I don't get it, you'll die. Do you understand that?"

Chalmers's head dropped. "Yes," he whispered. "Yes, goddammit. I believe you. Jesus Christ, let's get this over with."

Matt released the man's wrist. As he did, Chalmers lurched forward, grasping the rail of the deck, and vomited explosively over the side. He clutched the wooden railing tightly as his stomach heaved, until at last he could bring up no more. Wiping his mouth he slowly straightened up. "My God," he murmured, looking down at the wet stain spreading across the front of his trousers. "I've pissed myself too." He raised his eyes to Matt's. "Okay, you bastard. What do you want to know?"

"Let's start with something easy," said Matt. "Why'd you try to kill me?"

Chalmers took a breath. "Killing you wasn't my decision," he said slowly. "I argued against it, as a matter of fact."

"Argued with who?"

Chalmers hesitated. "Don't get me wrong. I just meant—I mean, this is complicated, it's not easy to explain, and—and I'm afraid of what's going to happen now, of what they'll do."

"Who are 'they'?"

Chalmers shook his head. "That's what I'm afraid to tell you," he whispered. "You've got no idea—"

Matt moved in close. "Mr. Chalmers, let me ask you something. Are you more afraid of them or of me? I assure you, I can get very, very scary in a very short time, if I have to."

Chalmers looked from side to side and seemed to come to some sort of decision. "What the hell," he said at last. "All right. How much do you know about the Ragnarok project?"

"A little," Matt said. "Why don't you tell me more?"

"It's our biggest contract at TransCentury—we've got fifty million dollars tied up in this. We got the contract five years ago for the basic R and D on software systems for the guidance component of Ragnarok; what they call Odin. I'm not a goddamn tekkie—I don't understand half the stuff in the reports—but we put a lot of money into developing artificial-intelligence systems that were small enough to fit into the missile." He looked up. "And it worked. We did it."

Matt raised his eyebrows. "Not according to what's on that tape."

Chalmers let his breath out. "Yeah, well, that's something else altogether. Something's fucked up somewhere, and if you find out what it is, tell me and we'll both know. Up until last week Odin was working perfectly." He grimaced. "Now this. If we don't turn this thing around, and fast . . ." his voice trailed off.

"What happens then?" asked Matt.

Chalmers's expression was agonized. "The goddamn company goes under, that's what happens. This is a performance contract, for Christ's sake—we either come up with a system that works, or everybody's out on the street tomorrow."

"Is that why you tried to kill me? Because of the tape?"

Chalmers passed his hand over his face. "Look, you gotta believe me, it wasn't my idea. This is the absolute truth, I swear. Look at me, for Christ's sake. Do I look like a hit man? Jesus, man, think about it."

Behind them, on the mountain road, headlights swept the ridge. A car's engine slowed, then speeded up again. Matt relaxed; if anybody caught a glimpse of them, they would just be two men talking on the deck in the evening.

"Whose idea was it, then?"

Chalmers took a deep breath, and let it out slowly. "Takashi. Takashi Yamashita. One of our . . . partners."

"Guy with black leather gloves?"

"Yes. He—he was here earlier."

The Dragon. Matt remembered the face behind the dark glasses in the limousine. The look the man had given him just after he'd shot Farron Lascelles in the head. "Takashi killed the biker?"

Chalmers nodded. "Yeah." His head dropped. "Yeah, that's what he said. He called me, later. Said he'd had to, ah, terminate the guy he'd sent to whack you out."

"*Terminate?* That's the word he used?"

Chalmers nodded. "His English is okay, but I think he must have spent a lot of time watching spy movies or something. He talks like that sometimes."

"How'd he find my motel room?"

Chalmers shrugged. "Said somebody told him where you were staying."

A chill coursed through Matt. The only people who'd known his whereabouts were at the Jefferson Institute in Washington.

Chalmers spread his hands helplessly. "I don't

know any more than that." He paused. "I learned a while ago not to ask the guy too many questions."

"What about Martha Larsen; the journalist who died in the car wreck. Did Takashi kill her?"

Chalmers hesitated. "I think so." He sighed. "Probably. Shit, I don't know. Did you know her?"

Matt nodded. "Tell me how she died."

Chalmers looked off into the night. "I didn't even know about this one until after the funeral. You ever see our test site out north of Barstow? No? Well, it looks like a wilderness, but it's not. We've got the place seeded with people-sniffers, the kind of stuff they used on the Ho Chi Minh Trail in Vietnam. One of the sensors picked up a signal late Saturday night, and they called me at home. I called the security chief and told him to check into it. Sometimes we get a coyote or a cougar, stray dog, stuff like that, sets off the alarms. They usually send a tracker up the trail. The next day I hadn't heard from security, so I called. They said that Takashi had handled it, so I put in a call to him. He didn't get back to me until the next day. They'd had a slight security problem, he said, but he'd taken care of it himself. That's what he said." He paused. "And the next morning I read about the funeral in the papers."

"Let me get this straight," Matt said. "This guy Takashi does security jobs for you? Without your permission? Who's working for who here?"

Chalmers spread his hands. "Look, you've gotta understand something—I didn't have anything to do with—with what I'm about to tell you." He wet his lips. "Defense contracting is a shitty business, okay?

Companies like TC've got virtually no chance in the market, the way things are these days. IBM, Zenith, all the big guys, they can just roll over you. They do it lots of different ways. They steal your people, they undercut your prices, they change the software specs, all that sort of shit. TC was a small company up until about five years ago, doing maybe five million a year, most of it for specialized markets like plant robotics, medicine, stuff like that.

"And then we had a chance to make it, big-time. Government contracts are hard to get, but once you're on the track, you're an incumbent, if you see what I mean. So when the contract to develop Odin came out, we bid on it. Problem was, we underbid, just to see if we could get it. It's, ah, pretty standard practice to come in with a low bid, and then to go back and hike it up, giving them a bunch of bullshit about increased costs, all that sort of thing."

"And?"

He paused. "It didn't work. Two things happened. First, most of our suppliers for components were also, in some sense, our competitors. They knew that if we blew this contract, we'd never get another. So little by little the prices for system components began to go up. Certain parts were 'unavailable' or 'discontinued' when we ordered. Shipments came in late, orders were mislaid, or incorrectly filled. It was a goddamn nightmare, I can tell you."

"You said two things happened. What was the other one?"

Anger clouded Chalmers's face. "The goddamn government changed the fucking rules, that's what.

Because of the recession, the Congressional investigations, all that shit, the Pentagon started looking the contracts over *very* carefully. We applied for cost adjustments, and they were turned down. We couldn't believe it. The Odin contract is a fixed-fee deal, which means that we're obliged to deliver, whatever it costs us, and if we don't, we have to pay back all the money."

"So what did you do?"

Chalmers looked at him. "The only thing we could do, mister. And I'm not proud of it, but there you are. I mean, we're all just trying to make a living, right?" He dropped his voice. "We went offshore. We went to the fucking Japs. And they bailed us out."

"You mean a Japanese company supplied you with the parts you needed?"

"Exactly. Dirt cheap, high quality, and right on time. We couldn't have done it without them."

"What's the company in Japan?"

"Shima Industries. It's a big outfit outside of Tokyo; they specialize in subminiature components and custom-designed software programs. When we set up the deal for the components, I went out there for a couple of days to meet Yoshi Itoh, the big boss. Guy's rich as hell, flew me over in his own corporate jet."

Matt frowned. "But this is a defense contract, right? Classified documents, restricted access, special personnel clearances, that sort of thing?"

Chalmers nodded unhappily. "You got it. We let 'em in and didn't tell the Pentagon. So now Itoh's company is involved in the most secret project that the country's got, they got guys over here practically running the show—"

"Guys like Takashi?"

Chalmers nodded. "Itoh gave us a couple of 'technical assistants.' Takashi's the muscle. A guy named Kanji's the brains."

"And what exactly do they do for you?"

"They don't mess around with the project, not directly. But they're just, you know, *there* all the time. Watching. Talking with each other in Japanese.

"They also fix things if anything goes wrong. Kanji's a genius, in a way—he's made some real improvements in the peripheral systems. He fixes other stuff too. Like one time I mentioned to Kanji that one of our American suppliers was shorting us on shipments. He got Takashi to pay the guy a visit, and everything's been just fine since then. Except that a week or so later I find out the guy'd spent a couple of days in the intensive-care ward.

"We had a minor labor dispute a couple of months ago, just a couple of hotheads in the shipping section. This kind of stuff happens all the time, usually we just go down there and straighten it out over a couple of beers. This time Takashi took care of it. The two guys disappeared and two more guys showed up the next day to take their place. Nobody knows where the other guys are—they moved out of town according to the phone company."

"So what's going to happen to Odin now?"

Chalmers grimaced. "We're gonna deliver on the contract," he said. "No other choice; we have to. We've got less than a month until we have to test in front of the Pentagon. That's the big one—Secretary of Defense will be there, plus a group of bigwigs from Europe. If we show 'em a missile system that works, we're set for life. If we blow it the way we did the other day—well, the game's all over."

His head came up. "We can't let that happen. We developed the core architecture for Odin before the Japs got involved, and that's the most important part of the system. So we'll go over Odin centimeter by centimeter, circuit by circuit. We're gonna run through the programming line by goddamned line. We're going to look at every damned one of them until we find the glitch."

"Sounds like a hell of a lot of work," he said.

"We'll have help," Chalmers said bitterly. "Lots of it. From our Japanese partners. Whether we want it or not. That's what Takashi was over here telling me tonight."

"Sounds like you got lucky."

Chalmers glance was aggrieved. "You call that lucky? What we've already done on this contract is so illegal that we could all go inside for ten years. We're about to let foreigners inside goddamn Odin's *brains* now—I'm no lawyer, but that's probably treason." He shivered. "I just hope we can keep the whole thing quiet." He looked bitterly at McAllister. "But I don't suppose there's much chance of that now."

"None at all."

"So what happens now?"

"You come back with me to Washington," Matt said. "Tell the people in the Pentagon and the CIA everything you know. Maybe we can get control of this thing. Maybe it's not too late."

"No." The voice came from behind Matt, flat and authoritative.

Matt turned to see a figure in the doorway. He held an Ingram, its silencer giving it the look of a short, thick piece of pipe. Matt had seen both the man and the weapon before, he realized. In the parking lot of the motel, earlier in the day.

"Takashi." Matt's voice was soft on the evening air. "The Dragon."

"*Hai.*" The man stepped forward and gave a slight bow, his dark eyes never leaving Matt's. "Mr. McAllister. You know my professional name, I see."

"How'd you know where I was staying?"

Takashi smiled. "A mutual friend told me," he said. "He also told me about your videotape. I tried to get it, but I clearly underestimated your abilities. So I am truly pleased to see you here."

He moved forward, onto the deck. "Where is the tape?"

"Somewhere safe," said Matt. "Not here." As he spoke he felt the tape's compact bulk in the pocket of his jacket, where he had put it hours before.

Chalmers stepped forward. "Don't be a goddamned fool," he said quietly.

Takashi swung his gaze to Chalmers. "You have disappointed me, my friend. I have been listening to you tell this man all about our arrangements. These were private matters, Mr. Chalmers. Between business partners only."

Chalmers took a deep breath. "This doesn't make any sense. We can't keep on this way. I—"

Takashi shook his head. "We can and must. You no longer control the situation. You have no power to stop us."

Chalmers's voice was defiant. "The hell I don't. I'm through with this."

"I'm sorry to hear that," Takashi said calmly. "I had hoped you would be able to help. I regret to have to say good-bye."

Chalmers backed up against the deck's railing. "What the hell are you saying?" he whispered, his hands held out in front of him as if warding off evil spirits.

The Ingram coughed three times.

Chalmers shuddered under the impact of the bullets, folding softly to the deck.

Takashi swung the weapon around, but Matt's arm was already in motion. The hunting knife flashed through the air, embedding itself in the fleshy part of Takashi's upper arm.

The Japanese screamed and fired the weapon in a long-drawn-out burst, but muscular reflex sent the shots wide. That was all the time Matt needed. As Takashi pulled the knife from his arm and fumbled with a fresh clip for the Ingram, Matt sprinted to the edge of the deck, vaulted over the rail, and sailed out into the darkness below.

14

Two gut-wrenching seconds of free fall, and then Matt hit the ground, legs buckling, rolling twice, vanishing into the scrub at the base of the deck. He'd had a split-second window of opportunity, and he'd taken it without hesitation. His last, fleeting thought as he'd vaulted the railing had been a fear that he might break his leg. Jump, his instincts commanded; you'll die if you stay here. *Move!*

And he had moved.

He rose to a crouch, shot a glance upward, ducking as rounds from the Ingram whipped through the branches around him. The bastard can't see me, he thought; he's firing blind. But even so, I've got to get out of here.

Ahead lay the canyon slope, overgrown with

small trees and underbrush. He plunged straight down into the thicket, just as a fresh burst from Takashi's weapon slammed into the ground behind him.

Three hundred yards from the house he paused, letting his breathing return to normal, listening for sounds of pursuit. He kept his mouth open slightly, eyes moving constantly, looking for movement at the corners of his vision. He saw nothing, heard nothing. It didn't mean he wasn't coming, he thought.

After a moment he struck out again, working his way silently down the canyon wall. He had no idea where he was going, but right now that didn't matter. If he didn't know where he was headed, then it was unlikely that Takashi would be able to figure it out either. Right now the most important thing was to put distance between himself and the Japanese killer, as fast as possible.

He looked up at the sky, found the pole star, and oriented himself. If he kept walking in this direction long enough, he knew, he'd eventually run into Highway 101. And long before he did, he'd have figured out what to do next. He took a deep breath and pushed on through the night.

As he loped through the dark, he thought. Several pieces of the puzzle had come together tonight, with a resounding thump. Takashi had sent the biker to kill him earlier, and when that had failed, he'd executed the biker to keep him from talking. Just as he had murdered Rollie Chalmers only minutes ago.

And how had he traced Matt to the motel? he wondered. A call, Chalmers had said. From Washington?

It had to have come from the Jefferson Institute, Matt thought grimly, remembering how he'd called there earlier in the day, looking for Buttons. Teddy had promised to relay the message. So both Teddy and Buttons had known where he was.

And earlier, Matt had left a message for Buttons, about the videotape itself.

It had to have been Buttons, then. But why? What was the connection between his friend and a Japanese *yakuza* killer?

Good question, he thought. But no answers. Not yet.

He settled into a loping stride, moving easily through the trees, with just enough moonlight to show him the way. From time to time he paused, listening for sounds of pursuit. There were none.

What now, McAllister? he asked himself. What's the next step? He ran the events of the past few hours back in his mind. He'd witnessed two violent deaths, met a Japanese hit man with whom he'd had a brief but very intense relationship, and been shown the outlines of what was clearly a major scandal. This was no longer about Marty and the circumstances of her death, but something much bigger, much more dangerous.

If Takashi and Buttons were talking to each other, then the *yakuza* knew how to find him. And he would come, as surely as the dawn. He needed time, he thought. Time to think, time to spread out the pieces of the puzzle, to find the patterns. To plan his next moves.

Whatever he did now had to be done very carefully, he knew. He needed a safe place to think, somewhere out of the way. Where no one could find him.

Toad Hall.

Nodding to himself he moved silently through the moonlight forest, headed for the distant lights of the freeway.

Overcast and humid, the day threatened rain as Matt walked slowly from the terminal building at National and got into his rental Chevy. His ankle still hurt, but seemed to be recovering fast. His legs and arms were covered with bruises, and he had a series of small but noticeable scratches and abrasions on his face and neck. Nothing like running at high speed through scrub brush at night, he thought, to test what shape you're in.

He had been lucky, he reflected, to get out alive. Getting out of the canyon had been a close thing, but not as bad as it might have been. There had been times in the past, he remembered, when death had been closer, the long walk home harder. He shook his head. It wasn't supposed to be like this anymore, though. He'd left that life behind, or so he had thought. He gunned the engine, heading out of the parking lot and onto the highway, toward Toad Hall.

He stopped just once to buy groceries and call Ace Emerson in California. Ace buzzed with the news of Chalmers's death, but went silent as Matt began to talk. "If Takashi makes the connection between us, he'll kill you," he concluded. "So forget you ever knew me, okay?"

"Don't I wish." Ace's voice was hushed. "Take care of yourself, man."

That evening Matt lit a hurricane lamp and sat on the front porch of the isolated mountain cabin, listening to the peepers celebrating the advancing springtime, feeling the night's comfortable cloak around his shoulders, absorbing his fears and tensions.

He rose at dawn, made breakfast, and was on the road by eight. He drove north to Frederick, found a space for his rented Chevy in an alley off East Patrick Street, and walked two blocks to the public library.

The library, a handsome two-story modern brick building, had an on-line computer and a store of microfiche records. Thanks to the miracle of fax, modem, and CD-ROM, even a relatively small library could access enormous databases and information nets. Although the electronic vaults where information lay stored were hundreds and even thousands of miles from the tiny Maryland town, Matt was able, within an hour, to start the dot-matrix printer at his elbow churning out citations.

The elderly librarian sighed when Matt presented his slips. She looked him up and down, and finally nodded. "You look like a decent young man," she said at last. "I'm going to do something that is quite against all the rules, but I'm going to do it anyway. I have arthritis and today I'm tired. I spent most of last night watching the Academy Awards on the television, which by the way was the high point of my week. But disappointing nonetheless, and I stayed up well past midnight. Don't let anyone tell you that the elderly need less sleep; some do, some don't. I'm one who does, and I just plain don't feel like trudging down those stairs today and rooting around in a pile of dusty magazines. So I'm going to let you do it, provided you're very careful to put everything back just as you find it."

She cocked a bird's bright eye at him. "Do we have a deal?"

Matt grinned. "We do."

"Good." She began to walk toward the stairs. "Remember what I said—put everything back where you found it." She unlocked the basement door. "Down you go, then," she said. "Let me know when you're finished."

It was dark and cool in the basement, a faint odor of mildew and stale air over everything. Matt found the periodicals stacks without any difficulty, and ran his hands down the shelves until he located the issues he was looking for. Taking an armload of magazines and a stack of spools, he moved to the microfilm reader in the corner.

He concentrated first on TransCentury Systems. From half a dozen articles he learned how the company had started, how it had developed from a specialty software company to a manufacturer of components and whole systems, and finally, how it had entered the defense contracting business, winning the coveted Odin contract for Ragnarok.

The story that unfolded was an old and familiar one. A young firm, high on ideas and short on procedures, made it on the sheer strength of its dreams and a better product than anyone else was producing. At which point the corporate equivalent of the Peter Principle kicked in. Overextended, TC began a desperate search for funds, and finally struck it rich through the efforts of Roland Chalmers, who'd received a personal profile in a recent issue of *Forbes*. Chalmers, the article said, was a wizard at raising cash and making deals, and although the article confessed that no one really knew *how* Rollie had pulled TC's chestnuts out of the fire, they were lavish with their praise. "Rollie's magic wand," the article concluded, "has turned TC from a frog into a handsome prince once more, and even though we don't know how the man does it, plenty of firms wish they, too, had his magic touch."

So no one knew about TC's shadow Japanese partner, Matt thought. Not surprising, considering that all the work on Ragnarok was highly classified, and that even the suspicion of Japanese financial involvement would trigger an immediate investigation.

But there was more here, more that he was missing. Something bigger; something that would cause a Japanese company to send a professional hit man thousands of miles. Something that required a *yakuza* to keep an eye on everything that moved in and out of the test site.

Something that would provoke an instant response if necessary, and lead to quick death.

The answer, he decided, must lie with the Japanese company itself. He picked up the next pile of magazines. If he looked long enough, he'd see the pattern. There'd be *something,* no matter how small. In his experience there was always something, if you looked long enough, that would illuminate the shadows.

But what illuminates, he reminded himself as he threaded the microfilm reader, can also burn.

He read through the morning and into the afternoon, forgetting lunch entirely. Shima Industries proved to be somewhat of a rarity on the Japanese industrial scene; a stand-alone firm that had never become part of the larger *zaibatsu* constellations of Japanese companies all doing business in related areas.

Shima specialized in two areas: software programs; and highly miniaturized components, mainly chips containing preloaded programs. Shima sold very little to the United States. Most of their production went to the domestic market, although the company did export programs and components to Europe and various parts of Asia.

Shima was owned by Yoshi Itoh, an elderly millionaire who at eighty-something was still actively in charge of the company. His nephew, Kanji Nakamura, ran the research-and-development department. Matt paused; the same Kanji Nakamura who now shadowed the TC operations in California? Nakamura, thirty years old, had trained at Berkeley and MIT, and after graduation had spent five years in the United States working for Microsoft before finally returning to Japan to join his uncle.

And now he's back again, thought Matt.

He rubbed his eyes. Nearly four o'clock. One

more spool to go, he told himself, and then he'd break for coffee. He began to scroll, searching for the correct date.

There it was; a Sunday *Times* business section feature about the Japanese computer industry, with Shima Industries as one of the two lead stories. The news story itself contained nothing new, nothing that Matt hadn't already learned, but this time there were photographs. He sharpened the focus and leaned forward.

The first photo showed Itoh, the elderly millionaire, making a speech somewhere. All that was visible was his upper chest and face, rising up from behind a tall podium. Small and thin, Itoh had a large nose, glinting wire-rimmed glasses, and the sort of grin that made you think of dentists.

Matt glanced at the second photo, looked again, and peered closely at the screen, adjusting the focus again. The picture showed Itoh seated at a banquet table, peering out from behind an impressive array of plates and glasses. The caption read: "Self-made millionaire celebrates eightieth birthday, sixtieth year in business." Behind him stood half a dozen dark-suited men holding glasses in what looked like a toast. He felt the hair on his neck begin to rise. No doubt about it. One of the men was Takashi, the *yakuza* killer. The Dragon.

It was definitely him, Matt decided; standing close behind the old man and slightly to his right. Matt could even see his leather gloves.

He turned the page to the second article. This one concentrated on the role of Japanese research

universities in the government-funded Sixth Generation Project, focusing on the development of neural
networks for computers.

Matt scanned it quickly. There were more photographs, including one of a group of academic researchers in a laboratory. The people in the picture
were mostly young Japanese, dressed in lab coats and
carrying clipboards.

And one of them was Yuki, the woman whose
life he had saved.

He looked again to make absolutely sure. No
doubt about it, he thought, and there was her name,
Yukiko Matsushima, in the caption. She was described as a "mathematical theorist specializing in
computer systems." A man in academic robes was
smiling and bowing as he presented her with a large
bouquet of flowers.

He ran up the stairs and out of the building,
ignoring the elderly librarian's shout. A break, he
thought; at last, a break. Yukiko Matsushima is a
computer expert, and right now, she's sitting in
George Washington University Hospital.

And we've already been introduced.

15

H e'd set a record for the drive back to Washington, and now he moved down the hospital corridor at a fast walk, a large carton of takeout teriyaki in his hand. He entered Yuki's room, stopping abruptly when he saw the empty bed. Nancy Okamoto, the Japanese-American nurse who had spoken with him earlier, looked up from her chart.

"Oh, hi," she said. "We were looking for you earlier."

"You were?"

She nodded toward the empty bed. "Yuki was. She wanted to say good-bye."

"Good-bye?" Matt blinked. "You mean she's gone? But—where?"

"To Japan, of course." She looked at him. "You

didn't expect her to stay in the hospital forever, did you?"

"Well no, but—I guess I didn't expect her to get well so soon either."

The nurse nodded. "She's strong and very healthy. That helps a lot, you know. Her bruises have almost disappeared, and the stitches came out yesterday. She discussed it with the doctor, and told him that she'd rather be at home. He gave her permission to travel, and her reservation came through yesterday afternoon. She left a couple of hours ago." She looked at the bag in Matt's hand. "What's that?"

He held up the bag sorrowfully. "Teriyaki to go," he said. "She wanted some Japanese food. What do I do with it now?"

Nancy Okamoto laughed. "Leave it here," she said. "We all get hungry late in the afternoon." She opened a drawer, took out a folded piece of paper, and handed it to him. "She left this for you."

Yuki had written: *Thank you again, dear Matt. I hope to see you again, in Tokyo perhaps. I will always remember you. Good-bye. Yukiko Matsushima.* The writing was small and precise, curiously formal.

He turned the paper over in his hand. "I can't believe she's gone so soon."

"She was homesick, Mr. McAllister. She'd had a very bad experience, and she was far from home. Wouldn't you want to get back if it was you?"

"Of course." He cursed inwardly as he walked slowly back down the hall. Yuki was gone now, thousands of miles away. A great lead, he thought, and now it had evaporated like smoke on a summer breeze. He thought of her, sitting in the plane on the long trip back to Japan, and realized that his emotions were driven by more than frustration. He had been looking forward to seeing her again.

He got back into his car, slammed the door angrily, and sat thinking for a moment. What now? He had to find out what was going on with Buttons. This wasn't the time to confront him directly, not until he knew more. Maybe, Matt thought, it was time to search Buttons's office, see what he could turn up. He started the engine.

Ten minutes later he parked the rented Chevy on Jefferson Place, three doors down from the institute. Using his key he let himself in quietly, hoping that everyone had gone home for the day. He wanted to avoid Buttons until he'd had a chance to investigate his office.

As he mounted the stairs, however, he met Nigel, coming the other way.

"Good God, Matt, is that really you?" Nigel's voice was jovial, but his expression showed concern. "We've all been wondering where you'd got to. You've just missed Buttons, which is lucky for you, bucko, because he's in a filthy mood, and you're mainly to blame. He's been worried sick about you. Where on earth have you been?"

"That's a long story," Matt said.

Nigel was pulling on his jacket. "Well, let's hear it over a drink, what do you say? I'm meeting young Theodore at Lynch's in twenty minutes. He's giving me the redrafts of the Ragnarok chapters. Why don't you come with me now?"

He opened the door and sniffed the air. "Decent enough evening. It's just down the street. Shall we walk?"

Matt paused, considering. There'd be time later in the evening to search the office. "You're on," he said.

Ten minutes later they entered the ground-floor bar of Lynch's Public House, one of the ephemeral Washington bistros that seemed to Matt to sprout like mushrooms after a rain. In the past few months Lynch's had become Nigel's favorite after-work watering hole.

They sat comfortably at a back table, glasses in hand. Matt had spent most of the walk over sketching out to Nigel the events of the past few days, the details of his return trip to California: his brush with death at the hands of Farron Lascelles, the murder in the parking lot, and later on, the violent and bloody end to the evening at Chalmers's house. He omitted mention of Ace Emerson.

When he had finished, Nigel raised his glass. "Here's to absent friends," he said quietly. "I don't think we'll ever get over the loss of Marty, you know."

He took a drink and leaned forward. "This is a most horrifying story, Matt. Almost unbelievable. Frankly, I was beginning to think you weren't coming back. I take it your videotape's safe, after all that?"

Matt nodded. "But there's something I need to

tell you," he said. "Takashi—the Dragon—found me because someone here tipped him off."

"Here? What on earth do you mean?"

"Someone at the institute." Briefly, Matt related his telephone call to the institute from his Los Angeles motel room, and Chalmers's remarks later that night, just before he died.

"And I remember something else," Matt added. "When I got the tape in the mail, I called Buttons and told him."

Nigel's expression was troubled. "And what exactly did Buttons say?"

"I didn't actually talk with him. I left the message on his voice mail. Did he say anything to you?"

Nigel shook his head. "Not a bloody word. My God, Matt, do you seriously think—"

"Mr. Hastings?" A waiter had appeared at Nigel's elbow, a portable telephone in his hand. "Call for you, sir."

"Excuse me, Matt." Nigel took the phone, listened, and said, "Yes. Come round now. I've got Matt with me, we're in the lounge bar." He hung up.

"It's Theodore," he said to Matt. "He's on his way here." He sipped his drink. "But let's get back to this business with Buttons. Very worrying, Matt." He pursed his lips. "Very worrying indeed. I have no idea what to tell you, except to share something with you that I hope you won't pass on."

"Of course not."

Nigel dropped his voice. "Buttons is a bit strapped financially these days." He nodded. "Yes, once again. More than a bit strapped, actually. He—

ah—has borrowed substantially from his options with the institute, to the point where I had to have a fairly stern heart-to-heart with him last week. I believe that what he's done is technically embezzlement, but of course, I have no intention whatever of treating it that way."

"You're kidding," said Matt. "He hasn't mentioned anything about this to me."

"I'm sure he hasn't," murmured Nigel. "He's very embarrassed about the entire thing, I think. I gather he's made some spectacularly bad investments in the past year or so." He sighed. "As you'll recall, it was his general lack of ability in the area of money management that brought me into the institute a few years ago."

"You think he's getting money from the Japanese?"

Nigel frowned. "Can't rule it out, can we?"

"But how does that connect with his involvement with TransCentury? With this Japanese *yakuza*? Isn't that improbable?"

Nigel laced his fingers around his glass. "Not entirely. In the past ten years there has been a clear pattern of involvement of certain Japanese concerns with various American organizations—especially research, public relations, and policy bodies. Some of it has been fairly aboveboard and straightforward." He paused. "And some of it has not been."

"So he's been bought?"

"It's a strong possibility. Our report, when it comes out, will have a determinant effect on how the world's buyers see the technology behind Ragnarok.

Our assessment of the missile's capabilities and its reliability will induce potential buyers to make up their minds, one way or another." He cocked his head like a bird. "Who stands to lose if Ragnarok is successful?"

"The Japanese, obviously. But it's still hard to believe that they've got Buttons in their pocket."

Nigel shook his head slowly. "Ah, Matt. Until just now I wouldn't have thought it remotely credible. But if we put what you've just told me together with what I know of the man's financial predicament?" He grimaced. "I rather think the facts speak for themselves."

They were interrupted by the appearance of Teddy, flushed and perspiring. "Hi, Matt," he said, sliding into the seat next to him. "Jeez, what—"

"Never mind all that," said Nigel crisply. He pushed his glass forward. "We're dry here. Can you be a helpful lad and bring us three more drafts?"

Nigel nodded appreciatively at Teddy's retreating back as he headed toward the bar. "Fine fellow, Theodore. He's still a bit wet, you know—they all are when they get out of graduate school—but he's coming along. By this time next year I believe he'll have actually learned how to think a bit." He leaned forward. "I don't know what the *hell*'s happened to graduate education in this country, to tell you the truth. All I know about are its products, and most of 'em are bloody awful. I blame the tenure system, actually: bunch of overpaid ignoramuses far too concerned with puffing themselves up and asserting their authority over a bunch of kids. No wonder they never learn to take initiative. Never really learn how to *learn,* if you think about it."

He paused. "But not Teddy. He's one of the better ones, and we're lucky to have him. Although"—he frowned—"I sometimes wonder if the lad isn't a bit too clever for his own good."

A moment later Teddy returned with three pint mugs dripping cold foam. "Ah, that's wonderful," breathed Nigel. He took a drink and cleared his throat. "This, ah, Japanese. The *yazuka,* or whatever they call them—"

"*Yakuza,*" said Matt.

Nigel waved his hand. "Whatever," he said. "This sounds extraordinary. Are you sure of all your facts here? I mean, do you really think this man will actually try to hunt you down?"

"I'm sure of it," Matt replied. "He's a professional, and absolutely ruthless. He killed Roland Chalmers with barely a second thought to keep him from talking to me. Earlier, he shot the biker, once he saw that his plan to kill me had failed. He's a trained assassin, and he's hunting me." He paused. "I expect him to show up anytime now."

"Gosh," said Teddy, eyes round. "Do you really—"

"Hush," said Nigel impatiently. He turned back to Matt. "Look here, old boy. Isn't this stretching things a little too far? Do you actually think he's going to come all the way here?"

Matt returned his gaze steadily. "I'm sure of it. I've got the one thing he's desperate to lay hands on.

The videotape of the Ragnarok launching. Incontrovertible evidence of a conspiracy."

"Hmm." Nigel stared at the beer in his mug. "What do you intend to do now, Matt? Need a place to stay? We've got a guest bedroom out in the studio you can use."

Matt smiled. "No, thanks. I've already made arrangements."

Nigel nodded. "Of course. Well, you certainly know how to take care of yourself." He paused. "What about the videotape? We could put it in the office safe, you know."

Matt shook his head. "It's safe, Nigel. And the less you know about it, the better."

Nigel frowned. "I'm sure you're right." He rose. "Still, if you need anything . . ." He let the end of the sentence trail off.

Matt shook his hand. "Thanks."

Nigel glanced at his watch. "The good woman's waiting," he murmured. "I'd best get a cab. I'll just collect my coat." He moved off toward the cloakroom.

Teddy held up Matt's keys. "Your car's parked behind the office; I put it there on Friday. I'll bring it around for you if you like. I think Susie left her compact in the glove compartment the other night."

Matt nodded. "Go ahead. I'll swap you my Chevy for it."

Teddy flashed a grin. "No problem. Give me two minutes." Then he was off, practically running through the lobby.

Nigel returned, shrugging into a lightweight

Burberry. "One thing," he said to Matt. "Have you given any thought to how you're going to handle this? I mean, aside from self-preservation?"

"Some," said Matt. "But I'm open to suggestions. Got any ideas?"

"Here's one, at least," said Nigel. "Don't go to the police. Not yet, at any rate."

"I hadn't even considered it," said Matt. "The last thing I want is to be mixed up in yet another murder investigation. The California Highway Patrol would just love that, I'm sure."

"Quite right," said Nigel. "But on the other hand, you've got to tell *someone* about this, about what you think is going on. You're walking on a razor's edge. So here's my idea: I have a friend on the Senate Armed Services Appropriation Committee, and I think you ought to see him. He's out of town this week, but I suggest we both talk to him as soon as he gets back. I think that's the right way to approach this."

Matt frowned. "Why not just go straight to the Pentagon?"

Nigel shook his head. "Not wise, in my opinion. The Pentagon may itself be compromised here in some way." He grasped Matt by the elbow. "This is clearly a conspiracy, Matt. But we have no idea how extensive it is, or where it may lead. No, the best course is to push this thing as quietly as possible onto someone else's plate, and then to forget about as much of it as possible."

"But what about Marty? You're not saying that I

just *forget* about the fact that Takashi killed her, are you?"

"Not at all," replied Nigel. "I'm suggesting instead that you let someone else bring the man to justice, that's all. It's murder. And it will be investigated, once the facts are known."

He gave Matt's arm a squeeze. "That's our role now, Matt. Making the facts known. Come on. Teddy should have—"

A dull boom rolled into the quiet bar, rattling windows and the bottles on the shelves. "What on earth was that?" said Nigel, counting out bills and laying them carefully on the table. "It almost sounded like—"

Matt was already running toward the door. From outside, somewhere on the street, came the faint sound of screaming.

He came down the steps, blinking in the sunlight, to face a roaring inferno and a wall of dirty, billowing smoke. From somewhere inside the flames came a crackling sound, like bacon frying in a pan.

Nigel was right behind him. "Good God," he whispered, pointing to the flaming mass in the middle of the street. "It's Teddy. In your car."

Matt ran forward, pulling spectators roughly aside, moving closer to the burning car. The trunk of the Miata had been blown off, as had one of the doors. The tires were little more than liquid puddles of black now.

Kept at bay by the intense heat, he stared helplessly as he heard the first of the sirens approaching.

*   *   *

'The police think it was a thermite grenade," Nigel was saying. "Whatever that is. Are you familiar with these things?" His voice sounded very far away.

Matt gripped the telephone receiver tightly. "I am," he said. "Did they tell you anything else?"

"A bit. The thing was made in Belgium, apparently, but the bomb specialist I talked to said they're quite common here. It was hooked to a sort of trigger device that went off after the car began to move. Something about a mercury vibration sensor, I believe."

"That makes sense," Matt said. As he spoke, he kept his eyes on the street, searching for movement. He stood in the telephone booth in the Safeway parking lot off Wisconsin Avenue, a few blocks from his own house. He had spent the last two hours scanning the neighborhood, noting the cars and pedestrians, fading back into the shadows when patrol cars approached, searching the passing faces for some sign of Takashi.

"They're looking for you, you know."

"Who?"

"The police, of course." Nigel's voice was disapproving. "They want to talk to you. About the explosion. You've put me in an awkward position, Matt. They naturally wanted to know where the owner of the car was. I had to tell them that you'd simply disappeared. That sounded pretty damned stupid, if you don't mind my saying so."

"Can't be helped," said Matt. "I don't have time to talk to the police right now. I've got other things on my mind."

"Such as what?"

"Staying alive. You don't think the cops are going to be able to stop this guy, do you? He wants me dead, Nigel, and he's good at what he does. If I stay out in the open, he'll get me. I need to buy time, get things straight in my head. Then I'll figure out the next move. This is between me and Takashi now."

"Matt, I don't think this is wise. Not wise at all. Let me help you. If you need a place to stay—"

"Thanks, but I'll be fine." He paused, glancing at his watch. "Listen, gotta go do some things. I'll be in touch."

"Matt, wait. I—"

Matt hung up.

Pushing open the door to the booth, he walked across the parking lot and into the warren of streets beyond, his eyes darting from side to side.

Nine o'clock now, time to make a move. Time to go on the offensive; take the war to the enemy. He'd figured out what to do next. Now he just needed one or two things.

So it was time to break into his own house.

16

Matt circled his block three times slowly, scanning the area carefully, his eyes moving ceaselessly from side to side, up and down. Nothing suspicious, nothing out of place. Just the ordinary comings and goings of upper Georgetown on a weekday night; students heading down to the bars and restaurants on Wisconsin Avenue, elderly residents out for an evening walk, occasional cars and taxis.

But Takashi was somewhere close by, he felt sure. He had to be. And right now he had the advantage, because he'd know that sooner or later Matt would have to come home, back to where he lived. So let's get this over with, he thought, and be on our way.

He slipped into the alleyway behind his house,

walking softly past the parked cars and the high wooden fences walling off each narrow town house from its neighbor. Garbage cans stood like mute sentries beside each wooden door, waiting patiently. A short distance ahead a gray cat gazed at him with flat yellow eyes, twitched its tail once, and melted back into the shadows.

He paused at the entrance to his own gate, listening, watching. Seeing nothing but shadows and the familiar outlines of his garage, he eased open the gate and crossed the yard to the basement storm door.

His house keys were fused metal now, blown up along with Teddy in the explosion that had destroyed the Miata. But like all forgetful homeowners Matt had locked himself out too many times. He'd long ago stashed a key to the basement.

Now he felt along the upper ledge of the foundation, feeling the thick dust of decades coating his fingers. There it was. "Come to Papa," he whispered, as he drew the key out and blew on it to clear the dust.

Working quietly, he inserted the key into the lock of the bulkhead door and turned it carefully, holding his breath. It was unlikely that the house was booby trapped, but not impossible.

And if it *was* booby trapped, this was where it would blow.

The lock squeaked quietly and then opened. Matt unhooked the lock from the latch and slipped inside the basement.

He shivered as he crouched in the damp blackness, waiting for his eyes to adjust to the dim light. After a few moments he pushed forward off the balls of his feet, moving quietly and slowly, one step at a time. Easy does it, he thought. Get in, get a few items, and get out again. As quickly and as quietly as possible.

He paused again at the foot of the basement stairs, listening. The old house sometimes creaked and groaned to itself at night, but now it lay as silent as a graveyard at midnight. Almost as if it were waiting for something. Reaching into his shoulder bag he carefully removed the penlight and cupped it in his hand, ready for use. He took a breath and started up the stairs.

Into the kitchen now, his breathing coming a little more rapidly, the blood coursing through his system with strong, almost audible heartbeats. Stop worrying, he told himself. Five minutes, and you'll be done. Breathe normally, for God's sake; you'd think this was the first time you'd done this sort of thing.

It wasn't the first time, not by a long shot, Matt reflected grimly. But no matter how many times he did it, it never seemed to get any better.

He glided silently through the dark kitchen and out into the tiny dining room, skirting the table as he did so, brushing lightly across the back of the china cabinet. Easing up now, coming into the living room, and to his right, the stair landing. Careful, he told himself; here's where the floor creaks. He stepped cautiously onto the first of the treads, hearing the ancient boards sigh faintly. Shifting his weight slightly he took the stairs one at a time, holding his breath each time he set his foot down.

Grasping the rail he continued up the stairs, willing his breathing back to normal. Halfway now. Three quarters now. Almost there now.

He cleared the stairs and stood at the top of the landing, wiping sweat from his forehead. This is crazy, he told himself. There's nobody here. What the hell are you going through this silly charade for? If Takashi *had* been in the house, he told himself, he'd have attacked you by now. Calm down and just collect what you came for.

He walked to the end of the hallway, past his bedroom, past the spare room and the tiny bathroom adjoining it, to his study. Pale, ghostly light filtered through the curtains from the streetlamp outside, making the interior of the small study glow with a muted silver halo.

He paused at the doorway, watching for movement, and then moved to the desk. The bottom drawer slid out smoothly. Matt turned it over, found the release catch with his fingertips, and swung the false bottom compartment cover back, smiling faintly in the darkness as he felt the outlines of his getaway kit, a leftover habit from his Coyote days. Everything was there: passport, traveler's checks, and his around-the-world airline ticket. He reached into his jacket pocket, took out Marty's videotape, and slipped everything into the shoulder bag.

He was turning to start back downstairs when he heard a sound.

He froze, hair rising on the backs of his hands. There it was again. A faint electric current passed through his body. He moved silently to the doorway of his study, listening, his mind already beginning to weigh the options.

The sound had been that of breaking glass. Coming from the basement. And now there were quiet footsteps, coming slowly up from the cellar.

Someone was in the house with him.

No prizes, Matt thought, for guessing who it was.

Matt took two steps back into the study. Groping behind him with one hand he eased open the closet door. Reaching into the back of the closet he closed his hand around the twelve-gauge pump shotgun that he'd attached to the wall with clips. The weight of the gun was reassuring, but it wasn't loaded.

Not yet.

Transferring the shotgun to his other hand he fumbled for the box of shells on the shelf beside the gun rack. Season's come a little early, Matt thought grimly, as he found the heavy shells and loaded them into the gun.

A faint creak drifted up from the stairwell. The bastard was coming up to the second floor. Matt moved back to the doorway and listened, his eyes probing the darkness of the hallway, searching for a target. If I can't see him, he thought, I can't shoot him.

The shotgun held six shells, each capable of killing an intruder. A man hit full in the chest at close range with a load of number-four buckshot would be nearly ripped in half, and even at thirty feet it would still stop someone dead in their tracks. As quietly as he could, he opened the choke on the shotgun, widening the blast diameter. Since he'd be shooting blind, he reasoned, he needed all the spread he could get.

Adjusting the strap of his shoulder bag he blinked into the darkness at the top of the stairs. Where the hell was the bastard? He knew that he had a second, two at the most, to bring him down once the action started. If I don't get him first, he thought, he'll surely get me.

So let's get him.

Reaching back he felt with his fingertips along the shelf of his bookcase for his camera. He'd bought the expensive Nikon last year, and his one regret was that he hadn't used it more often. With a pang he remembered that there was an undeveloped roll of film inside, containing pictures of Marty.

Keeping his grip on the shotgun with one hand, Matt carefully probed with his fingers until he found the Nikon's timer button. The camera had come equipped with all kinds of useless gadgets, most of which he'd never used. One of them was a motorized film drive connected to the powerful built-in flash. If he pushed the timer all the way down, Matt knew, the motorized drive would expose frame after frame of film until the camera was empty.

And for each frame the flash would automatically fire.

Matt tried to remember how many exposures were left in the roll inside the camera. Doesn't matter, he decided; one flash is all I need.

Holding the Nikon he depressed the timer lever with his thumb and took a deep breath. Once he let go, he would have very little time. He hesitated, peering out into the darkness. Do it now, he told himself. Every second's delay is working against you.

He eased himself out of the doorway, moving his head from side to side. He could see nothing in the pitch blackness of the hallway. Unless he's got infrared, Matt thought, Takashi can't see anything either. So on that score we're even.

Time now to change the odds.

He set the camera face up on the floor by the doorway to the study, released the lever, and in two silent strides moved into the tiny bathroom. He turned, bracing himself against the wall, and brought the shotgun up.

Seconds later the first flash went off. Matt got a strobe-lighted glimpse of Takashi, crouched at the top of the stairway, pistol in hand, eyes wide in surprise.

Matt fired, pumped, and fired again. The noise inside the bathroom was deafening, the atmosphere lit by successive flashes as the camera snapped one exposure after another.

Matt changed his body angle, pumped another shell into the shotgun, and peered out. The hall was deserted, smoke from the shotgun eddying in and out. Where's he gone? he wondered. Where's the bastard gone? The hair began to rise at the back of his neck. The camera on the floor kept flashing all the while, keeping time with the pounding of his heart.

As if in slow motion he saw an arm appear from around the corner of the bedroom, the small, dark, spherical object leaving it, spinning slightly as it came toward him.

He knew what it was before it hit the floor at his feet. Reaching down with one hand he scooped the grenade up and sent it back down the hall, following it with another blast from the shotgun. Wiping sweat from his forehead he turned, glancing up at the bathroom window. Behind him the grenade detonated with a roar and a flash of light, the blast pushing him as if with a giant hand.

No time to think now, only seconds to get out. He reloaded the shotgun and fired three times into the glass-brick window of the bathroom, blasting a wide hole through the wall, feeling the cool, blessedly fresh night air hit his face.

He put two more quick shots into the window to widen the hole, and heard a thump at his heels as another grenade hit the floor behind him.

Dropping the shotgun he grabbed a handful of towels from the rack, threw them over the bottom of the opening to protect himself from the jagged glass, and heaved himself through.

It was a straight drop to the ground fifteen feet below, and he took it hard, turning as he fell and rolling twice on the hard asphalt. Above and behind him sections of wall and window blew outward as the second grenade's blast lit up the night.

Matt crawled to his feet and wiped blood and sweat from his forehead. He still had his bag containing the videotape. He checked his trousers and found the passport and money intact. His house was on fire now, the entire structure burning, and from somewhere off to the right near Wisconsin Avenue, Matt could hear sirens, several of them, approaching.

Time to get moving. Hunched over, he moved rapidly away from the growing circle of firelight, back into the darkness and safety.

As he jogged down the street, Matt felt a strange yet familiar exhilaration: the feeling he'd had often in the past as he changed from being the hunted into the hunter. Time to stop running, he told himself. Time to go on the offensive, hit them where it will hurt the most.

And you know exactly how to do that, don't you? Never mind Takashi; go for the head. Find Yoshi Itoh. And when you do, he told himself, you fix things, then and there. Just the way the Handyman used to do it. No muss, no fuss. No more problems.

No matter what it takes.

17

Matt called Nigel from the departure lounge, using one of the new video phones. The conversation did not go well.

"People have been looking for you, Matt. The police, to be exact." Nigel's furious face glared at him from the tiny liquid-crystal screen. "Seems your house blew up earlier tonight amidst a volley of shots. Now, get round here straight away and perhaps we can straighten this mess out."

"Flight 703 for Seattle and Tokyo is now ready for immediate boarding. Will all passengers holding seats in rows thirty-five through sixty please present their boarding passes at gate number ten. To repeat,

flight 703 for Seattle and Tokyo is now ready for boarding."

This was a waste of time, Matt thought. "Nigel, the less you know the safer you are," Matt said. "I'll get back in touch." He broke the connection. Behind him the departure gate light had begun to flash.

Time for one more call. He zipped his credit card once more through the slot and punched in Yuki's number in Tokyo, reading from her card. The video screen cleared, flickered, and suddenly flashed a photograph of Mount Fuji over three lines of Japanese characters. There was a hum and click, and Yuki's recorded voice came on, speaking Japanese.

Shit, thought Matt; a damned answering machine. He waited for the beep. "Yuki, it's Matt. I'm flying to Japan tonight. Call you tomorrow." He cut the connection, scooped up his bag, and headed for the gate.

He spent the next twenty hours in a cramped seat wedged deep in the tail of the huge Boeing 777. They stopped in Seattle to refuel and take on passengers, and then the big aircraft climbed back into the sky, turned its nose west, and began the long haul across the Pacific toward Japan.

Matt fell asleep thinking about the events of the past twenty-four hours. How had Takashi known so much about his movements? It was almost as if the killer had read Matt's mind. Or Buttons's, Matt thought bitterly. No matter; it would take Takashi time to catch up with him now, and by the time he'd figured out where Matt was headed, it would be too late. Matt patted the videotape in his jacket pocket. Once he reached Japan, Yuki would be able to help him find Yoshi Itoh. And Itoh, together with his nephew Kanji, were the keys to the puzzle.

He dozed fitfully as they thundered on through the night, the aircraft rolling gently under him, generating dreams of sailing with Yuki on a calm sea.

The big JAL jet banked sharply, its engines altering pitch as the flaps lowered and the warning lights came on. The aircraft shuddered and seemed to hang motionless for a second before sinking swiftly through the cloud layers. Raindrops streaked the window as Matt, bleary-eyed, saw the island of Honshu slowly materializing below him.

He saw a gently rolling landscape under low clouds. In the small compact villages tile-roofed houses huddled tightly together, surrounded by green geometric fields. The cabin crew bustled down the aisles, checking the passengers, collecting the debris of the long crossing.

What now? Matt asked himself. All I've got is a name. Yoshi Itoh, multimillionaire head of Shima Industries. Not much to go on, but it'll have to do. Yuki should be able to help me.

He reached inside his bag and pulled out Marty's videotape. And I've got one other thing, he reminded himself. Something that will either keep me alive, or get me killed in short order. All depending on what I do next.

So what's it going to be? Matt rubbed his temples, trying to clear the cobwebs from his mind. First a hotel and a hot shower. Then about twenty hours of interrupted sleep. And when he woke, he'd give Yuki a call. And after that he'd phone the U.S. embassy and see if Tommy Clegg was in.

Tommy Clegg had been one of the original Coyotes, back in the old days, and Matt seemed to remember hearing that he'd wangled himself a desk job in the Tokyo mission after a hijacker's bullet had taken away half his liver. Might be nice, he thought, to have a drink with Tommy and talk about old times.

And then?

He sighed and pulled his seat upright. And then, old son, you'll do what you always do. Get out on the street, show your pretty face. Shake the bushes, make a little noise.

See what jumps out.

He resumed staring out the window. Fewer fields now, more houses, many of them with distinctive blue tile roofs, their ends turned up in vaguely Asiatic fashion. Billboards in Japanese, low-storied factories, more power lines, and then they were coming in, racing fast over a golf course. Tarmac suddenly appeared under the wheels.

A hard bounce and a squeal of tires, and they were down. The engines blustered into reverse thrust as the airport terminal building came up on the left side.

"—to Tokyo's Narita Airport, where the temperature on the ground is seventy-eight degrees with some rain, and the local time is five P.M. Passengers with

*connecting flights internationally or domestically,
please contact our service agents in the lounge. All
other passengers must clear immigration and customs
here. Welcome to Japan."*

The announcement was repeated in Japanese,
the woman speaking in a high, chirpy voice.

The plane nosed to a stop, and bells chimed
softly. Matt groped for his shoulder bag, shaking his
head to clear it. Maybe bed first, *then* a shower.

He joined the passengers shuffling toward the
door. Now it begins, he thought.

Crowded, busy, and drab, the terminal seemed filled
with endless streams of people flowing through fluo-
rescent-lit corridors on automatic walkways. Overhead, large advertisements featured Japanese cameras
and electronic equipment.

Matt was suddenly aware of how few westerners
there were in the airport. He was bigger and taller
than practically everyone, and as he shuffled toward
the immigration checkpoint, he began to feel somehow out of place and time. Jet lag, he thought. Some
sleep and I'll be fine.

The immigration checkpoint consisted of a line
of plastic booths with signs in English and Japanese.
Matt dutifully got into the "Foreign Passports" line,
waited his turn, and eventually handed his passport
over to the blue-uniformed woman behind the
counter. She checked his landing form perfunctorily,
glanced at his passport photo, and flicked her eyes up
to check his face against the image before her. Tap-

ping characters into the computer beside her she hit the return key and waited. Matt stood comfortably, whistling softly through his teeth, watching her.

He saw her expression change as she glanced down at the screen. She frowned, tapped in more keys, and frowned again. Her eyes came up to meet his. "Mr. McArrister, where do you stay in Tokyo?" She formed the words slowly and distinctly, as if with effort.

Matt gave her a relaxed smile. "I don't know yet. Thought I'd find a hotel once I got into town."

She nodded, picking up the telephone beside her. Speaking softly into it she glanced again at him. She listened intently for a moment. *"Hai,"* she said finally, replacing the receiver. Then she seemed to shut down, her hands on the counter in front of her, one of them still holding his passport, her eyes expressionless.

"We wait," she murmured.

Stay cool, he told himself. He glanced from side to side, estimating distances, noting what was in his immediate environment, even as he decided to do nothing.

Two blue-uniformed airport police materialized behind him, one on either side. They wore pistols at their belts, the flaps covering them unbuttoned. A rapid-fire exchange of Japanese took place between one of the cops and the immigration official, ending in an expression of surprise and raised eyebrows.

The man asking the questions walked around behind the counter and peered at the computer screen for a moment, and asked another question.

"Hai," the woman replied. With a short bow she gave Matt's passport to the policeman.

"You come now," he said. Matt saw that his partner had moved around behind him, standing a few paces off, watching carefully. Matt moved back a step and saw both men shift position, covering him.

"Come," the first policeman repeated doggedly. "No problem. You come."

Here we go, Matt thought; time to turn into the Ugly American. "What the hell's going on," he said, raising his voice. "What do you mean, 'no problem'? Why are you stopping me? Hey, bud, talk to me!"

The second policeman moved up and took Matt gently by the arm. Matt recognized the move—a standard come-along hold using firm but light pressure. It could be transformed in a split second into a bone-snapping grip, should the suspect refuse to cooperate.

Matt sighed as he let himself go limp. I'm not in this goddamned country ten minutes and I'm in trouble. Out of the corner of his eye he spotted one of the cabin attendants from his flight. "Hey!"

The attendant turned, her almond eyes widening with surprise.

"Can you help me?" Matt indicated his two uniformed companions. "They don't speak English very well, I'm afraid. Can you find out for me what they want?"

She took in the scene for a long beat, then nodded. Walking over to them she bowed slightly to the older of the two policemen, speaking to him in low tones. He answered her abruptly, almost gruffly, and she drew back visibly, glancing from the policeman to Matt and back again. Another exchange ensued, and this time the second policeman chimed in.

I'd give anything to know what the hell they're saying, Matt thought bitterly. It wasn't just that he didn't understand—literally—a word of Japanese. Matt couldn't even tell what emotions were being expressed as the people in front of him talked.

Finally, the cabin attendant turned to him. "I think there is some problem," she said, embarrassment written all over her face. "These are policemen. They say that they must take you to their, ah, place—"

"Station," said Matt. "The police station?"

"Ah, yes. Thank you." She bobbed her head quickly, like a bird. "They will take you to their police station in Tokyo. They have received information about you from the United States. They must, ah, keep you until they can contact the police in Los Angeles." She paused. "That is what they say."

Los Angeles? There could be only one reason, Matt reasoned, why the L.A. cops would be looking for me. I'm now a suspect in Chalmers's murder.

To hell with that, he thought. I'll have to find some way out of here. He looked up at the corridor. Another plane had just landed, and the passageway overflowed with arriving passengers, all of them exhibiting the unmistakable signs of a transpacific journey. There were several hundred of them, a mixed crowd of Japanese and westerners, all shapes and sizes. And among them, someone he recognized.

The Dragon.

Dressed in a sharkskin suit, carrying a fashionable soft-sided leather briefcase, Takashi Yamashita walked toward several men waiting at the immigration barrier. They stood almost at attention, their hands straight down at their sides. As he approached they bowed deeply several times.

Jesus Christ, thought Matt. He's here. Not fifteen feet from me.

Just then the *yakuza* caught sight of Matt. He stopped in the midst of his greetings to his colleagues, a smile spreading across his face. He took a step across the distance that separated them and raised his gloved hand in an unmistakable gesture of greeting.

Then Matt was being guided, gently but firmly, through a side door, and up a flight of steps. He twisted his head to catch one last glimpse of the Dragon staring after him, the smile still on his face.

Matt's mind raced as he was frog-marched down a long corridor. How the hell did the L.A. cops know I was coming to *Tokyo*? And how did *Takashi* know I'd be here? None of this makes sense. Nobody knew I was coming here.

Not true, he reminded himself. Nigel knew.

He drew his breath in. Well, I'll be damned, he thought.

The pattern of the last twenty-four hours fell suddenly into place. It had been Nigel all along, Matt realized; he had been blind not to see it. Anyone could have retrieved messages from the voice-mail system at the institute; Nigel had obviously monitored every message. And his story to Matt in the restaurant just before Teddy's death had been painfully thin, nothing more than a ploy to buy time until Takashi could kill him.

I've got to get out of here, he told himself. He turned to one of the policemen. "Where are we going?"

"Office. You wait. No problem." The two cops were handling him with professional ease, keeping him moving smoothly down the stairs, into another corridor, and around a corner.

They opened a door and pushed Matt through. Inside was a desk, two filing cabinets, half a dozen chairs, and a telephone. A holding room, Matt thought. Or an interrogation cell.

Get out *now*, he told himself. Takashi's less than a hundred yards away, probably on his way here now. *Move!*

Matt acted almost by instinct. Driving the point of his elbow into the gut of the policeman to his right, he used his momentum to continue the spin, bringing his left foot up as he turned and snapping it outward. The heel of his shoe caught the second policeman squarely on the point of the jaw, knocking him backward into the air. The first policeman was coming up off the floor now.

Finish it, he told himself. Finish it and get out.

Matt clasped his hands and brought them down hard on the back of the man's neck, driving him flat.

Then he was out of the room and sprinting down the narrow corridor, eyes darting from side to side, seeking an escape route. Within seconds, he knew, the alarm would bring dozens of police to the scene. He needed to make a move, and make it now.

He raced past metal doors with Japanese characters painted on them, giving no clue as to what lay on the other side. Up ahead he spotted another door, this one with the international symbol for a stairway. He slowed, tried the door, and when he found it was open, pushed inside.

Leaning back against the door he paused, panting, while he considered. A broad flight of concrete steps led in both directions. Up or down? he asked himself.

Down, he decided. He needed to get out of the building, out of the airport, away from the area altogether. The important thing was to get away, put distance between himself and the police. Only then would he have time to think out his next moves.

He charged down the stairs, pulling open the door at the bottom, emerging into a large, crowded hall filled with thousands of departing passengers. Better, he thought, but not good enough. Within minutes they'll have this place cordoned off. They're probably already looking for me. He forced himself to adopt a normal walking pace. Running would just make him easier to spot.

Almost everyone was Japanese. Here and there a lone westerner moved through the crowd. I'm going to stand out like a beacon, Matt thought, unless I can think of some way to divert their attention. He began scanning the crowd, looking for what he needed.

He found the hat first, piled on top of a baggage cart beside a sleeping family. It was a large cloth cap, and he took it as he walked by, putting it on after only a few paces. Change the profile, he told himself;

alter the gestalt. His next acquisition was a shapeless overcoat, picked casually from atop a pile of baggage being pulled by a sweating, overweight foreigner in a track suit. He put it on and pulled the cap farther down over his eyes.

They're looking for somebody they've only seen for a few seconds, and if there's any truth to the belief that we all look the same to them, now's the time to make it work for me, he thought.

Now to get out of here. He had several thousand dollars in cash and traveler's checks, but no Japanese money. No time for formalities, he thought; we'll just have to wave greenbacks at a taxi driver and see what he does.

He spotted signs for the exit, and a sign in English reading TAXIS—LIMOUSINE. Just in front of the automatic doors a policeman stood, hands folded behind his back, rocking back and forth on the balls of his feet. As Matt watched, his radio squawked, and he responded, his eyes flicking across the crowd as he listened to whatever was coming across on the speaker.

Damn. Time for a diversion. Scanning the area, Matt saw signs for the toilets, off to the right. He headed in that direction. Looking neither to the right nor the left he walked straight through the door to the men's room, noting with relief that the area was empty. Going straight to the basins he began pulling wads of paper towels from the dispenser and stuffing them into the trash bin. When he'd filled it half full, he dragged the bin into one of the stalls. He locked the door behind himself, pulled out his Zippo, and set the towels on fire.

When he had it burning well, he hopped up on the toilet seat, levered himself out of the booth, and dropped lightly to the floor. The room was already filling with smoke. Time to move along, he told himself. He had, he estimated, only minutes before they closed the airport down completely, looking for him.

He didn't intend to be there when that happened.

On the way back to the exit doors Matt noticed a fire extinguisher on a wall bracket, and beside it an alarm handle. He grasped the red handle and pulled. From somewhere behind him a bell began to ring.

Time to leave, he thought, adjusting his cap down over his eyes. The policeman who had been standing under the exit door was coming forward now, a look of puzzlement on his face as he held his walkie-talkie to his lips and mumbled something into it. He passed Matt without so much as a glance, hurrying toward the fire alarm.

Off we go, he thought. Pushing through the doors he emerged into the sunlight and heat outside. The air reeked of kerosene and automobile exhaust. Directly in front of him an airport coach was loading up. Two uniformed porters lifted baggage into the lower hold of the big bus, while in front of the open door the driver collected tickets from a line of passengers.

Too risky, Matt decided; too many people. The airport was going to be cordoned off soon, and then the call would go out. He didn't want to be trapped on a bus when that happened.

To his right a line of taxis waited, their drivers reading newspapers and smoking behind the wheel. Matt walked over to the first one, a big late-model black Toyota. The driver, a young Japanese with shoulder-length hair, saw him coming and stubbed out his cigarette butt and folded his newspaper.

Matt leaned down. "Do you speak English?"

The driver's face split in a broad grin, revealing metal teeth. *"Eigo wa wakarimasen, baka-mono."*

Something hard poked into Matt's kidney. "He says he doesn't speak English, Mr. McAllister." Takashi's voice was soft in his ear. "But I do. Get in, please. And stay quiet."

18

They sped along a broad freeway headed, as far as Matt could tell, toward Tokyo. Late-afternoon traffic was heavy, with a large number of double-tandem trailers and buses. The man with the metal teeth drove professionally, weaving expertly in and out of the slower traffic. They entered a built-up area, with electric power lines and factory buildings stretching far into the distance. From time to time Matt could see what looked like a private house or small apartment building, but most of the area was devoted to manufacturing, a bleak, strictly utilitarian landscape of concrete, metal, and wire.

"How'd you find me?" said Matt at last. "How'd you get here so fast?"

Takashi chuckled. "This man flew me here," he

said, indicating the driver. "He's Mr. Itoh's pilot. As soon as I knew where you were going . . ." His voice trailed off.

"Nigel told you, didn't he?"

Takashi nodded. "Yes, of course." He shifted position, still keeping the pistol jammed against Matt's ribs.

"And were you responsible for arresting me? Are you and the police together in this?"

Takashi pursed his lips. "Not exactly. We do not really control the police; we merely have . . . influence. It was important to Mr. Itoh that your movements be tracked once you entered Japan. The easiest way to do that was to tell the immigration police. We therefore informed them of the murders in California. Once you were in custody, we would have used our . . . associates to search and interrogate you. And later, when we wished, we could have gotten you released by our lawyers." He smiled. "You very nearly spoiled the plan. But this way is even better. No explanations needed."

He sat back on the seat. "After my last attempt to kill you—in your house—I decided that chasing you was a waste of time. It is hard for me to admit this. I am not used to such . . . difficulties with those I decide to kill." He touched his arm where, days before, Matt's knife had struck him. "You are clever, Mr. McAllister, and very resourceful. I came to the conclusion that perhaps I would not be successful after all. So when you escaped from your house, I consulted with my colleague."

"Nigel."

"Yes. We discussed the problem of your death, and he advised me that it might be easier to dispose of you in some other way. The important thing, he said, was to keep you from telling others what you know. His idea was that sooner or later he would be able to kill you himself."

He laughed then, a short barking cough. "But *my* idea was that you might eventually come to Japan, looking for me. We are similar in many ways, Mr. McAllister. I think I can imagine how your mind would work. Two hours later he called to tell me that he had spoken to you. I left immediately for Japan, hoping to see you here. And so in the end I was right, wasn't I?"

They rode in silence for several minutes. Finally Matt spoke. "What happens now?"

"I'm going to kill you. But not yet. Mr. Itoh would like to see you first. So we go now to his office in Shinjuku."

"Is that what you do for Itoh? Kill people?"

Takashi's eyes met his. "I am a businessman, Mr. McAllister, a valuable and trusted associate of Mr. Itoh. Business has many different sides. Many kinds of people contribute to its success."

Not much to say to that, Matt decided, as he gazed out at the urban landscape rolling by beyond the window of the taxi. They had reached the city proper now, the streets choked with late-model cars, nearly all of them Japanese. Those few autos that were *not* Japanese were Mercedes, Jaguars, Bentleys, or BMWs—the cream of the European crop. On the sidewalks crowds of people walked purposefully along, all of them well dressed, the men in dark business suits, the women in equally formal professional attire. Nearly everyone Matt saw carried a briefcase of some kind.

If you looked carefully, however, you could see signs that the Japanese miracle hadn't been totally successful, Matt thought. Mixed in among the affluent crowd were men and women dressed in cast-offs, bent over, carrying untidy bundles of rags and paper, just like their American counterparts.

The shops and stores looked bright and new, crowded together under garish neon signs with huge Japanese characters. Up above the street level huge billboards advertised soft drinks, electronics, and food. Some of them were animated, and once Matt saw an entire section of the side of a building composed of huge television screens. As he watched, a woman in a kimono raised a soft-drink can, smiled brightly, and began to speak. Talking billboards? Why not? he told himself. It's Japan, after all.

Everywhere there were people moving, advancing smoothly along the sidewalks and crossings. There was none of the bustle and confusion of Africa and the Middle East here, Matt thought. Instead, people seemed to be isolated, steering expertly through a field of obstacles on their way to myriad destinations.

Few genuinely tall buildings were in evidence. Instead, most construction seemed to be ten stories or less in height. Although the shopfronts and some of the ubiquitous billboards showed considerable art and ingenuity, the architecture itself seemed drab and uninspired, composed of featureless concrete slabs, almost as if the city had been constructed using huge versions of a child's plastic building-block set. Nearly everything looked to be of recent construction. Matt remembered reading about the earthquakes and the bombings during World War II, when vast firestorms had raged through Tokyo.

The big Toyota stopped in front of a tall sky-scraper complex of two enormous glass towers. Takashi concealed his gun. "Get out," he said. "It's time to see Mr. Itoh."

Matt nodded.

They left the car and entered a large modern lobby. There were few people in evidence, and those in uniform bowed low as Takashi approached, their faces carefully blank. They stopped in front of a bank of elevators, and Takashi extracted a metal card from his pocket and inserted it in a slot beside the door. With a hiss the doors parted.

"Inside."

The elevator chirped something to them in Japanese, a woman's voice in a high, childish register. The doors whispered shut. He pressed a button, and the elevator began to move. It accelerated quickly, then slowed, and stopped smoothly at the thirtieth floor. It spoke again in Japanese as the door opened to reveal a long deserted hallway stretching out before them.

"Out," said Takashi, prodding Matt with the barrel of his automatic. "All the way to the end. Mr. Itoh's waiting."

The offices were empty. Of course, thought Matt, it's Sunday. The door was open to the office at the end of the hallway, and as Matt approached it, he could hear classical music coming from inside. He stopped at the door, hesitating.

"Inside," Takashi ordered.

Two men stood by the enormous windows, coffee cups in their hands, gazing out at dusk falling over the vast Tokyo skyline. Beethoven's *Symphonie Pastorale* crashed from tiny speakers mounted high up on the wall. The older of the men turned as they approached, reaching out with a hand to turn down the volume on the stereo at his side. He set down his coffee cup and approached, staring intently at Matt, frank curiosity in his eyes.

Yoshi Itoh looked every day of his eighty-odd years, Matt thought. His thin white hair was combed straight back from his forehead. On his upper lip a razor-thin mustache gave him an almost military bearing.

Itoh's eyes were alert, his frame erect. He stared at Matt for almost a full minute, letting his eyes move over his face. Finally he murmured something softly, and stepped back a pace.

The second man came forward. Overweight, with a pleasant round adolescent's face and lank hair that needed cutting, he looked like an Oriental whiz kid. His clothes were expensive but casual, his tie loosened at the neck, his jacket rumpled. Whereas the older man exuded discipline and tradition, this one appeared relaxed, almost sloppy, his thick black-rimmed glasses giving him the air of an amiable bookworm.

"He says he's impressed." The fat boy's accent was pure California.

"What?"

"Mr. Itoh says he's impressed. He didn't think you'd get this far." He gave a tiny bow. "I'm Kanji Nakamura, by the way."

Matt looked at him carefully. "The computer wizard. Mister Fix-It for TransCentury. I've heard of you."

Itoh spoke then, a short question, accompanied by a sharp movement of his head.

"He wants the videotape," said Kanji.

"Doesn't he speak English?"

"Not a word. But I do, as you see." Kanji grinned. "Berkeley, then MIT. Came back here five years ago." He shook his head. "Seems like yesterday. I miss it sometimes."

"And you've been working for Itoh ever since?"

"Mr. Itoh's my uncle, Mr. McAllister. And my *sensei*. He put me through school. It must have cost him, oh, close to half a million. And now I'm paying him back."

He moved to Matt and began to go through his pockets. He pulled out Matt's passport, ruffled the pages, and popped it into his own pocket. He found Matt's wallet, deftly plucked the cash from it, and gave it back.

"You won't need the money anymore, McAllister," he said with a grin. "This is going to be what you'd call an all-expense-paid vacation." He zipped open Matt's bag and peered inside. "Ah, here we are." He took out the videotape and passed it to the old man, who nodded in satisfaction, turning back to Takashi.

Kanji rubbed his hands together. "Well, that's that," he said. "The old man wanted to get a look at you, but he was mainly interested in the videotape." He looked at Matt thoughtfully. "It would be interesting to know exactly where you heard of me, and how much you know," he said. "But all that's water under the bridge, as they say. You'll be history in an hour."

"What happens then?"

He smiled again. "I can get back to work. It's a great job, actually. My uncle's got money, ambition, and power. I can have anything I want. Anything I need to do my work."

"Which is what, exactly?"

Kanji smiled, showing large white teeth. "Cracking it, Mr. McAllister. Figuring out how it all fits together." He watched Matt's face. "You know anything about quantum physics, the theory of everything, that sort of stuff? No? Doesn't matter. It's pretty simple: physics is about how the world works, and mathematics describes the patterns underlying physical laws. Follow me so far?"

"I'm struggling," Matt said. "But I'm just about able to keep up."

Kanji nodded. "Sense of humor, oho. Very good. Okay, computers generate the math that explains physics. And"—he grinned in triumph—"software programs enable the computers to operate. So it's all connected, see? It's not really different things at all;

it's just one big thing. And once we figure it all out, we'll have a theory of everything!"

"And what happens then?"

Kanji shrugged. "Who the fuck cares? Figuring it all out is the fun part. What people actually *do* with it doesn't really interest me at all."

He glanced at Itoh, who had retired to a corner with Takashi and was engaging him in quiet conversation. "I think my uncle—if he's still alive by then—plans to use it to make a lot of money and eventually take over the world or something, but hey, that's only his agenda, right? Me, I'm just interested in figuring it out. Science is a lot like magic, you know. Pretty soon we'll be able to do practically anything we want. And it's all happening right now."

His eyes shone chipmunk-bright behind his glasses. "I want to be a magician, Mr. McAllister."

A faint flush had appeared on his cheeks. "Everybody in the computer business knows we're close, and everybody wants to get there first. It's like that in science—you're either a leader or a follower. Either you discover a new paradigm, and everybody else plays catch-up, or else somebody else makes the discovery, and you and a whole bunch of other losers spend your careers filling in the blank spaces for somebody else." He grinned. "You can either be an artist or you can do the paint-by-numbers. Remember what Oppenheimer and his buddies said about atomic fission? It was a 'sweet' problem. Well, this is too. We've got the reach and the speed, and we're going to get there. Very soon now."

"So how does all this connect with Ragnarok?"

Kanji glanced at Itoh and back again. "That's what I've been trying to explain to you, McAllister. Ragnarok's just a rocket, but its brain, Odin, is much more than that. Odin is an enormous step toward the theory of everything."

An almost dreamy look came into his eyes. "Odin's system architecture is wonderful; the best in the world. The Americans have always been very, very good at making things, and in Japan we've always been very, very good at figuring out what to do with those things. Odin is the breakthrough that everybody's been waiting for in artificial intelligence. With what's inside Odin people will be able to do things you've never dreamed of. Completely automated factories. Computer-controlled highways. Communication systems that are a hundred times more efficient than what we're using today."

He paused. "It's worth hundreds of billions, obviously. Whoever develops a workable AI system first will dominate the world market for ultrasophisticated software systems for decades to come. There are only two contenders: the Americans and the Japanese." He smiled at Matt, his eyes moist and friendly. "But only one of us can win."

Matt nodded. "So you're going to steal it."

Kanji threw back his head and roared with laughter. "Steal it? No, Mr. McAllister. That idea never crossed our minds."

"What are you going to do, then?"

"It's already done." Kanji folded his hands and spoke quietly. "All we have to do now is wait." He turned as Itoh and Takashi came forward.

Itoh and Kanji exchanged several sentences in low tones. Itoh glanced once at Matt, nodded briefly, and said, *"Wakatte imasu. Ko shite hoshii."*

"Hai." Kanji bowed, stepped back a pace.

Takashi pulled his leather gloves on and took Matt's elbow. He bowed to Itoh. *"Aitsu nesaseta ato, karada wa do surun no yo?"*

The old man's face seemed to stiffen then, as if he had been insulted.

From behind them Kanji's voice came. "Do with the body?" he said in English. "Whatever you decide. Hell, just get it done, okay?"

As Matt was led out the door, Kanji smiled at him. "Don't worry," he confided. "The man's an expert. You probably won't feel a thing."

19

The big Toyota slid quietly back into the Tokyo traffic. From behind the tinted windows the world looked like a silent movie as they moved through the evening streets.

How much time have I got? Matt thought. The interview was over, the business done. All that remained now was to find a quiet place to do the killing. He was conscious of Takashi's pistol, its muzzle resting gently against his ribs.

He sat quietly in the backseat, thinking about death and how it would come. His, or Takashi's. One or the other was highly likely within the next few minutes.

He considered his options. Both Takashi and his driver were armed, both were expert in the use of violence. Either man, he knew, would kill him instantly if trouble threatened. So the problem was really quite simple.

He either had to kill them first, or get away.

Getting away might be easier, Matt decided. He stopped thinking about the two men in the car with him and began to concentrate on his surroundings. Night had fallen, and the crowds on the sidewalks had thinned somewhat. He had no idea where he was, but his location didn't really matter. He was looking for cover, for places to go once he got out of the car. He needed a park, a sports field, or an open-air market—something that would give him room to move, places to hide. Something he could lose himself in, where they would have to come after him on foot, one by one. Something like—

The subway.

He saw the lighted sign, the stairs heading downward, the people coming out clutching their parcels and newspapers. The entrance was going by on their right. And now the Toyota was slowing, stopping for the traffic light at the intersection.

Now or never, he thought.

Time seemed to slow down, stretch, as he began his series of moves. Half a deep breath to start with, as the car stopped completely at the intersection. Focusing, drawing in, and then two movements at once, smooth and powerful, the breath exploding from his lungs in a cry as he grasped Takashi's gun hand at the wrist, at the same time driving the flat of his other hand into the man's Adam's apple.

The silencer made a sound like an air gun as

Takashi got off a wild shot into the upholstery and fell forward, clawing at his throat. Matt leaned forward, grasping the seat belt in his hand and pulling it up and across the neck of the driver, reaching over and pulling the chrome-plated pistol from his shoulder holster at the same time.

Gun up, a quick glance at Takashi, and three shots in a triangular pattern against the side window of the Toyota, the safety glass frosting over instantly. Then up with his shoe, punching out the glass in big chunks, clearing a hole. In a second he was squeezing through the window, pushing desperately now, kicking back with his feet as Takashi made a desperate grab for him.

He broke free, falling backward onto the street amid a blare of horns and screech of brakes as cars swerved. He hit the pavement hard and felt the precious gun slide from his grasp and skitter under the car. No time to get it now, he thought, scrambling to his feet as the Toyota's doors opened.

He bolted, broken-field running through the busy traffic toward the subway entrance, gasping for air, expecting a bullet in his back any second. He took the steps at the entrance three at a time, hurtling headlong down the narrow tiled corridor, pushing others out of the way, *moving,* desperate to escape.

He reached the bottom of the staircase, a T-junction, signs in Japanese pointing in both directions. Matt didn't have time to think; he chose the tunnel with the most people in it, and began to race down it. Don't look back, he commanded himself;

don't wonder about how close behind they are. Don't think about when you'll feel the first bullet hit.

Slightly curved, the tunnel stretched for over a hundred yards. Matt sprinted around the end to find it opening up into a large public space. He stopped, leaning against a wall to catch his breath, and looked around.

He had no idea what he should do next, or even where he should go. His only desire was to put as much distance between himself and his pursuers as he could in the shortest possible time.

Wherever he was, he thought, it was *busy*. Thousands of people milled about the underground hall, while above them yellow and white lighted signs in Japanese pointed in all directions. Shops and boutiques set into the walls were doing a brisk business. For a place with so many people, Matt thought, it was amazingly clean.

A sign in English above his head said MARUNOUCHI LINE THIS WAY, and he followed it, plunging into the heart of the crowd, letting them sweep him along the corridor, down yet another level, into the subway itself.

He stopped just before the turnstiles, staring at the enormous map of the subway system on the wall in front of him. Above the names of the stations were numbers, which Matt assumed indicated the fare. Beside the map was a bank of what looked like slot machines, into which travelers were feeding coins, punching numbers, and taking small cardboard tickets as they emerged from the slot below. He fumbled his wallet from his coat, and then remembered that he had no money. Kanji had taken it all, even the traveler's checks. He'd left only the credit cards.

He saw a woman behind a magazine counter, and approached her. She bowed as he approached, her eyes wary. *"Hai!"*

Here goes nothing, Matt thought. "Money," he said, holding up his credit card and speaking slowly and distinctly. "I want money. Can you help me?"

She looked flustered. *"Sumimasen,"* she murmured, giving another small bow. *"Wakarimasen. Mo ichido o-negai shimasu. Motto yukkuri itte kudasai."*

Sweet Jesus, thought Matt. I can't understand a word she's saying. He waved his credit card at her. "Credit card, see? I want money. Japanese money."

Comprehension broke over her face like a wave. *"Chotto matte kudasai, o-negai shimasu."* And with that she scuttled off, beckoning to another woman at the other end of the counter.

The second woman came forward. Sizing up the situation she shook her head, and smiled regretfully. "Not possible," she said in heavily accented English. "Sorry, not possible."

"Look—" Matt began, and then, over the woman's shoulder, he spotted Takashi and the driver emerging from the tunnel. The driver caught sight of Matt, grabbed Takashi's arm, and together the two men began to run toward him.

"Shit," muttered Matt, turning away, back toward the turnstiles, where uniformed attendants were punching tickets. Moving fast he pushed past them and onto the platform, ignoring their angry exclamations.

Wide and clean, the platform teemed with passengers, most of whom had arranged themselves neatly in groups behind painted lines on the floor, presumably where the subway cars would stop. Overhead signs in English and Japanese announced the arrival of the next train in sixty seconds.

Matt pushed to the center of the platform, stopped, and waited, glancing up and down the track. A group of sweaty Japanese kids in dirty baseball uniforms stared curiously at Matt, whispering to each other. He felt a tap on his shoulder and turned to see two blue-uniformed policemen beside him. One held a printed sheet, while the other spoke softly into a walkie-talkie.

The first policeman bowed. "*Chotto sumimasen,*" he murmured. "Passport, please."

"Passport?" Matt fumbled in his pockets. "I— I'm afraid I've left it behind. Yes, it must be back at the hotel. Sorry."

The policeman frowned. "We go to your hotel," he said finally. "I need to see the passport." He spoke English slowly, as if to a child. A crowd gathered around them, silent, watching carefully, keeping a safe and respectful distance.

The man who had been listening on the walkie-talkie suddenly looked up at Matt. "*Hai, wakari mashta,*" he said into the mouthpiece. He turned, murmuring something in a clipped, low voice to his companion.

"*So desu,*" said the first policeman, snapping

open the holster on his revolver. Just then Matt caught sight of Takashi and the driver, bursting onto the platform at the far end.

"Sorry," whispered Matt, as he caught the first policeman across the Adam's apple with the flat of his hand, snapping the man's head back hard.

He then turned, driving his fingers into the second policeman's solar plexus.

The crowd broke in panic, scrambling back, some of the passengers screaming in fear and confusion. At that moment Matt felt a building vibration as the train approached through the tunnel. And from the corner of his eye he saw Takashi running forward, his hand going into the pocket of his jacket.

Matt didn't stop to think. He turned, took three quick steps, and launched himself off the platform and onto the tracks, directly into the path of the oncoming train.

Cool and damp, the subway tunnel was a twilit world, lit by dim bulbs set along the ceiling every ten yards. Matt tried desperately to control his breathing as he moved crabwise along the wall, keeping well back in the shadows. He paused, listening, hearing nothing but the dripping of water far off in the darkness.

He had taken a hell of a chance jumping out in front of the approaching train. A close and desperate gamble, but it had paid off. He had landed on his feet scant yards in front of the train, gathered himself, and vaulted over the low concrete barrier onto the parallel rail.

The oncoming train had blared past, its warning horn echoing in his ears. Temporarily hidden from sight Matt had taken advantage of the few seconds of cover to dodge into the parallel tunnel, seeking distance and darkness. He heard shouts behind him, then nothing. Fighting to keep his breathing under control he pushed on deeper into the underground maze.

He was safe for the moment, but trapped, trapped like a rabbit in its burrow, with the ferrets on the way. He had no idea where the tunnels led, no clue as to where his survival lay.

Get out, he thought. Get out and get away. But how? And to where? In the dim light he could see no air shafts, no inspection ducts. No way to reach the surface.

In the distance he heard a rumble and a whoosh. Turning, he caught a glimmer on the damp wall of the tunnel, a faint glow that seemed to grow in intensity. Another train, he thought. Another train's coming.

He shrank back into a recess set into the wall. As the train rumbled closer, a wild thought took shape in his brain. It would be difficult and dangerous, but perhaps his only route out of the tunnels to freedom.

The train's dual headlamps stabbed the darkness as it thundered around the curve. Matt could feel vibrations through the concrete as the subway train bore down on where he crouched, hiding.

He burrowed farther back into the recess, seeking the safety of the shadows. The timing for this had to be perfect, he thought, watching the lead car approach. He had seconds to decide.

As the train came abreast of him, Matt straightened and began to run alongside it, scant inches away from the rocking metal of the cars as they swept past. He ran doggedly, willing his legs to move faster, searching for a handhold as the cars flashed by.

The last car was coming up now. Matt glanced left, looked again, and finally spied what he needed: a chromed handrail, above a footplate at the end of the last car. As the handrail came alongside he seized it, swinging himself up.

Standing on the footplate he gulped air into his tortured lungs. Had anyone inside the train seen him? The interior of the train was lighted, the outside of the tunnel dark except for the illumination bulbs set into the ceilings. Everyone was seated, facing forward, and no one appeared to have noticed.

So far so good, he thought grimly. Gripping the top of the handrail tightly he began to pull himself up, reaching the top of the car just as the train approached the next station. He saw white columns flashing by, yellow signs, and crowds of people waiting at the platform's edge. Scant inches lay between the top of the car and the high-voltage cables overhead. He flattened himself along the top of the car, just under the cables, hoping to make himself invisible to the people waiting on the platform below.

The train sighed to a halt, doors opening to the sound of chimes. Matt lay perfectly flat, motionless, holding his breath. If anyone had spotted him climbing on board, now was when they would say so. Two uniformed policemen stood in the middle of the platform, watching the passengers carefully. Neither one glanced up. If they had, they would have seen Matt's eyes staring back at them from the top of the subway car.

With a hiss the doors closed. A few seconds later the train moved off.

The top of the train was smooth stainless steel, with an air-conditioning unit in the center of each car. Matt hung on desperately as the train flashed through the tunnels. He had no idea where the train was going, when it would stop next, and where in the vast night-time sprawl of Tokyo he would be. Exhausted and hungry, he desperately needed food and rest.

Only one certainty kept him going: if the Dragon ever found him again, he would kill him on the spot.

Sensing the train slowing once more, Matt flattened himself. As the station lights approached, he saw people waiting patiently for the train to stop, lined up obediently behind the painted lines on the station platform, clutching shopping bags and briefcases, staring straight ahead. None of them gave the top of the railway car so much as a passing glance.

The chimes bonged softly, the doors hissed shut, and the train moved off once more. Glancing ahead Matt saw open sky, and realized that the train was coming up from underground, emerging into the open night air.

They moved up onto an elevated track now, and Matt saw the nighttime city taking shape around him. He had quick impressions of crowded streets, lines of cars and trucks, their yellow and red lamps making snake-patterns in the streets, pedestrians thronging the sidewalks. The buildings were garishly lit, their stories-tall animated advertisements casting pulses of colored light out into the night. He clung to the car as it rocketed on through the city.

It seemed like an eternity until the next stop. Finally, he could feel the train slowing, rounding a long curve, coming up to meet the platform lights ahead. Gathering his strength he got ready.

As the train slowed by the platform, Matt edged closer to the far side. The train stopped, the doors opened, and people began to pour inside. Matt glanced down once to get his bearings, let go, and slid over the side of the car down onto the roadbed below.

He landed off-balance, twisting his ankle painfully. Stifling a cry of pain, he hobbled off as quickly as he could into the darkness on the far side of the train, putting distance between himself and the platform lights and the people.

Across a second set of tracks was a low wall, and beyond it, darkness. Matt lurched across the rails and hauled himself up on the concrete parapet. He rolled over it and down into the darkness beyond just as the train behind him closed its doors and began to pull out of the station.

The night was quiet, and there were no enemies in sight. Matt closed his eyes, turned to huddle against the concrete, and drifted unsteadily into unconsciousness.

* * *

He awoke with a start, his heart thudding heavily through his ears as he turned on the wet ground, his eyes probing the darkness. Something had brushed against him, awakening him. His hand snaked out and fastened around a scrawny ankle. He pulled hard, and with a shriek of fear the man who had been crouching beside him crashed to the concrete. Matt got a blast of cheap whiskey mixed with fish sauce as he pulled his companion close.

His eyes widened at the sight of a foreigner, and he began to jabber incomprehensibly. Just a half-drunk bum, Matt thought disgustedly, noting the stinking rags. He patted the man down and retrieved his wallet and watch. Then he gave him a sharp cuff on the side of the head and sent him scampering into the darkness.

Matt lay back, staring up at the stars, letting his ragged breathing return to normal. He was in a vacant lot of some kind, the ground cold and damp, smelling of oil, excrement, and cinders.

The lights of the city blazed on the periphery, the noise of the traffic on the overpass muted and low. From behind him he heard the muted sound of the underground train moving off from the station platform.

He rose to his knees. He was weak with hunger, dizzy with fatigue. He checked his watch; not yet midnight. He had to find a place to spend the night, a place where he could think, rest, and collect his wits. Above all, a place where he could get food.

Yuki.

Of course, he thought, relief washing over him.

Yukiko Matsushima. Her address and telephone number were in his wallet. Or had been, he told himself.

On the ground around him he saw bits of paper, and realized that the bum who'd tried to rob him had emptied his wallet, looking for cash. Cursing, he bent to pick up the scraps—receipts, scrawled shopping lists, business cards—scattered across the damp, stinking ground.

Yuki's card was nowhere to be found.

Cursing, he clambered to his feet, pulling his filthy jacket closed. Favoring his tender ankle he began to hobble off toward the lights at the edge of the lot, trying to remember what Yuki had said to him on the day she'd given him her card. "My apartment is easy to find. It's in Shinjuku, that's a kind of neighborhood. You look for a big camera store, it's called Yodobashi, and I am five doors away."

Find a telephone, he told himself. Find a telephone, get her number. He staggered out of the vacant lot, across a wide intersection, and into a maze of busy streets. I've got no money, he thought; no passport. Both the cops *and* the gangsters are looking for me. If I can't find Yuki soon, I'll be dead.

The late-night district he had entered seemed populated mainly by middle-aged men in business suits, most of them drunk, their sweaty faces illuminated by the garish neon of wall displays reaching halfway up the sides of the tall buildings. Huge red, blue, and green video screens carried a parade of images and messages in large Japanese characters six feet high.

Music blared from every shopfront and bar, and in front of some, men and women with microphones kept up a nonstop patter at high volume, enticing customers inside.

Matt gazed curiously at the sea of faces in front of him, receiving blank stares in return. One or two people glanced curiously at the tall foreigner in the tattered, filthy clothes. Then they moved quickly aside and passed by, not glancing back.

Halfway down a side street he found what he'd been looking for. The bright green telephone on the wall was unmistakable, and on a chain Matt spied what could only be a city directory.

Thank God, he murmured as he picked it up. Then he realized that both the directory and the instructions for the telephone were written in Japanese.

He pawed through the pages, searching in vain for a section in English, French, or *any* European language. He wiped his eyes, trying to focus in the dim light. If only the damned streetlight wouldn't blink, he thought. Something was wrong with the bloody streetlight. It wasn't bright enough, and—and it was going off and on. Blinking. He raised his head.

Shit, it wasn't a proper streetlight at all. It was some kind of a goddamned advertising sign. A huge red neon sign, and it was blinking on and off, directly above him. The shop below it was closed and shuttered, the street nearly deserted, but the damned neon sign kept blinking on and off.

Matt stood in the middle of the street and stared at the sign, nearly three stories high, as it broadcast its simple message into the night.

On and off.
Off and on.
In English.
YODOBASHI CAMERA.
Well I'll be damned, he thought.

20

Yuki lived in a ground-floor flat tucked away behind a late-night convenience store with a large MILD SEVEN awning outside and a row of vending machines selling everything from cans of hot coffee to fifths of whiskey, lined up against the wall like off-duty robots. Although the entrance door was on the noisy street, a long and narrow corridor led back behind the store to where she lived, and Matt had the impression of being in a quiet, safe nest, far away from the bustle of the street.

She had opened the door cautiously, her eyes widening in surprise as she took in his appearance. "Matt-san . . . is it really you? What on earth has happened to you?"

Relief washed over him. "Kind of a long story," he said. "Mind if I tell it inside?"

She had bowed then, and stepped back. *"Dozo go-yakkuri,"* she murmured. "Please come in."

She led him into a tiny living room, where all the furniture seemed to be no more than six inches off the floor. Wincing with effort, he lowered himself onto a couch, bending his knees awkwardly in the unaccustomed posture.

Yuki's face still showed sleep, but she was fully alert as she looked at him now with wide, serious eyes, taking in his ripped and ruined clothes, his bloody hands, his bruises.

"Look, I—"

She put soft fingers to his lips. "Not yet. Get clean first, then some food. Then we can talk." She took his hand and pulled him along behind her through the tiny apartment. At the end of the corridor was a bathroom, shiny with tile and chrome. Yuki opened a cupboard and took out a towel, frowning. "Not big enough," she said. "But okay for now." She peered into the cupboard again, shaking her head. "Damn."

"What are you looking for?"

"Something for you to wear," she said. "Your clothes are filthy. Nothing of mine will fit you, obviously, but—ah, here it is." Triumphantly, she pulled out something that looked like a striped hospital shift. "Perfect."

Matt grasped the thin fabric. "What is it, a bathrobe?"

Yuki smiled. "Sort of. We call it a *yukata*. It

belonged to an old boyfriend. I hope you don't mind."

She looked at him and frowned, wrinkling her nose. "There's the shower; soap's inside." She pushed him forward gently. "And leave your dirty clothes on the floor, okay?"

Afterward, his hair and skin scrubbed long and hard, he told her everything, starting with the evening at Marty's apartment after he'd taken her to the hospital. Leaving nothing out, he went through the escalating sequence of violence and mystery that had brought him to her door.

Yuki stayed silent throughout. "I can hardly believe this," she said at last. They sat across from each other in the tiny living room, Matt on the low couch, Yuki curled up on the cushions, her long legs tucked under her. On the low wooden table between them sat a bottle of Suntory whiskey, two glasses, and the remains of a large sandwich.

Matt sat awkwardly, trying to preserve some sense of modesty. His thin cotton *yukata* barely covered him, and seemed in constant danger of falling open. Yuki's shower had been no bigger than the one on Buttons's sailboat, but the water had been hot and plentiful, and he had spent a good twenty minutes letting his muscles relax under the pounding water.

Matt nodded. "I really don't believe it myself," he said, feeling the unfamiliar whiskey start to warm his body. "But it's true. All of it."

She shook her head. "You know, I never expected to hear from you again."

"Likewise," said Matt. "But I'm very glad I'm here."

More than I ever expected, he admitted to himself. Seeing Yuki again had reminded him, forcefully, of how attractive she was. She was taller than she had appeared in her hospital bed, her legs long and slim, her body well proportioned. He found himself remembering the soft brush of her lips on his face when she'd kissed him in Washington. Although it had been only the briefest of contacts, he recalled it vividly now.

Attractive wasn't the word, he decided. She was stunning. Her long hair, pulled back with a simple jade clip, cascaded down across one shoulder. She wore no makeup, but had somehow managed to scrub the sleep from her face while he had been in the shower. Her bruises were almost gone, Matt noted. The classic oval of her face framed wide and lovely eyes.

Quite a change, he thought, from the battered woman he'd taken to the hospital that night.

He leaned back. The alcohol had relaxed him, and the food rested comfortably in his stomach. In minutes he would probably begin to run down, like a watch, and fold into a tiny ball on the couch.

Yuki pursed her lips. "I am glad, too, Matt. But now we have to think what to do." She picked up her whiskey glass and took a small sip. "Tell me about this man you call the Dragon." She dipped her finger in the whiskey and began to draw on the shiny surface of the low table. "This character is *ryu*, and it means 'dragon.' If Takashi Yamashita is really a *yakuza*, then he may use the name 'Dragon' professionally. His employer, Yoshi Itoh, is very rich and *very* powerful. Itoh is rumored to be connected to one of the large organized crime syndicates, the *Yamaguchi-gumi*. If so, Takashi is not the only *yakuza* who are looking for you, Matt. Everyone in the syndicate will be helping them."

"When I met Itoh, there was a third man in the room as well. Kanji, Itoh's nephew. He spoke good English. What do you know about him?"

She looked up. "That is Kanji Nakamura. He's famous, a kind of genius, really. The newspapers call him the Japanese Einstein. He has invented some very sophisticated software for the company. We use some of it at my university, in fact, to do our research on neural computer networks. If Kanji worked for us, we would be much farther along with our work than we are. But Itoh is his uncle. And Kanji would prefer to work for Itoh, I think."

"Why is that?"

"Because they are both the same, even though fifty years separate them. Itoh is of the oldest generation of Japanese businessmen. The generation that made it possible for us to go to war; the generation, too, that helped Japan recover from the war, and rebuild its industry and its economy. Itoh is a strong-willed man, Matt. All his life he has tried to become as strong as possible. Kanji is a scientist, but he has the same drive that Itoh does: to control, to dominate."

"And now they're trying to sabotage Ragnarok."

Yuki nodded. "It looks that way. And I doubt that you can stop them. You are only one person, Matt. Yoshi Itoh is the head of a very large company. He has connections to everyone in the government. If the *yakuza* are working for him, then I understand how they knew to stop you at the airport. The *yakuza* have connections with all the powerful people here. They tap telephones; they intercept mail. The group is like a giant spiderweb, what you call an old boy's network." She paused. "But how did they find out you were coming to Japan?"

Matt gave a thin smile. "One of my colleagues at work told them. A man named Nigel Hastings."

She put her glass down. "A person in your own office? Why would he do this?"

"Money. Everybody needs it, and these days the Japanese have it. Nigel's not too different from TransCentury Systems, I guess. And the Jefferson Institute operates pretty much the way TransCentury does, if you think about it—it survives by selling things to other people, in a highly competitive market." He shrugged. "Nigel got a better offer, that's all."

He leaned back on the sofa. "What the Jefferson Institute will write about Ragnarok won't be the last word, but it will be the first. And for that reason it's going to be very influential. Like the first reviews of a new book or movie—everybody's going to want to know what we think."

Yuki nodded. "And if people don't want anyone to know the bad news . . ."

"Right. Did Itoh promise Nigel a fat grant if he'd

slant the report? Is he somehow making money on the side with this? Who knows?" He paused. "It would have been easy for Nigel to pass information to Takashi. The phone system in the institute isn't secure; anyone can retrieve voice-mail messages. He heard my message to Buttons about the videotape, and he picked up the address of my motel in California the same way. Later, he heard the flight announcement when I called him from the airport."

"But why did he blow up that person? The one in your car."

Matt shook his head. "I think that was a miscalculation. The bomb was meant for me. It didn't occur to him that Teddy might bring the car himself."

"So what are you going to do?"

Matt leaned forward. "I've got an old boy's network of my own. An old friend of mine works at the American embassy, and I thought I might give him a call. Back in the days when we used to work together, he was pretty good at finding stuff out. I want to find out more about Takashi. And about Itoh and his whiz kid, Kanji."

"And what will you do with what you find out?"

He flashed her a tight smile. "I'll fix things—make everything okay again. That's what *I'm* good at."

At ten o'clock the next morning Matt and Yuki sat facing each other in the apartment's tiny kitchen. He had a cup of strong coffee in front of him, his second, and held the telephone to his ear as he watched her delicately forking rice and dried seaweed into her mouth with a pair of wooden chopsticks.

"American embassy, good morning."

"Tom Clegg, please."

"That'll be the Economics Section. One moment, I'll see if he's in."

A buzz, a click, and then a familiar voice came on the line. "Clegg."

"Tommy, this is Matt McAllister."

"McAllister? Well, I'll be damned. Where you calling from, Handyman? Christ, it must be what, five years?" Cowboy Tommy Clegg's West Texas drawl was deep and rich, just the way Matt remembered it, as familiar as an old pair of shoes.

He felt his spirits start to rise. In the old days Tommy Clegg had been one of the best Coyotes in the business, and a damned good friend. Cowboy Tommy had worked a different beat most of the time, usually Europe or the Far East, but their paths had crossed often, and once, in Beirut, they'd done a three-month assignment together. It had wound up with the two of them racing through the war-torn city together at night, scant blocks ahead of Syrian troops, trying to get to their safe house behind the green line before they were randomly killed by one of the hundreds of mortar shells exploding all around them. "I don't mind the thought of a bullet with my name on it," Tommy Clegg had said later, sipping straight gin in the bunker, two floors under the street. "It's the sonofabitch that just says, *To whom it may concern,* that gives me the shits."

"Great connection, Handyman. You sound like you're practically next door."

Matt cleared his throat. "I'm in Tokyo, Tommy."

"Well, hell, boy, what you doin' here? Thought you was through with the business." He pronounced it *bidnez*.

"Long story, Cowboy," Matt said, finishing the last of his coffee. "It's why I called, in fact. We have to talk."

There was silence for a moment. "You, ah, wanna come in, that it?" Tommy Clegg's voice had dropped a register and gone soft around the edges. *Coming in* meant coming to the embassy and sitting down in the "bubble"—the secure room inside the walls, where no one could hear you, and where the place was swept for bugs daily. The place where the really important conversations took place.

"No," Matt said. "Not that. Outside. Somewhere open, somewhere public. You live here, I don't. Pick someplace."

The line hummed quietly. "Ueno Park," Tommy Clegg said at last. "Up by the National Museum. Nice big open place, got a big pool with ducks, all that kinda shit, everybody goes there in good weather to eat lunch. I'll be sitting on one of the benches by the fountain at one o'clock. That suit you?"

"Ueno Park," Matt repeated. "One o'clock. Come alone, Tommy."

"I know the drill, Handyman," Clegg said. He dropped his voice. "You gonna tell me what the hell this is all about, partner?"

"When I see you, Tommy," Matt said.

"Better be good," Clegg murmured, and hung up.

It would be good, Matt thought, as sat staring at his coffee cup, thinking. It would be damned good.

Just the sort of problem the Cowboy liked.

"If you're going to Ueno Park," Yuki said, breaking his spell, "then you're going to need decent clothes. The ones you arrived in are ruined." She got up. "There are a couple of places down the street. I can pick up what you need. I'll just get some money."

"Wait. You don't have to—"

She grinned at him. "Take a look at yourself, Matt-san. Would you rather walk around like that?"

She came back a moment later, shrugging into a fierce-looking leather jacket, a Marlon Brando classic with silver snaps and buckles, and holding a black-visored helmet by the strap.

"Be back in about an hour." She opened a closet, took out a pair of heavy motorcycle boots, and stepped into them, buckling the straps. "There's more coffee if you want it. Rice in the bowl."

She put on her helmet, pushing her long hair out of the way, smiling as she caught his glance. "This is my secret identity, Matt. I'm not really a professor at all, you see, but one of the *bosozoku.*"

"The what?"

"*Bosozoku.* The thunder clan. It's what we call bikers in Japan."

She opened the back door to the flat, revealing a powerful red-and-black Kawasaki GPz 400 crouched in the alley. It had a racing cowling and upswept twin pipes. She hopped aboard, touched the starter button, and its throaty roar exploded in the confined space.

"Back soon." She gunned the engine, popped the clutch, and roared out of the alley into the sunlit street beyond.

21

A little after noon Matt found himself perched precariously on the pillion seat of the big Kawasaki, his hands tight on Yuki's waist, as she roared expertly through the Tokyo traffic. Her long hair billowed back from under her helmet in the slipstream, tickling his nose.

They weaved left and right, dodging cars, trucks, and pedestrians in the crowded streets. This was nothing like an American city, Matt thought. Like New York or Boston it had the same crowded, bustling near-chaos atmosphere, but none of the open frustration and annoyance, the blaring horns and shouted curses, that seemed so much a part of an American traffic jam. Drivers sat quietly in their cars, expressions impassive, waiting for lights to change and lanes to clear. All the while blue-gray fumes rippled upward from thousands of exhausts.

Yuki sped smoothly through the congestion, weaving back and forth across the lines of waiting vehicles, matching speed and movement to the rest of the motorcycles and scooters also playing bob-and-weave.

They sped past featureless blocks of concrete and glass. Modern Tokyo was carpentered and utilitarian, almost sterile, Matt thought, hardly designed for people at all. Here and there he caught glimpses of green space, of open areas and, once in a while, the upward curve of a traditional tiled roof.

Twenty minutes later Yuki steered her motorcycle up on the sidewalk and stopped. "Here we are," she said, taking off her helmet and shaking her long hair loose. "Ueno Park."

Matt dismounted and looked around. To his right was an imposing older traditional structure, very wide, with a massive tiled roof with upswept ends. "The National Museum," Yuki said, following his gaze. "Lots of old paintings, swords, and things like that." She wrinkled her nose. "They made us go there frequently when I was small. I've not been inside since." She smiled. "The best part was the restaurant. After we looked at all the things in the museum, the teacher would take us there for ice cream. That's what I remember most." She turned the other way. "This is the park entrance. Shall we go in? It's nearly one o'clock."

Matt shook his head. "Not yet. Let's walk around a little bit. I want to get a look at things."

Arm in arm they began to walk along the park's perimeter. Matt kept his eyes busy the whole time, taking in the details of the wall around the park, the placement of the trees and buildings, the roads and paths leading in and out.

Pedestrian and vehicular traffic was light along the side roads, and he briefly scanned the parked cars and the faces of people passing by. In front of them a group of Japanese men in virtually identical drab business suits trudged along in herdlike fashion, led by a woman with an imperious voice and a brightly colored flag mounted on the end of a thin metal baton.

"Salarymen on vacation," murmured Yuki. "They all dress the same; we call it the *dobu-nezumi* look. It means 'brown rat.' "

They had turned the corner now, and were heading parallel to the park wall, along a narrow sidewalk above a bustling commercial district. "Ueno Station," said Yuki, pointing down at the congestion. "And across the street is Ameyoko-cho Arcade."

The street below was choked with goods trucks, and on the sidewalks crowds of people milled in and out of what looked like hundreds of small shops, each with its garish neon sign above the entrance. An elevated railway ran through the midst of the bustle, with electric trains moving in both directions. He thought of his wild ride through the subway the night before and shivered.

They walked slowly up the hill into the park, passing benches and groups of people talking and eating ice cream in small groups. To the right stood a small shrine, with a statue of what looked like a samurai warrior walking a dog.

Yuki pointed ahead. "The fountain is just up here, Matt. Do you want me to come with you?"

"No," he said. "You'd better stay on the sidelines." He looked ahead to where the park opened up. "I can take care of things from here, I think. Go back to where you parked your motorcycle and wait for me there." He squeezed her hand. "I'll be fine."

She shivered. "I hope so." She reached up and drew his face down close and gave him a light kiss on the cheek, so soft it felt like the brush of a butterfly's wing. "Be careful, Matt." Then she turned and walked away, not looking back.

The fountain area was essentially a rectangle, trees and a low wall forming the sides, the middle dominated by a square-edged pool in which hordes of ducks swam to and fro, bobbing for breadcrumbs.

Small groups of Japanese schoolchildren, in black, military-style uniforms with brass buttons and visored caps reminiscent of the last century, sat on the grass sharing their lunches from small lacquered boxes, carefully picking out choice morsels with their chopsticks and offering them around, trading with each other. Several mothers pedaled bicycles through the park, their children stuffed into carrier baskets at the front.

Small kiosks sold cigarettes, newspapers, and candy. Nearby, a man fed popcorn to the pigeons, letting the birds perch on his shoulders and arms. A knot of Japanese cub scouts looked on delightedly, clapping and laughing. Elderly men sat on the benches and played cards, large bottles of Sapporo beer beside them.

Matt found Cowboy Tommy Clegg halfway down, sprawled across a bench. The two men recognized each other immediately. The Cowboy spoke first. "Hello, Handyman," he said, his wide grin spreading like the sunrise across his seamed face. "We got a lot to catch up on."

He hoisted himself upright and patted the bench beside him. "Take a pew, old son, and let's talk."

Tommy Clegg hiked up his trousers over the tops of his hand-tooled lizard-skin cowboy boots and blew cigarette smoke through pursed lips. He flipped over the pages of the yellow pad he'd been using to take notes on. "Christ, Handyman, sounds like you've had a hell of a time." He shook his head. "Anything more you want to tell me?"

Matt shook his head. He'd spent the last twenty minutes outlining the last week of his life to the person who'd been his closest associate in the old days, holding nothing back, omitting no detail. It was all out now, all of it, everything from Marty's clandestine tape of the Ragnarok launch to his meeting last night with Yuki. "That's it, Tommy," he said. "There's nothing more."

Tommy Clegg looked at his watch. "Okay, Handyman. Where do you go from here?"

"I need to find the Dragon," said Matt. "Get the videotape back. Then you have to help me run this back through channels to Washington, flash priority.

Tommy, this thing is big, and we haven't got much time. I've got an idea of where—"

Tommy's big hand came up. "Whoa up, hoss. Not so fast. Got to be careful here. We don't want to get the cookie-pushers involved, do we? Now, I've heard of this guy Takashi. And if half the stories are true, he's meaner'n catshit on a pump handle. The Dips wouldn't know the first thing about how to handle this." He smiled broadly. "Hell, not only don't they *know* nothin', they don't even *suspect* much."

He hunched forward on the bench. "See, you've just told me a story most folks would find a little hard to swallow. To hear you tell it we've got a conspiracy involving a major Japanese corporation, a U.S. defense contractor, and God knows how many other people"—he cocked an eye at Matt—"including maybe one or two of your own buddies, all of 'em out to get you."

He slapped his knee. "Why, shit, boy, we got something for everybody here. Japanese gangsters, motorbike assassins, things that go bang in the night . . . Hell, you ought to be able to get movie rights."

He leaned forward. "Tell you what. How about you come back to the office with me, just for a bit. Have a little debriefing session with one or two of my colleagues; talk the situation over with them. Then we'll all decide where things go from there. How's that, Handyman?"

Matt shook his head. "You and I are field men, Tommy. You *know* we haven't got time for a dog-and-pony show around the conference table."

Tommy Clegg sighed and sat up, looking from side to side. "So what the hell *do* you want?"

"Money, Tommy. And a safe house. Somewhere I can hole up while I finish this thing."

Clegg shook his head. "No can do, Handyman. Things don't work that way anymore."

Matt stared at him. "Jesus, Tommy," he said. "Just a couple of thousand, just for a week or so. It won't take any longer than that. What's the problem?"

Clegg looked at him with mournful, hound-dog eyes. "*You're* the problem, Matt."

"What are you talking about?" Matt's voice was a whisper.

Clegg looked down, made a note on his yellow pad. "Even before you called, I saw your name in the morning catch." The *catch* was embassy slang for the overnight collection of classified cables that Tommy Clegg read first thing each morning. "Didn't say a hell of a lot, tell you the truth. Wanted to know if anybody out here'd seen you, that's all."

He cleared his throat. "So I punched your name into the net. Things are a whole lot better organized in the business than they were a few years ago, partner. Don't take but a few seconds now, what with the computer network they use." He paused. "Came up with a whole shitload of flags."

Matt sat frozen, listening, while his eyes darted around the park.

Tommy Clegg made another note on the pad. His voice came like a sigh, a soft whisper through the forest. "They want me to arrest you, Matt. They got a lot of questions for you, starting with a couple of murders in California, a car bomb in Washington, plus some shit about burning down half a block of Georgetown or something." He glanced over at Matt. "You been a damn busy boy, Handyman."

"Tommy, listen to me. None of that is important right now. I told you, they're after me. They've—"

"Damn straight they're after you. I don't know about the *yakuza*, but your own doggone *government*'s after you." He tapped his pencil on the pad lying across his knees. "They got a team of gentlemen, no shit, flying in this afternoon from Okinawa, just to see you, Handyman, and they want you to be there for the party."

He tapped his pencil again, harder this time. "I don't know what you done back home, boy, but you got a lot of people's BVDs in a twist."

He was slapping the pencil down on the pad hard now, angrily. "Dammit, Handyman, you listening to me? *Look* at me, boy, don't just stare off into space like some pumpkin-eater."

Something in the man's tone made Matt glance at him. He saw Clegg's eyes, burning with intensity, lock on his and then flick downward, twice.

The message was unmistakable. *Look down.*

On the pad lying across Tommy Clegg's knees, he had written in large block capitals: RUN. GET OUT NOW.

He looked up at Tommy Clegg, saw him nod once, his lips pressed together tightly. "Jesus Christ," breathed Matt, rising to his feet.

There was movement at the corner of his eye,

and the sound of approaching footsteps. He cursed silently. Of course. They would have hidden in the shrubs beside the pond. It should have been obvious.

An American emerged from around each side of the bench and walked out onto the gravel to either side of him, blocking his way.

"Too late. Shit," murmured Tommy Clegg. "I'm sorry, Matt." He got slowly to his feet, put his hand out, and started forward. "I just wanna tell you—"

He stopped abruptly, a puzzled look on his face. As Matt watched, a red stain blossomed on his shirt-front, growing rapidly. Clegg's expression went from puzzlement to pain, and then he collapsed at Matt's feet.

Matt looked beyond Tommy Clegg's body to see Takashi, his Ingram up and ready, standing ten yards away.

From somewhere behind them a woman screamed.

"What the fuck?" mumbled one of the Americans, turning, his hand snaking up inside his sport jacket. Takashi fired twice, the gun making hardly any noise at all. The first shot went wide, but the second blew the back of the man's head off, spraying blood and bone chips into the passing crowd.

As the panic began, Matt could see at least four other Japanese closing in from the sides. The second American had disappeared somewhere out of sight, but Matt could hear shots coming from behind him, and Takashi, his eyes still fixed on Matt, hit the ground, rolling quickly to the side.

Matt stooped and fumbled under Clegg's jacket,

finding the small automatic tucked under his belt at the small of his back. Agents weren't supposed to go armed in foreign countries without special authorization, but Tommy Clegg, Matt remembered, hadn't been much for the rules.

As Matt straightened up, he could see Takashi in a crouch, bringing his arm up across his knee to steady the barrel of the Ingram. Matt, fumbling with the safety, had no time to bring his own weapon to bear. Takashi smiled, his dark glasses glinting in the sunlight, and Matt saw his finger tighten on the trigger.

Suddenly, with a roar, Yuki swept up behind Takashi on the Kawasaki. Her boot caught the *yakuza* squarely on the side of the head, sending him sprawling. The Ingram clattered to the ground.

She skidded to a halt in front of him. "Hurry," she gasped.

Matt caught a last glimpse of Takashi's face as he rose from the ground, his features contorted with rage. And then they were off, blasting through the panic-stricken crowd, headed for the exit and safety.

Yuki drove the heavy Kawasaki with reckless skill, roaring along the park's gravel path as Matt craned his neck, glancing back at the chaos behind them. Two of Takashi's men stood in the classic firing stance, squeezing off rounds methodically, ignoring the crowd around them. Two other men were running after the motorcycle, losing ground fast as Yuki accelerated. Matt twisted awkwardly in the pillion seat, Clegg's pistol raised and ready, trying to get a shot at one of their pursuers.

Weaving and skidding they tore out of the park and down a sidewalk leading to the main road in front of Ueno Station. Pedestrians scattered, yelling in fear and anger, as they bumped down the broad steps and onto the main intersection. Brakes screeched and horns blared, and then, miraculously, they were through and into the narrow passage of the Ameyoko-cho Arcade, swallowed up by the crowd of shoppers.

Yuki slowed the big motorcycle to a near crawl as they moved through the throng, letting it envelop and hide them. As she drove, Matt kept glancing backward, searching for Takashi's men. He stuffed Tommy Clegg's pistol under his jacket.

As the minutes passed, he began to relax. When they had covered another two hundred yards, he tapped Yuki on the shoulder. "Pull in," he said, indicating one of the numerous narrow alleyways leading off from the main shopping street.

A moment later they coasted to a stop behind a stack of vegetable crates, the tang of fresh radishes and onions strong in Matt's nostrils. She shut off the engine, and then all that remained was the ticking of the hot metal, punctuated by their hoarse breathing.

"My . . . God," she said after a moment. "Was that the Dragon? He—he nearly killed you." She caught her breath. "But who were the others—Americans?"

Matt nodded. "They were there to take me in. Takashi and his friends got there first, that's all."

"Take you in?" Her eyes were wide.

"The intelligence boys want to talk to me," Matt

said quietly. "Seems the police in Los Angeles and Washington are also looking for me, so they're naturally curious." He paused and took a deep breath. "Tommy was bait. They had two men hiding in the bushes. He tried to warn me, but it was too late."

"But Takashi—"

"—must have been watching the whole thing," Matt said. "Once he saw what was happening, he moved in. They went for Tommy first, to distract the other two guys. They knew if they shot the leader, the two honchos would stop whatever they were doing for a few seconds, and that would give them time to kill me." He paused. "And they would have, if you hadn't come along."

"It was like a bad dream, Matt." She spoke in hushed tones. "When I left you, I walked back to the motorcycle, and rode it up to the park entrance. I could see you in the distance, talking to that thin man with the boots."

She shivered, and wrapped her arms around herself. "Then I saw four Japanese get out of a big Toyota. They stopped at the entrance of the park, looking carefully around. One of them had leather gloves, just as you had described."

"Takashi."

"Yes, Takashi. They pointed at you, and then they began to walk forward. I saw the man with the gloves take a gun from under his coat." She looked up at him. "That's when I started the motorcycle. I didn't know what I was going to do, but I knew I had to do something."

"You did very well," he said. "I'm alive because of it."

She frowned. "But, Matt, there's something I don't understand. How did Takashi and the others know where you would be? They came straight to the park, almost as if they knew. How did they do that?"

"Simple, I'm afraid. Takashi's men must have had a tap on Tommy Clegg's phone. And probably on every other phone in the embassy as well."

She drew in her breath. "Is that possible?"

Matt gave a short laugh. "Technically, it's no problem. A ten-year-old could do it. But it means that Takashi and his boss are a lot better connected than I thought. They've got their people everywhere."

"You can't go back to the embassy again, can you?"

"No, I can't. And we can't go back to your place either." He peered out of the alley at the crowds passing by. "They've got the license number of your bike. It won't take them more than half an hour to trace you and get your address."

She looked at him. "Are you serious?"

"I didn't want you mixed up in this, but it's too late now." He put his hands on her shoulders. "They'll kill us both if they find us. We've got to hide somewhere, somewhere they won't think to look."

She thought for a moment. "I know a place," she said at last. "Outside Tokyo, in the countryside. We would be safe, I think, for a few days at least. Until we can plan what to do next."

Matt nodded. "We're going to have to leave

your bike here. A woman and a foreigner on a red motorcycle are just too conspicuous."

She looked at her motorcycle sadly. "I guess you're right," she said finally.

They hid the motorcycle carefully behind a stack of empty boxes. Then they walked out of the alley, blending into the crowd. As they approached the taxi stand, Yuki said, "What if we see them again, Matt? What are we going to do?"

He patted the lump under his shirt where Tommy Clegg's automatic pistol lay. "We negotiate with them," he said. "In the only language they understand."

22

"I think you can take your mask off now."

Matt nodded, slipping off the white cotton surgical mask he'd been wearing for the past four hours, letting the fresh wind from the lake blow against his face. The speedboat, a fast-moving Yamaha inboard with twin Volvo Penta engines, roared over the lake's rippled surface, heading for the far shore. He kept his Pittsburgh Pirates baseball cap pulled down low over his ears, his collar up, and his dark glasses on.

The mask had been Yuki's idea; a simple way to disguise Matt's *gaijin* features, using something worn by thousands of people in Tokyo every day: a cloth face-mask, widely believed to protect the wearer against cold and flu germs.

Matt and Yuki had spent four hours on a combination of trains, cog railways, and even a funicular to reach Ashino-ko, a high mountain lake nestled among wooded peaks. He'd kept a lookout the whole way for any signs of the *yakuza,* but saw nothing suspicious. Maybe, he thought, just maybe, they were safe.

Yuki took his arm. "Look, Matt." Behind them and to their right Mt. Fuji rose up, majestic and bare. "We are lucky," she said. "Fuji-san cannot always be seen. There are usually clouds."

Matt nodded and turned his eyes back to the lakeshore, scanning the approaching shoreline. Wooded slopes dropped steeply to the water's edge, the trees thick and tall along their sides. He could see no houses, no roads—no evidence that humans came here at all.

Except, Matt thought, for the tiny jetty poking out from the cove ahead. He shook his head in admiration as they drew closer. The boat landing was small and well concealed, almost camouflaged. Now, as they slowed, Matt could see a gravel trail leading up from the jetty into the trees.

Matt and Yuki stepped off the boat, and a moment later, with a roar, the speedboat headed back across the lake. Matt pointed up the trail. "What's up there?"

Yuki's eyes sparkled with mischief. "A surprise." She took him by the hand. "Come, let's find out."

The air was cool and invigorating as they walked up the trail. As they entered the forest, Matt felt his tension slipping away, little by little. It was quiet in under the trees, and even the birds seemed to have muted voices. Yuki walked in front, her long black hair swaying gently from side to side. They walked quietly, without talking, neither one wishing to break the mood, until, after several minutes, they rounded a bend in the trail and emerged into a small clearing.

There, under the evergreens, stood a one-story wood-and-tile building, so carefully designed and constructed that it seemed to be a part of the forest itself. As they came closer, Matt saw that it was larger than it had at first appeared, and was in fact a rather rambling structure, with strange turns and angles, as if it had evolved naturally over a long period of time.

He looked at Yuki, a question in his eyes.

"A *ryokan*," she said. "What I think you call an inn. It is very peaceful here, very relaxing. My parents used to bring me here when I was small, during school vacations. I have not been back for many, many years. In fact, I was afraid that the place might no longer be here."

She took his hand. "Come on; let's go in."

They crossed the small private garden, shielded from the path leading up to it. Carefully trimmed shrubs were laid out in seemingly random but somehow thoughtful patterns, interspersed with narrow gravel walking paths. At the door they were greeted by an older woman dressed in the traditional kimono and obi, her hair elaborately arranged and lacquered.

"*O-tsukara-sama deshita.*" She bowed deeply, and Yuki did the same, replying in the same low voice. Yuki and the woman held an animated conversation, during which the woman's eyes moved to Matt several times. Yuki then asked a question, and the old woman answered with a short statement and a nod of the head.

Yuki turned to Matt, smiling. "We're in luck; they have room." She paused. "I told her you're my husband. It will make everything a lot simpler. She was worried that you might not feel comfortable here."

She took Matt's hand. "So now I will teach you how to behave. Take your shoes off here"—she indicated a pile of street shoes just beside the door—"and put these on." She picked up a pair of wooden sandals. "You must do this every time you go in and out."

Matt viewed the pile of shoes doubtfully. "Don't they worry about people stealing their shoes?"

Yuki made a face. "Really, Matt. Just the sort of thing a *gaijin* would say. Now come on."

The manager led them down a long corridor to the room at the end. She opened the door to reveal a small room, sparsely furnished, but with a large picture window giving them a spectacular view of the lake and Mt. Fuji beyond. Yuki clapped her hands in delight. She turned to the manager, bubbling her thanks, and with much bowing and smiling the manager finally retreated back down the corridor.

They were alone. Matt entered the room and immediately cracked his head smartly on the top of the door frame. Yuki stifled a storm of giggles. "The door is telling you to take your slippers off, Matt."

"Again? I just put these on."

Yuki indicated the large tatami mat on the floor. "You only wear socks inside the room," she instructed. "That is the way it is done. There are other rules about feet as well. When you go in the toilet, you put special sandals on. And if you want to walk in the garden outside, they will give you traditional *geta* sandals to use. Don't look so confused," she said. "That's just how we do it in Japan. And that's how you should do it too."

She turned and spread her arms wide. "What a large room," she said. "Six mats. Wonderful."

Matt grunted. By American standards it was almost tiny, but he'd begun to get used to the scale of Japanese society. A small vestibule gave onto the main room itself, divided by sliding paper shoji screens into living and sleeping areas.

The decor was simple, almost stark. The room's few pieces of furniture hugged the floor: double futon sleeping cushions on a slightly raised wooden platform, a low table with cushions instead of chairs, and a television on its own low stand. Apparently, thought Matt, you were meant to live at floor level in these places.

At one end of the table Matt saw a game board, dozens of small round ceramic pieces lined up on the crosshatched surface. Yuki caught his glance. "That's a Gō board," she said. "Like chess, but not really."

Cupboards against one wall contained shelves and hangers, and Yuki was already busy unpacking their single traveling bag and arranging its contents carefully.

On the other side of the room was a tiny alcove,

almost a shrine, containing a scroll painting deco-
rated with wispy calligraphy. Beside it were two
doors.

Matt opened one of the doors, finding a toilet
enclosure so tiny that he doubted that he could fit
inside without squeezing sideways. He shook his
head and closed the door. The second door, however,
contained a surprise: a relatively large room containing a spacious, deep, tiled bath, looking somewhat
like a small, square swimming pool. A bench sat
along one wall, and there were several water taps and
several wooden tubs, together with a set of scrub
brushes and several large sponges.

Yuki appeared behind him. *"O-furo,"* she said.
"Japanese bath. For later. Japanese take their bath in
the evening, before dinner. Let's unpack, and then
take a walk."

Outside, the air was turning cooler as the afternoon
wore on, and the scent from the evergreens was fresh
and invigorating. Yuki led Matt on a narrow trail
along the lakeside, through the woods. They walked
for perhaps fifteen minutes in silence, listening to
birdcalls and the rustling of the breeze through the
treetops. To their left the water of the lake sparkled
invitingly. They passed only one other couple, obviously students out for a weekend, who greeted them
happily with bows and smiles.

After a time they came to a cove, with several
large rocks jutting out into the lake. Holding hands
they gingerly walked out on the largest of these.

There they sat, staring out across the mirrorlike surface of the lake, the forest at their back.

The scene was quiet and peaceful. Far down the lake Matt could see a white excursion boat moving slowly along. Across the lake, closer to them, the red *torii* of a shrine rose up out of the lake waters themselves. And behind, in the distance, towered the almost perfect cone of Fuji-san itself, bathed in late afternoon sunshine.

Yuki sat, her hands clasped around her knees. "It's beautiful, isn't it? I can remember so clearly the times I came here as a child. There are other lakes in the area around Fuji-san, but I always liked Ashino-ko best." She turned to Matt. "Do you like it?"

He nodded. "It's very restful, very quiet."

"Yes." She smiled. "And a good place to hide, too, I think."

They sat facing Fuji-san, their legs dangling over the edge of the rock, their feet brushing together lightly from time to time.

"I sometimes wonder if I belong here," she said at last. "Perhaps that is why I am not married." She spoke in a soft, quiet voice. Matt listened, saying nothing.

"I could not imagine myself living with some salaryman in a small apartment somewhere. Waiting for him to come home late at night. People work hard in Japan, Matt. Too hard. Many die of *karoshi*, of overwork."

Her hand crept into his. "But few people are challenged here; few Japanese ever get a chance to really do their best. This is a good country to be ordinary in. But not to be too different. The freedom that Americans have, the life I grew to know there, frightens many Japanese. We must always maintain *tatemae,* what you would call 'face,' and practice *jishuku.*"

"*Jishuku?*"

"Self-restraint." She shook her head. "When I came back here from California, I knew then what my life was going to be like. I was what we call *shokuba no hana,* a flower of the workplace. I was pretty, and of the right age. The next step would be marriage to a salaryman and then straight into the cemetery of life."

"The what?"

She smiled. "*Jinsei no hakaba.* That's what some people today call marriage. Anyway, I cannot accept that. I sometimes feel that I would be better off in a country like America." She turned to him. "But I am not American, I am Japanese. And this is where I live."

She swept her hand across the tableau in front of them. "This is my country, Matt." She turned to face him, her eyes dark and serious. "This is the only place on earth that the Japanese can call home. And although it is beautiful, it is a poor land."

"I'd hardly call it poor," Matt said.

Yuki shook her head. "The wealth you see here comes from hard work, not from natural resources. We have no minerals, no steel, no oil. Nothing but rice." She tapped her forehead. "And what is in our heads."

She took his hands in hers and looked into his

eyes. "Matt, try to understand this. We're not like America, all those different kinds of people. We are all Japanese, all related to the emperor. We were an isolated kingdom until the last century. And then we realized that we could no longer ignore the world around us. And so we began to send people, our young people, out into the world, to learn from it, to bring back whatever would be useful to us.

"Yoshi Itoh and others of his generation knew that Japan must be strong and clever to survive in a hostile world, and so they set out to industrialize us. They saw the war as a way to open up markets and to secure our influence all at the same time."

She looked away. "They were wrong, of course. The war was a disaster. Japan was crushed by the Americans and their allies, her land occupied, her political system changed, and the emperor himself brought low. I was not even born, Matt, when the bombs fell on our cities, when Hiroshima and Nagasaki were destroyed, but I grew up under the occupation, and I know what the people felt. It is complicated, Matt, not easy to explain, especially to an . . . outsider."

Matt sat quietly, not speaking.

"The Japanese have prospered enormously as a result of the war. They know the war was wrong, and although they will not say so openly, most people are deeply ashamed for everything that happened." She looked at him with a small smile. "If you get to know us, Matt, you will learn that we are ashamed for many things; that we are often fearful of giving offense, or seeming to be clumsy or ignorant." She paused, staring out at the quiet surface of the lake, the water turning golden in the light of the setting sun.

"The Americans were not a bad thing for us, really. They gave us a kind of democracy, they helped us rebuild, and they seemed to really like us." She took his hand. "But nothing had really changed, you see. That was what people here realized after a time. Japan was still without friends and allies, without markets, without raw materials. We had tried war, and now we had to try something else."

"Economic domination," said Matt.

"No," Yuki said quietly. "Not domination. Security. Japan needs economic security. And we must do this for ourselves—no one will do it for us."

"So Itoh's just working out a kind of national destiny, is that it?"

"Matt, please." Her eyes were imploring. "Itoh loves his country, as I do. But he is wrong to do this. He has forgotten his honor. He wants to win too badly. He wants to take the prize, however he can. And if that means sabotage, then yes, I think he would do it."

"Then I have to stop him."

"How? We can't go to the police, or to your embassy. The one man who could have helped you there is dead. We are being hunted by the *yakuza*, and sooner or later they will find us. What can you do?"

"Find Itoh," Matt said.

She shook her head. "That's nearly impossible, Matt. Itoh's practically a hermit. You were lucky to see him at all the other day. Most of the time he lives alone, in his castle outside of Tokyo."

"A *castle*?"

Yuki nodded. "Truly. The original walls and main building are from the time of the Tokugawa. They say it resembles Edo-jo, the old castle that stood where the Imperial Palace now is. It is famous, even marked on some tourist maps." She caught Matt's glance. "Matt, be sensible. Suppose you could confront Itoh—what good would that do you?"

"If I can get to Itoh," he said, "I ought to be able to find Kanji. Somehow, I think he's the key to what they're planning. Once I have him, maybe I can get somebody in Washington to listen to me."

"What about Takashi? To get to Itoh you will have to deal with him."

"All the better. He's tried to kill me half a dozen times in the past week. I'd like to even the score a little." He paused. "Besides, he's got my videotape. I need it back."

She turned to face him in the twilight. "Matt, this is very dangerous. Forget Takashi; forget the videotape."

He cradled her face in his hands. "I need it, Yuki. If I'm going to convince people in Washington, I'll need the tape." He stared out across the lake. Lights were coming on in the shrine on the far shore. "In two weeks there's going to be a public test of Ragnarok. Whatever these guys are planning is going to happen before then. To stop the test I need evidence. The videotape will help, but what I really need is a warm body. Kanji's or Itoh's."

"But, Matt," she said, "you're talking about kidnapping. That's illegal."

He laughed then. "Yuki. Who ever said we had to play by the rules?"

They fell silent, each lost in private thoughts. Finally Matt stretched. "I'm getting hungry," he said. "What time is dinner around here?"

"In about an hour," Yuki said. "We have enough time, I think."

"Time? For what?"

Yuki took his hand. "An old Japanese custom," she said. "Come on."

Yuki and Matt stood naked on the tiles of the *furo* bath, Matt feeling awkward and uncomfortable, trying to keep his eyes off Yuki's slim form as she instructed him in the finer points of Japanese bathing.

"Americans use the bath for washing," she said as she filled a wooden bucket from the tap set into the wall. "This we consider barbaric. No Japanese would think of getting into the bath dirty." She finished filling one bucket and started another. "So we wash first, outside the tub. Much better this way, don't you think?"

"Sure," mumbled Matt. He was relaxing a little now, but was still self-conscious. She had led him back along the path to the *ryokan,* where they had bowed effusively once again to the manager, exchanged their shoes for sandals, and, at the door to their room, changed the sandals for bare feet. Yuki had then explained, without a trace of embarrassment, that although some *ryokan* had communal facilities, this one was even more luxurious; their room had its own private *o-furo*. Before Matt could open his mouth, she had wiggled out of her jeans and was slipping off her blouse.

"Come on," she'd said, grinning. "I hope you realize you're not the first man I've seen naked. Or the first *gaijin*," she'd added mischievously. "And surely you've seen women before."

"Ah, absolutely," Matt had said, somewhat dazed, as he gamely reached for his belt buckle. She'd peeled off her underwear, walked to the door to the bath and opened it, looking at him expectantly.

Now she sat him down on one of the low wooden stools, pinned her hair up out of the way, and began to pour hot water over him. When he was thoroughly wet, she took a bar of strong-smelling soap from the shelf and began to lather him, punctuating the soap with fierce intervals of scrubbing using a rough sponge.

"Easy," grunted Matt.

"Be quiet," she murmured. "Just relax; this is good for you. *Gaijin* don't know much about bathing, in my opinion. So pay attention to what I'm doing. When I'm done with you, you can do me."

It was part washing, part massage, part scrubbing. Yuki worked quietly and expertly, covering his entire body with thick lather, scrubbing him down, and rinsing him off with hot water. It was definitely erotic, he decided, but oddly comforting at the same time. He found himself relaxing, luxuriating in her touch, in the counterpoint of textures and pressures as lather, sponge, and water alternated across his body.

Finally she was done. Matt thought that he had never felt so clean in his life. "Now me," she said, sitting down on the stool and presenting her back.

Matt knelt and worked the lather over her body, feeling the hard muscles under the softness of her skin. Although Yuki was slim and light, Matt realized that she was well muscled and in excellent physical shape. When he had rinsed her back, she reversed her position on the stool. "Do the front now."

He looked down at her, feeling his pulse begin to pick up the pace. Her breasts were perfect, surprisingly full, the nipples large and deep pink. His eyes rose to her face, to her wide, almost luminous eyes.

"Ah, look," he said. "What are we getting involved in here? I, ah, mean, I think—"

She put a finger to his lips. "You probably think too much, Matt-san," she said. "So stop thinking for a while, okay?" She picked up the sponge and handed it to him. "It's just a bath, you know. Don't scrub too hard here," she added, indicating her nipples.

Matt bent to his work, carefully lathering her from neck to toes, reciting multiplication tables in his mind as he fought to control his body's impulses. If Yuki was aware of his efforts, she gave no obvious sign, but he detected a slight crinkling of her eyes that might have indicated amusement. Her own breathing was steady and regular, and she nodded approvingly as he scrubbed her with the rough sponge, and then rinsed her off with one bucketful after another of hot water.

Finally, he was through. She stood up. Her skin, like his, shone wetly. "Now we are clean," she said. "Time for the bath." They entered the deep tiled bath carefully, for the water was quite hot. "Like a hot tub in California," said Yuki. "You can sit along the side. Here, come this way."

In a moment they were seated facing each other, only their necks and upper shoulders out of the water. Small drops of sweat beaded Yuki's forehead and upper lip as she smiled at Matt. "Nice," he said, feeling the tension in his body begin to melt away under the water.

"Umm," she said, bringing her hands up the sides of his arms until they rested on his shoulders. "Japanese people try to do this every day. We cannot understand people who bathe as you do, in their own dirty water. Do you like the Japanese way?"

"So far," said Matt. "What happens next? Does somebody come in and whip us with tree branches?"

Yuki laughed. "That's Finland, I think. No, here we just stay in the bath until we are relaxed and happy. Then we get out and have our dinner."

Matt realized with a start that he'd forgotten all about his stomach. His hunger returned with a jolt as he realized that neither of them had eaten a thing since breakfast, long ago, in Yuki's Tokyo apartment.

"What's for dinner?" he asked teasingly. "Hamburgers?"

She made a face. "Of course not. This isn't America, you know."

America seemed very far away right now, Matt thought, and very strange. Here, in a deep bath, hold-

ing a Japanese woman whom he hardly knew lightly
around the waist, hiding in a country whose language
he could not speak and whose customs reflected no
familiar logic—*this* somehow felt right, felt almost
normal. I must be going into culture shock, he
thought. Either that, or I'm dopey from too little
sleep.

Yuki was looking at him with an amused expression on her face. "Homesick, Matt?"

He ran his hands up her ribs and placed them
gently on her shoulders. "No. This feels like where I
ought to be right now, to tell you the truth."

"Good. Because it's where *I* want you to be."

Matt looked at her. "Look, I don't think—"

She brushed his lips gently with her fingers.
"Matt, do me a favor, okay? Shut up for a little
while. *Don't* think. Just enjoy what's happening here,
whatever it is."

Matt swallowed, nodded, and took her slim
body in his arms. She turned, leaning back against
him. He held her lightly, both of them nearly buoyant
in the steaming water of the bath.

Her voice when it came was dreamy, almost a
whisper. "I'm a grown-up woman, but sometimes I
think I'm still a little girl. Just like men are really little
boys a lot of the time." She turned to him, laced her
arms around his neck, and drew herself closer. "Little
Japanese girls are like other little girls, Matt. They
read fairy stories and they dream of heroes, what we
call *tateyaku*. And later on they realize that there
aren't many heroes in the world." She kissed him
softly on the cheek. "You're a hero, Matt. You saved

my life. And now you are fighting for your country, against a dragon, just like in the stories. If you win, we will have peace. If you lose, our countries may be at war."

"I'm not—"

"—a hero? Yes, you are, Matt. A real, live hero. And I am an ordinary woman doing an ordinary job in a dull and overcrowded city. Since you arrived, my life is very different. But this will not remain so. I know who I am; I know who you are. We live in different worlds, not just in different countries."

"Not so different," murmured Matt.

"Yes." She looked up at him, tears starting in her eyes. "And this *is* a fairy tale, Matt. Like a fairy tale it will end, very soon. And I will never see you again. But for now let us enjoy our time together." She looked into his eyes. "And while we are together, I will help you, Matt, as much as I can." She moved back, away from him. "Let us finish now," she said. "It's time for dinner."

She rose, gleaming, out of the steamy water, pulling him up behind her. After they had dried themselves with thick towels, she picked up a thin cotton bathrobe lying neatly folded on a side table.

"Here is your *yukata*," she said, tossing it to him. "It is how we dress for dinner in Japan. Put it on and tie it with the obi. Oh, yes—make sure you put the left side over the right."

Matt did as he was told, lapping left over right, tying the black belt at his waist. "Why left over right?" he asked.

"Because done the other way, it's for dressing the dead."

Dinner had already been laid out in their room by the time they emerged from the bath. The Gō board had been pushed out of the way, and the low table was now covered with lacquered boxes of various sizes, set in precise alignment around a teapot and two cups. Napkins, chopsticks, thimble-sized sake cups and a small flower arrangement completed the picture.

Yuki showed him how to fold his legs in the half-lotus position that appeared to be the only way people could manage to eat at the table. Then she began to open the boxes, explaining to him what was inside each one.

It was a little like a culinary Christmas. *"Miso,"* she said. "A kind of soup. This is *sunomono*—vegetables." She opened another box. *"Tsukemono."* She made a face. "Very sour. And here is rice, *gohan*. And now"—she opened the largest of the boxes—*"sashimi*. I think you know what this is, right?"

Matt nodded. "Raw fish." He peered at the carefully arranged display of different-colored strips of fish. "But I have no idea what they are."

"This is *ika*, squid. And this, *maguro*—tuna. *Awabi* here and here, *ebi*. *Ebi* is shrimp, but I don't know the word for *awabi*."

Matt picked up a tiny piece and tasted it. "Might be abalone," he said after a moment.

Yuki shrugged. "Whatever it is, you will like it." She pointed to the various small dishes of sauces.

"Soy sauce, horseradish, other things. Try them all." She poured tea and picked up her chopsticks. "But we start with *zensai,* the appetizers. *Itadakimasu.*"

They ate slowly and carefully, as aware of each other as they were of the food. Matt had the same superficial acquaintance with Japanese food that most Washington dwellers had and was surprised to find the tastes new and exquisite. The hot sauces set off the raw fish perfectly, and Yuki showed him how to mix several of them for maximum effect. As they ate, she kept their teacups full. Once in a while she would select a particularly delicious morsel of raw fish, dip it into the sauce, and put it into his mouth using her own chopsticks.

It took them over an hour to eat, and when they were through, Yuki came around to his side of the table and opened the sake. Pouring them both tiny cups she raised hers in a toast. *"Kanpai,"* she whispered.

"Down the hatch," Matt replied, and drank the warm wine, looking into her wide dark eyes.

"Matt," she said at last, "I am afraid. I am afraid of what will happen if you go looking for Itoh. How will you know what to do? How will you succeed?"

He set his sake cup down and smiled. "Hell, I don't know," he said. "But as they say, desperation is the *real* mother of invention." He put his arm around her. "So I'll think of something, don't worry. I have to. Otherwise, I'll probably be dead in a couple of days."

Yuki shivered and drew closer to him, saying nothing. Silently, they both looked out the window at the night beyond. The moon had risen, making a silver trail across the placid water. Over it all they could see the bulk of Fuji-san rising into the ghostly half-light.

They sat together for perhaps fifteen minutes, their bodies warm and smooth against each other, until finally Yuki stirred. "Time for bed," she said softly. "Help me with the mats, please."

23

The futons were spread out side by side on a raised wooden platform. Matt and Yuki lay side by side in the darkness, only their hands touching. Matt could hear Yuki's soft breathing, aware of her warmth and her faint scent.

Her hand left his and touched his hip, soft as a feather, her long fingers tracing slow patterns on his skin. He felt his breathing begin to quicken, his heart starting to pick up the beat. A rustle in the dark, and she turned on her side, her lips inches from his.

"Matt-san—"

He reached over and pulled her to him, covering her mouth with his.

Matt found the unfamiliar contours of her body exquisite and exciting, her responses quick and ardent, as together they began the long, slow climb to passion's summit. Unfamiliarity and shyness fell away as they progressed, replaced with confidence and assurance. And when, much later, they both cried out into the night and were still, a bond had been forged that could never be broken.

They lay on their backs, fingers touching, letting their heartbeats return to normal. Finally, she shifted on the futon. "Are you all right? I haven't killed you, have I?"

Matt chuckled in the darkness. "I think I'm still alive."

She turned to him, her eyes shadowed. "I want to tell you many things, Matt. Romantic things. But right now I thought of something that is not romantic at all. It is about this missile." She paused. "I think I know what Itoh and Kanji may be planning."

"You do?"

"I don't think they really want to destroy Ragnarok. They want to control it."

Matt got up on one elbow. "And why would they want to do that?"

"To destroy the credibility of those who designed it. In your country there is a lot of opposition to this missile, I think."

Matt nodded. "Some people say it costs too much. Others say it'll never work."

"And some people also say that it is not possible to build a computer that thinks, isn't that so? And if there *was* a computer that could think, some of them would even be afraid of it, wouldn't they?"

"That's true," Matt admitted. "There are a lot of stupid people in the world, I guess."

"Maybe not so stupid," said Yuki. "I work in artificial intelligence at the university, and even I'm not so sure that we will ever be able to build an intelligent machine. People aren't so stupid, Matt—they just fear an intelligence that is different from their own. In many of your stories this is very clear. Think of *Frankenstein,* think of *The Terminator,* or any of the books and films of that sort."

Matt smiled. "Do you think Ragnarok is really a kind of Frankenstein's monster, then?"

"I think it could be," she said. "You said that during the first test, the one on videotape, Ragnarok destroyed its control center." She paused. "Suppose that someone had programmed the missile to do that? It wouldn't require much, you know. Two or three lines of code, and then a homing signal located in the bunker."

Matt turned to her. "But why go to the trouble, Yuki? Why generate a failure during a secret test? Why not wait for the big day itself?"

Her voice was soft in the darkness. "The Rule of *Ko.*"

"What?"

"The Rule of *Ko.* From Gō, the board game. Sometimes the two sides become trapped in an endless stalemate, where neither one can win over the other. When that happens, the Rule of *Ko* lets one of the players move away and start a new attack on another part of the board." Her voice grew intense. "Yes, that is how they did it. They wanted access to

Odin's system architecture. And since they couldn't get it, they found another way in. Didn't you tell me that some of the microprocessor chips are made by Itoh's company?"

"Only two. And they're apparently not crucial to the guidance system. They—"

"That's how they did it, then. They used a Trojan horse."

"A what?"

"A computer virus called a Trojan horse. A set of commands that enters an operating system under a disguise. Once it's in the system, it changes itself into something else. Like the Trojan horse in Greek history."

She sat up, pushing her long hair back over her shoulders, out of her eyes. "That's how Kanji must have set it up. I don't know what the original Trojan horse virus contained—whether it simply destroyed parts of Odin's operating system, or whether it contained countercommands of some sort. But whatever it was, it was introduced in a disguised form."

"In the microprocessor chips made by Itoh's company?"

"Yes. It could be easily done during manufacture. The chips would then be assembled as part of the missile. The Trojan horse would only begin its work once initial debugging tests were completed. No one would have suspected the existence of a malfunction until it was too late."

"And then?"

"They will be desperate to repair the malfunction before the public test takes place. TransCentury will have to go into the system, find the virus, and remove it." She gripped his bare shoulder. "And since Kanji is the person who designed the chips they got from Shima Industries, he is the only person who can fix things for them. But for him to repair the damage they will have to give him access to Odin's system architecture itself, the part of the missile that no foreigner has ever seen."

Matt thought back to the briefing around the table at the Jefferson Institute. "And if he can get inside Odin, he can rearrange things to make the missile do whatever he wants," he said at last. "The system has belief and motivation structures embedded in the architecture. If he can alter those—"

"—he could turn friends into enemies," Yuki finished. "Black into white, night into day. And if the architecture itself were changed, no one could tell that anything was wrong until the program was activated. And that will produce an even more spectacular failure, on the day the whole world will be watching."

"So a missile designed to protect us," Matt said slowly, "would kill us instead. Not by mistake, but by design—because it defined us as targets, enemies, threats." He heard Nigel's voice in his mind: *"It's quite important to have it clearly in mind who the real enemy is, isn't it?"*

"Yes," she said.

Matt was quiet, remembering what Rollie Chalmers had said to him that night on the deck of his canyon house. *"We're gonna run through the programming line by goddamned line. We'll have help, lots of it, from our Japanese partners. Whether we want it or not."*

"Kanji may have already gotten into Odin's core," he said. "I remember now what he said when we met in Itoh's office. 'It's too late,' he said. I didn't know what he meant at the time, but I do now. He couldn't get into Odin's head any other way, so he set up a malfunction in another part of the guidance system."

He looked at Yuki "The Rule of *Ko*, is it? In the States we have the same thing: we say, 'If you can't win the race, move the finish line.' Those bastards."

Yuki sat up, hugging her knees. "If I were Kanji, that would be my plan." She turned to him. "Kanji isn't like me, Matt. I am doubtful about artificial intelligence, but he is not. He believes in it, and he will try to do it. He sees, as many Japanese do, that computer science is an area in which we can compete and win against the West. It does not matter to the world whether they are American or Japanese computers. But it matters to people like Itoh and Kanji."

"And the stakes are a little too high for good sportsmanship." Matt looked out across the quiet, peaceful lake. "So he's turned Odin into a psychopath. With American technology discredited the market will be wide open for the Japanese. My God."

Her voice, when it came, was as soft as the wind's whisper in the trees. "What are you going to do, then?"

Matt turned, seeing her profile in silhouette in the darkness. "The Secretary of Defense and most of NATO's top brass will be there for the test. Jesus, it's going to be a killing field. I've got to find Itoh and Kanji before then."

Yuki gripped his arm. "Unless they kill you first."

"That won't happen." Matt's voice was harsh. "They've got everything to lose, Yuki, and I have nothing. It's not an even contest."

Yuki let her breath out and turned away, her back to him, lying quietly in the darkness. After a moment he sensed movement, heard a quiet sob, and realized that Yuki was crying.

He put his hand on her shoulder, half turned her. She lay on her back, eyes staring at the ceiling, the moonlight glinting off the tear tracks winding down her cheeks. "How can you be so sure that you will live?" she said angrily. "How do you know what will happen?"

She burrowed into his chest, sobbing. "I am so sad, Matt-san. Whatever happens, you will soon be gone from my life." Her voice dropped to a whisper. "When you meet the Dragon again, only one of you will survive. If you die, you are gone forever. If you win, you will return to America." She paused. "Either way, I lose you."

She drew him close to her, fitting her body to his, closing her eyes as she brought her face up for his kiss. "Can you blame me, then, for wanting this now?"

They made love again with quiet intensity, slowly and with great care, communicating by touch and whispers, letting their passion and need speak for itself. And when at last they were sated, they slept curled around each other, their breathing deep and even, as they drifted toward the morning and whatever the new day would bring.

Matt rolled over, blinking as the bright sunlight hit his eyes. He sat up, brushing sleep from his eyes. Yuki, naked except for a towel wrapped around her waist, her long hair a wild tangle, was opening the window blinds. *"Ohayo gozai masu,* Matt-san," she smiled at him. "It's a nice morning."

She came to him then, knelt, and kissed him. Finally, they broke away, gazing at each other. Yuki blushed. "Matt, what is it?"

"You're very beautiful," he said softly.

She laughed, a sound like temple bells. "I was wondering when you'd notice." She brushed his cheek mischievously with her nose. "I noticed *you* right away."

Matt sat up. "You did?"

"Sure," she said. "That second time you came to the hospital. When you brought the Japanese food. You remember Nancy Okamoto, the nisei nurse? She said to me, 'Your visitor—*kare-wa te hansamu-ne*—how handsome he is! Who is he, your boyfriend?' I was so embarrassed. But she was right—you were certainly handsome."

She pulled back and ran her hand over his cheek. "And you need a shave, Matt-san. Then you'll be even handsomer." She tickled him under the armpit. "Come on, get up, the sun's been up for almost an hour. I'll order breakfast while you shave."

Matt grimaced and got to his feet. "Hold off for

twenty minutes, okay?" He pulled on his trousers and began tying his running shoes. "I like to take a short run in the morning if I have time." He grinned at her. "Sharpens the appetite. I'll just do a half mile or so down the trail." He kissed her on the tip of her nose. "Eggs, bacon, toast, and juice, please."

Yuki laughed. "You're in Japan, remember? Rice, seaweed, miso soup, and fish." She noticed his expression and put her hand to her mouth to stifle a fit of giggling. "I will ask, Matt."

He kissed her lightly once again, pushed aside the shoji screen, and stepped onto the patio. The day was clear and bright, the air crisp and fresh. The lake's stillness was ruffled by a light breeze, and above it all Fuji-san rose up, dominating the skyline. Matt took a deep breath, and began to jog along the trail, into the forest, beside the lake.

A cushion of thick pine needles covered the trail. The terrain rolled pleasantly up and down, smooth enough to allow Matt to jog almost effortlessly. He felt rested and full of energy despite—here he smiled to himself—the fact that he hadn't actually gotten that much sleep. What had developed with Yuki had been a surprise, although a most pleasant and welcome one. He was still trying to figure out what it all meant, but time would provide its own answers, of that he was sure.

His immediate problem, he reminded himself, was how to find Itoh and Kanji, recover the videotape, and get back to the States without getting killed. Once he had the evidence, he could concentrate on telling people in Washington, people who would listen, about what was going to happen to Ragnarok, and stop the test before a lot of people died.

As he jogged, he ran it down in his head. On his own now, he had to be very careful. The Japanese police were searching for him. The American embassy as well; Tommy Clegg's death would have set alarm bells ringing all up and down the State Department.

So it was back to the old Coyote ways: the Handyman, on his own, headed barefoot and naked into the maze. The best kind of game, Matt thought grimly, with the highest sort of stakes. And no confusion about who'd won or lost. As Cowboy Tommy used to say, "good clean dog-eat-dog."

Slowing, he checked his watch. Fifteen minutes; a little over two miles if he kept to his usual pace. Time to be heading back. He turned on the narrow trail and picked up the pace slightly, feeling his leg muscles stretch in response.

The door to their room lay open. "Yuki?" Matt stepped inside to see the breakfast tray on the floor, tea and rice scattered across the tatami mats. "Yuki? Where are you? What's happened?"

The room was silent. In the corner Matt saw Yuki's *yukata*, thrown aside carelessly. Underneath it her suitcase lay open, with clothes spilling out. Yuki was nowhere to be seen.

"Yuki?" Matt's voice echoed in the empty room. "Yuki, where are you?"

Then he noticed the torn scarf on the futon, the

broken watchband beside it, the shoji screen ripped in two places, the door to the outside open, the gentle morning breeze drifting through. And pinned to the futon itself, a sheet of paper containing a single Japanese character, hastily scrawled with a felt-tipped pen.

Trembling, Matt picked up the paper and stared at it. The character was one he had seen before, one he knew the meaning of.

The Dragon.

24

Matt lay stretched full-length on the rooftop, scanning the castle walls through his binoculars. He had surveyed the building and its grounds for most of the day, and he was fairly certain now that he knew how he would enter the castle.

He was less certain of what he would find there.

He took the binoculars from his eyes, shifting uncomfortably on the rough gravel. Another three or four hours until sundown, he estimated. If he survived that long without being spotted, he had a chance to succeed. But with every minute that passed, his odds lessened.

He had left the *ryokan* immediately after finding Yuki gone. It was useless to search for her on the premises, he knew: the trail was clear enough.

Itoh's castle.

A trap, with Yuki as bait.

It must have been the boatman, Matt had decided. And once they knew where he was, Takashi had come for him. But an early-morning ambush had gone wrong, and Takashi had arrived to find Yuki alone in the *ryokan*. Rather than risk a surprise confrontation with Matt, the Dragon had used Yuki to draw Matt onto home territory, where he could kill Matt easily, at his leisure.

But Matt wasn't going to let that happen. Throwing caution to the winds he had taken Clegg's pistol, gathered up whatever loose cash he could find, and left the *ryokan* for Tokyo. Late that afternoon he had disembarked at Ueno Station, gone to the tourist information desk, and procured a map of Saitama Prefecture, with Itoh's castle clearly marked on it. He spent twenty minutes drifting among the shops surrounding the station area, browsing through the merchandise, adroitly shoplifting the few small items he needed. Then he entered the alleyways of Ameyokocho, and retrieved Yuki's Kawasaki.

He waited until dark. Tucking his pistol into his waistband he started the big cycle and eased out of the alley. He remembered Yuki's warning: *"Takashi isn't the only* yakuza *looking for you, Matt. Hundreds of his colleagues are on the alert now."* Let them come, he thought grimly. It's all the same now, after all.

He found the castle before dawn, and by sunrise he was in position on the gravel roof of a nearby warehouse. He had seen Yuki twice so far, moving behind one of the castle's third-floor windows.

Her two appearances were anything but accidental, he knew. Takashi was showing her to him, making sure he knew that she was inside.

Making sure he'd come for her.

People in India hunted tigers this way, Matt thought. They staked a young goat or lamb out in a jungle clearing and waited, guns at the ready.

Well, here I am, he thought. But not quite ready to step into the trap.

He looked around at the scene below him. The castle lay in a parklike setting, a wooded estate covering twenty acres or more. The place must have cost him a fortune, Matt thought. The woods were probably equipped with surveillance devices; Matt had already spotted a video camera attached to a tree, covering the winding road leading through the park to the main highway. There would probably be others, but he was confident that he could spot them when it was time to move.

The park ended abruptly at a massive stone and tile wall that encircled the castle, protecting it from the outside. Thirty feet high, the top of the wall bristled with sharp iron and broken glass. A single portal, manned by security guards, seemed to be the only way in. Earlier in the afternoon Matt had carefully looked at every inch of the wall, searching for weak spots. He hadn't found any.

Beyond the castle Matt could see a private airstrip. A sleek Gulfstream jet was the only aircraft in sight, bearing Shima Industries' corporate logo on its side.

Matt turned his glasses away from the airstrip and back to the castle itself, moving the glasses back and forth over Itoh's stronghold. The castle was unlike anything else in Matt's experience, truly a fortress as far as he could see. Three stories tall, it had a wide overhanging tile roof reminding Matt of a temple or pagoda. The ground floor had its own sloped roof, jutting far out and covering a set of low windows with curtains. In the middle of the building a driveway ran straight into a set of wide doors set into the wall, clearly a gate of some sort.

The next story had a wide veranda with columns and a wooden railing. Windows here were larger, and through them Matt could see rooms with furniture and paintings.

The top floor was overshadowed by its wide tiled roof, its corners carved into elaborate patterns. A narrow walkway ran around the outside of this top floor, and only a few windows were evident. Behind one of these Matt again caught sight of Yuki, moving against the dark backdrop of the room.

He knew exactly where she was. Now he had to think of a way of getting her out.

And to do that he had to get inside the walls.

Just then the patrol reappeared, right on schedule.

Two men and four dogs, two animals to a man, patrolled the grounds. The men wore identical light-blue jumpsuits, pistols, and billy clubs at their belts. Their blue caps matched their jumpsuits.

The large, lean Dobermans tugged nervously at their leashes, turning their snakelike heads this way and that, eyes probing the shadows for prey. They moved silently and quickly over the ground, sniffing out the corners of the terrain. They had made two circuits already in the time Matt had been on the roof, and they would probably be on patrol through the night as well.

He could scale the outer wall without too much difficulty, he estimated, but once inside the perimeter he had no wish to confront the dogs and their handlers. Creating a diversion would enable him to deal with the patrols, but would also put the staff on alert, and make his job much harder in the end.

The best way, clearly, was to try and get inside without anyone knowing. And he thought he might have figured out a way to do that.

Three times in the last several hours Matt had watched delivery trucks pull up to the outer gate. Each time a guard would emerge from his kiosk, talk briefly to the driver, make a note on his clipboard, and pick up his hand-held radio. When he had received instructions, he would open the gate, waving the truck inside. Once the truck was through the outer wall, the inner gate opened automatically, swallowing the truck inside the castle itself. The check-off process was repeated in reverse before the truck was allowed through the outer gates again.

Matt edged back across the roof. He would wait until dark, he decided. Then he would make a move.

*　*　*

Nine o'clock now, fully dark. Matt lay quietly in the undergrowth beside the access road, waiting. His trap was ready.

An hour earlier he had foraged through the woods, avoiding the tripwires and motion sensors, searching for downed tree branches. He needed something large enough to stop a vehicle on its way into the castle, but not large enough to cause suspicion if the driver suddenly encountered it on the road.

The piece of wood he had found was almost perfect, he'd thought as he dragged it quietly into place. Then he sat back to wait.

It took longer than he'd thought. Nearly an hour passed before Matt caught sight of headlights swinging through the wooded park's curving road. He crouched low behind the bushes as the blue Mitsubishi panel truck came around the corner. The driver caught sight of the tree branch angled across the road, slowed, and stopped. Before his door was open, Matt was moving.

The driver and his companion took less than a minute to move the branch off the road and into the underbrush. In that time Matt had succeeded in slipping under the truck from the rear and attaching himself to the chassis, using his belt as a crude strap.

He tensed his muscles as he heard the truck's gearbox grind. If this doesn't work, he thought, I won't have a chance to try anything else.

The truck moved off into the night, approaching the castle's outer gate.

Matt held his breath as they were passed through. Beyond this gate was dog country, and if they sniffed him out, he had no chance to escape. But the exhaust fumes and general smell of the truck would, he hoped, disguise his own scent, or at least make it indistinguishable from that of the two men in the cab.

That was the theory, at any rate. He'd test it very soon.

They were moving into the buffer zone now, the truck grinding along slowly in low gear. A halt, a short conversation between the driver and someone Matt couldn't see, and then they moved forward again, through the inner gate.

Into the castle itself.

Under the truck Matt held himself in place by sheer willpower. They had entered a garage of some kind, stopping beside a large black limousine that was probably Itoh's personal vehicle. The two men stepped down, opened the back of the truck, and began stacking boxes against the wall.

He relaxed his grip and unbuckled his belt, lowering himself to the floor, feeling his abused muscles protest. He took a breath, and then silently and quickly rolled himself over and underneath the limousine.

Still flat on his back he peered out cautiously. Against one wall he could see shelves containing tools and what looked like spare auto parts. Against the other, the boxes—food supplies of some kind—that were coming out of the back of the truck.

And there, in the far corner, an open door.

The back doors slammed. The men were through unloading. One of them said something to his companion, making him laugh as he hoisted himself into the truck's cab.

A moment later they had backed through the doors, and Matt was alone. He moved cautiously out from under the limousine, checking his watch as he did so. Nearly eleven o'clock. Time to find Yuki.

Dark, quiet, and vaguely menacing, everything in the castle was somewhat larger than life, thought Matt, as he moved through the corridors, his pistol in his hand. He crept quietly down the ground-floor hallway, checking the doors as he passed, alert for the slightest noise or movement. Yuki had said that Yoshi Itoh lived alone, a virtual hermit, but Takashi was bound to be somewhere on the premises.

Perhaps stalking him even now.

But if the *yakuza* was nearby, there was no sign of him. Indeed, the place seemed strangely deserted. Something, Matt decided, was wrong. The place was too quiet.

At the end of the hallway, staircases led up in both directions, presumably to opposite ends of the hallway on the floor above. Between them a set of double doors lay partially open, light spilling from within. Matt crept closer, peering through the half-open door.

An old man in a kimono, his hair tied in a topknot, knelt before a low table. With a shock Matt realized that this was Yoshi Itoh, transformed from the suited businessman of a few days ago into a traditional sage, someone from the world depicted on the old scrolls that hung from the walls around him.

He sat, perfectly poised, before a low table, its surface gleaming with countless coats of lacquer. On the table beside him lay a flat ink pad, several large brushes, and sheets of large, heavy paper.

As Matt watched, the old man selected a brush, inked it carefully, and held it poised over the paper. He raised the brush like a conductor's baton, seemed to gather his breath, and then executed a single series of flowing, rapid strokes. When the brush left the paper, a complex Japanese ideograph had been formed. Itoh sat contemplating the character for some moments. Then he pushed the paper aside, picked up another brush, and began to ink it.

Matt withdrew into the corridor. Assuming that the old man was going to be occupied with his calligraphy for a while, he felt it was time to get things moving. He could always come back for Itoh later. He took the stairs two at a time, moving silently but swiftly upward. Where the hell was the Dragon?

The third floor was dark, the corridor smaller and narrower. Matt moved quickly to the corner room, where he had seen Yuki earlier in the day. He paused in front of the door, listening, and then tried the knob.

Locked. Matt fumbled in the pocket of his jacket, bringing out the set of tools he had stolen earlier, in the same shop where he'd picked up the binoculars. Setting his gun down he worked the screwdriver into the lock, applying upward pressure. The lock was old and simple, no trouble to pop, and in a few seconds he heard a satisfying snap as the bolt withdrew. He picked up his gun and braced himself.

Throwing the door open, he dived inside, gun up, presenting a minimal target, rolling fast to the side.

Nothing moved. In the middle of the empty room Yuki sat, bound to a chair with nylon rope, a tray of food beside her.

Matt got to his feet. He closed the door and then moved to Yuki. "Are you all right?" he whispered, touching her cheek.

She nodded. "I thought you'd never get here," she said. She lifted her face for a quick kiss. "Untie me, please. This is really uncomfortable."

Matt cut her bonds and helped her stand up. "Where are Takashi and Kanji?"

Yuki looked over her shoulder. "I haven't seen either of them today. The old man lives downstairs, I think. But there is another—a man with long hair and metal in his teeth. Very nasty. He—"

"Itoh's pilot," Matt said, remembering the ride in from the airport on the first day. "Okay. Anyone else?"

"I don't think so. There is a cook, I think, but she goes home at night. There are guards outside, Matt, with dogs. How did you—"

"Never mind that," he said. "We've got to get you out of here. But first I have to find the videotape. Any ideas?"

"Itoh has it," she said. "I saw it when they brought me here yesterday. The old man was looking at it downstairs."

Matt nodded. "Let's go get it, then."

* * *

The old man still sat exactly where Matt had left him. He turned as they came through the door, barely changing his expression as he caught sight of the pistol in Matt's hand.

"Forgive my impoliteness for not bowing," Matt said. "We've got a couple of things to discuss." The old man's eyebrows went up fractionally as Yuki translated. He nodded then, and murmured something in low tones.

"He asks you to state your demands," Yuki said.

Matt moved so that he could watch Itoh and the door at the same time. "First," he said, "I need the videotape that Takashi took from me on the first day." Itoh placed his brush carefully in its holder and gestured toward the far wall, where a wide-screen television and VCR sat incongruously between two antique wall scrolls.

Matt flipped through the cassettes in the rack, pulling out Marty's duplicate. "Did he erase it?" Itoh shook his head.

"Your lucky day, Mr. Itoh," Matt said. "Two more things, then. I need Takashi, and I need Kanji. Where are they?"

The old man's head came up as Yuki translated, and Matt caught the unmistakable gleam of triumph in his eyes. When he spoke, his voice was firm and defiant.

"He says Takashi and Kanji are not here," Yuki said. "They left last night. You are too late."

"Gone? Where did they go?"

"California."

Yoshi Itoh spat the word out. He turned to Yuki

and spoke in Japanese, gesturing to the bookcase on the wall behind him. She looked once at Matt, and then hurried over and began to paw through a stack of newspapers.

"Oh, my God."

Matt moved beside her. "What is it?"

"Look." She held out a copy of the English-language *Asahi Shimbun*.

As Matt moved forward to take the newspaper, he heard a noise from outside. Footsteps, approaching down the long corridor. Flattening himself behind the door he waited. The pilot entered, his eyes widening at the sight of Yuki. He stiffened as he felt the barrel of Matt's pistol dig into his back.

Matt disarmed him quickly. Then he fastened his feet together, using the belt of Itoh's kimono. The old man stood, trembling with anger, holding his robe together, as he watched Matt with careful eyes.

When he was through, he took the newspaper Yuki held out to him. Halfway down the front page the headline screamed at him: U.S. MISSILE TEST MOVED AHEAD.

He scanned the article quickly. Citing pressure from Congress the Pentagon had moved up the date for the Ragnarok test to the twenty-fifth, a full two weeks ahead of its originally scheduled time. Despite the change of date, the article continued, interest in the test was so high that European and Asian defense representatives were already on their way to southern California. The U.S. Secretary of Defense was expected to attend, as well as the Secretary of Commerce, the head of the Senate Appropriations Committee, and at least two of the Joint Chiefs of Staff.

Matt cursed inwardly. Takashi had outsmarted him brilliantly. He knew that Matt would assume that finding Yuki would also involve a confrontation with the Dragon. Leaving Yuki in Itoh's castle had given Takashi and Kanji time to get back to California for the test.

It hadn't been a trap at all, he thought bitterly; it had been a diversion. While he had been planning his assault on Itoh's castle, the Dragon was already on his way to California. Itoh had been left virtually unguarded because he was no longer crucial to the events unfolding thousands of miles away. The wheels had already started to turn.

Matt looked up, despair clouding his expression. "We're too late," he whispered. "The test is on the twenty-fifth. Today is the twenty-fifth."

"Not too late, Matt." Yuki spoke from his side. "It is one day earlier in California. The test has not yet taken place."

He looked at Itoh, who stood rigidly, no expression on his face. Then he looked at the pilot, lying on the floor with his feet lashed together.

"Okay," he said after a moment. "Let's try it. We might have just enough time."

Yoshi Itoh's big Toyota started immediately. As the automatic doors rumbled open, the pilot put the car in gear and they began to move out.

Matt and Yuki sat in the backseat with Itoh,

invisible behind the smoked glass. He held his gun trained on the old man.

He spoke to Yuki in a quiet voice. "Explain to the pilot once more. He tells the guard to open the gate right away. Anybody asks any questions, he answers them. And if he says anything he shouldn't, I'll shoot him first, right through the head. I've got nothing left to lose. Make sure he understands that. Make sure the old man gets it too."

She translated, her words coming rapid-fire in the darkness. Itoh stared at Matt, his eyes hooded and coldly neutral. *"Hai,"* he said after a moment.

The check at the gate was perfunctory. The two security guards snapped to attention, bowed, and as the gate opened, they waved the car through with a flourish. In less than a minute they had crossed the perimeter park and reached the intersection at the main road.

Yuki pointed to the left. "Tokyo is this way, Matt," she said.

"We're not going to Tokyo," said Matt. "Tell him to turn right."

"Where are we going, then?"

Matt pointed ahead half a mile, to Itoh's private landing strip, out to where the lights illuminated the sleek Gulfstream on its pad.

"We're getting out of here," he said.

They left the Toyota at the edge of the strip. Keeping his pistol out of sight inside his jacket, Matt prodded Itoh and the pilot toward the aircraft. It had started to rain lightly.

They clambered inside. "Do you know what you're doing?" Yuki asked him as they made their way forward, toward the cockpit.

"Not entirely," said Matt. "So if you have a better idea, I'd be delighted to hear it."

He handed her the driver's chromed pistol. "This may look like a flashy toy," he said, "but it will put a hole through Mr. Itoh very efficiently, if it's pointed the right way. I want you to tie his hands and feet together and get him comfortable. Then I want you to watch him very carefully. If he makes any funny moves, shoot him. Try not to put a hole in the side of the plane. I'll take care of the pilot."

Matt scanned the runway through the cockpit windows. No movement; everything was still. Five more minutes, he thought. That's all we need.

He settled himself into the copilot's seat and ran his eyes over the instruments as the engines warmed up. A state-of-the-art Gulfstream V, the plane had twin Rolls-Royce Tay turbofans and long-range fuel tanks. He flipped through the pages of the navigator's manual, noting range, cruising speeds, and fuel consumption rates.

Yuki tapped him on the shoulder. "Itoh says he will cooperate with us. He has no wish to die. But he wants to know where we are going." She paused. "And so do I."

"We're going to stop the test."

Yuki's eyes widened. "California? Can we really fly that far? Do we have enough fuel?"

Matt tapped the instrument panel. "We're showing full tanks. The listed range on this baby is 5,500 miles, plus or minus a safety factor. That's almost exactly the distance from Tokyo to Los Angeles. Better get strapped in. We won't be waiting for tower clearance." He prodded the pilot with the barrel of Tommy Clegg's automatic. "Get going."

Rain whipped past the windows as they took off, moving up and out, leaving the castle behind. In minutes they were flying across Tokyo Bay, their navigation lights strobing out into the blackness. Below them the city lights along the water's edge shone like a string of luminous pearls.

"Take a good look," said Matt. "We won't be seeing anything much for a while now." Then the nose tilted and the Gulfstream began to climb, pushing hard against the night, rushing to meet the sunrise.

25

The Gulfstream made landfall just south of Santa Barbara, helped by a tailwind, flying at less than three hundred feet to avoid coastal radar. After crossing the coastline it had flown straight east until Victorville, and then northeast toward Barstow. Matt rubbed the stubble on his face. Ahead of them the sun's light was harsh and blinding.

Itoh's Gulfstream boasted sophisticated telecommunications. As soon as they had come within range of the U.S. net, Matt had punched up Ace Emerson's number. When Ace came on the line, Matt handed the headset to Yuki. "Talk to this guy," he said. "Tell him your Trojan-horse theory. He's the only one who can tell us how to shut Ragnarok down."

When she finished, twenty minutes later, Matt

took back the headset. "Meet us in"—he checked the instruments—"about twenty minutes. Here's the location." He unfolded the navigation map and began to read off coordinates.

Strapped in tight, trying not to look at the pilot's white knuckles, Matt ignored the strident stall warning buzzer and the blinking LOW FUEL indicators as the Gulfstream dropped down toward the surface of Route 15, north of Barstow. They hit with a hard bump and a squeal of tires, and then they were down, wobbling along the roadway, coming up behind a line of cars with terrifying speed. The pilot pumped the brakes hard, easing the aircraft off the highway and onto the shoulder.

Matt emerged from the cockpit just as Ace pulled up with a screech of brakes, his face a grin from ear to ear. "Fuckin' A, man. You folks oughta think about joining the circus."

"Maybe after this is over," Matt replied. "This is Yuki. Yuki, Ace." He pulled the two Japanese out of the cockpit. "These are the bad guys. The old one is Kanji's boss. Also the Dragon's."

They bundled inside Ace's car. "Okay, campers," said Ace. "What now?"

"We've got to get inside the test site," Matt said. "Any ideas?"

"Yeah," said Ace. "Grow wings and turn invisible. The main gate's out, absolutely. They got guards everywhere, Secret Service, Army, all that shit. He pointed up the road. "I say we forget about the test site. Go for the tracking station instead."

"Tracking station?"

"Yeah. It's this cinder-block building a couple of miles away across the flats. They got a big diesel generator, a bunch of telemetry equipment, and a hard-wired link with the firing bunker. It's got its own entrance, couple miles up the way here."

"And they're hooked up to Ragnarok?"

Ace nodded. "Straight through the mainframe. They only cut the computer link a few seconds before lift-off. If I can get into the system before that happens, we've got a chance."

"Think you can do it?"

Ace smiled thinly. "Shit, I helped design the system, didn't I? Oughta be able to fuck it up."

He held up a computer diskette. "Didn't have time to get fancy," he said. "So I whipped up a little something before I left the house."

"What is it?"

"A logic bomb."

"A what?"

"Logic bomb. I get into the net, slip this baby into the drive, and hit return."

Yuki leaned forward. "You know the source codes, then?"

Ace smiled. "Know 'em? I *wrote* 'em, lady."

She nodded. "What did you use for the logic bomb? A recursive procedure?"

Ace looked at her with a new measure of respect. "As a matter of fact, yes. I—"

"Hold it," Matt said. "Is this a real bomb? How does it work?"

Ace grinned. "Relax, man, it's just a term. What's on this disk is about five lines of programming, what they call a recursive procedure. It'll send Odin into an endless loop, going back over itself again and again. And every time it loops, it'll send a string of data into one of the stacks in the programming."

Yuki nodded. "And the stacks will quickly fill up with nonoperating strings."

"She means 'garbage,'" Ace said. "In layman's terms, McAllister, Odin's brain will fill up with junk, and the whole shebang will just shut itself off. Oughta take no more'n three or four seconds."

Matt nodded. "Sounds like a plan. Let's go do it."

"Not so fast. First we gotta get inside the perimeter. *That's* the hard part. I've got my employee pass, but what the hell do we tell the guards about all the rest of you? It'd take a miracle."

Matt opened his mouth to speak, but just then a siren whooped right behind their car, startling everyone. Matt turned in his seat to see a county sheriff's car rolling up behind them, its light bar flashing.

"Damn," muttered Ace. "Shit about to hit the fan now, campers."

The patrol car crunched to a stop on the gravel. The door opened, and Sheriff Dan Simmons got out and began walking slowly toward them.

Matt watched him approach. "I believe our prayers have been answered," he said softly.

* * *

Matt slowed the patrol car as they approached the fence. Two armed soldiers stood on either side of the gate.

"You think they're gonna be okay?" Ace's voice sounded doubtful.

Matt reached up and adjusted Sheriff Simmons's hat. It was a size too big, but Yuki had fixed that with some wadded-up newspaper stuffed into the crown. The sheriff's shirt was also too big around the middle, but that didn't show as long as he was sitting down. He had his shield out on the dashboard, and Ace had his employee's pass in his hand.

Matt spun the wheel to avoid a gully. "No problem. These things have got bigger trunks than you'd think. I never thought we'd get everybody in there, though."

"Hope they can breathe with those gags on," Ace said.

"Don't worry about that. Worry about what happens now. Here we go."

He stopped the car and rolled down the window. "Howdy, boys," Matt said, hoping he'd hit the right mix of authority and bonhomie. "Open 'er up, willya? We got a coupla late arrivals here."

The lead soldier came forward and peered into the car. Regular Army, Matt noted with relief. That meant he probably wasn't from around here. "What's the problem, Sheriff?" His voice was friendly but guarded.

Matt tipped his hat back. "No problem," he said. "Just that we gotta get these two up to the tracking station." He revved the engine, waiting.

The soldier's face showed annoyance. "Nobody's supposed to come through after the first siren sounds." He looked at his watch. "That was twenty minutes ago. They're gonna be firing pretty damn soon."

Ace leaned forward. "Hey, jackass," he said, a hard edge to his voice. "There's not gonna *be* a test unless I get up there, you understand that?" He shoved his ID card in the soldier's face. "I'm the chief fucking engineer up there. Nobody pushes a button or pulls a switch until I say so, and if I'm not there in ten minutes, the Secretary of Defense is gonna be calling here to ask why."

He raised his finger in warning, his face tense with barely restrained anger. "I've had just about enough today. Freeway traffic, then a fucking breakdown. If it hadn't been for Simmons here"—he indicated Matt with his finger—"I'd still be back on the highway."

He pointed to the gate. "Now, open the damn gate, soldier, before I tear it off its hinges."

"Ah, right." The soldier was backpedaling fast, making frantic motions to his companion. "Okay. But, ah, sir, I've gotta take your names. Sheriff Simmons, right, and you're—"

"Emerson," Ace snarled. "*Doctor* Emerson, got that?" The gate was opening, and Matt started to inch the patrol car forward.

"Wait, what about the woman?"

Ace turned his head, shot a glance at Yuki. "Her? She's just my secretary, what the hell you think?" He tapped Matt on the shoulder. "C'mon,

Sheriff, let's get moving. Tracking station's still five miles up the road. Stand on it, willya?"

They rolled through the gate, picking up speed.

A low cinder-block building, the tracking station squatted in the middle of a flat barren area, several hundred feet above the valley floor. An array of cameras and satellite dishes cluttered its flat roof. In the distance Matt could see the test site itself.

As they approached, Ace was explaining the procedure to them. "See, a coupla minutes before they fire Ragnarok, they'll send a signal to Odin asking for a self-check. If everything's okay, then they'll start the countdown. The computer link is maintained right up until ten seconds before ignition, which is when the system arms itself. Once that happens, the mainframe logs off, and Odin's running on its own." He grimaced. "So we gotta get into the system before they light the burner."

He glanced at his watch. "Fifteen minutes, give or take. This is gonna be pretty goddamn close."

They pulled up just outside the doorway. "Stay here," Matt said to Yuki. He reached under the seat and brought up Simmons's service revolver. "Here," he said to Ace. "Take this."

Ace stared at the heavy gun. "Aw, shit, man, what do you expect me to do with this?"

"Nothing, I hope. Now, come on. Pretend we're bank robbers if it's easier for you."

Matt strode in through the main door, pistol held high, Ace close behind him. His eyes swept the room. Half a dozen technicians, headsets covering their ears, sat at a control panel running the length of one wall. Above them a wide picture window gave a panoramic view of the valley and the test site, several miles away. Unlike the day Marty's film had been shot, the test site was choked with people and vehicles. Two doors stood against the opposite wall; one bore an exit sign; the other DANGER—HIGH VOLTAGE.

Kanji Nakamura stood in front of a long table, printout sheets unfolded before him. He glanced up, looking at Matt with expressionless eyes.

"Shouldn't have bothered coming, Mr. McAllister. I told you in Tokyo—it's already done. You're too late."

Ignoring him Matt fired a single shot into the overhead lights. The noise exploded over the quiet murmuring of the printers in the corner, and everyone in the room froze. Kanji took a step backward.

"Time to shut things down," Matt said. "Everybody stand up. Move toward the center of the room. Come on, nobody's going to get hurt." There was a moment of hesitation, and then they started to move.

"Who the hell are you?" asked one of the technicians.

"Your guardian angels," said Ace, gesturing with his pistol. "Move it!"

"Hey, I know you," said the man. "You're Emerson. What the fuck—"

"Shut up," said Matt, motioning him back against the wall. "Now, listen to me." Matt raised his voice, speaking to all of them, but fixing Kanji with his eyes. "You're in no danger as long as you do exactly as we tell you. We're stopping the test." He pointed toward the window, out toward the test range. "The missile's been sabotaged."

One of the technicians looked at the large clock on the wall. "You're out of your fuckin' mind," he said. "They're going to launch in less than ten minutes."

Ace turned to him. "They gone to auxiliary power yet?"

The man nodded. "Five minutes ago. Final countdown's already started."

"Shit." He turned to Matt. "Gotta get into the system *now*." He went to the control panel, sat down, and began to access the mainframe, his fingers flying over the keyboard.

"Not so fast."

They turned. Nigel Hastings walked through the door. Takashi was one step behind him. He had Yuki by the neck, a pistol to her head.

"Saw you coming, Matt," Nigel said. "We were just settling in to watch the test. We nipped out the back door and got your lady friend out of the car." He smiled. "I must say, I'm surprised to see you. My colleague here"—he indicated Takashi—"thought you were still in Japan."

"Drop your weapons," said Takashi. "I can kill her with no trouble."

Matt nodded and took two steps backward, dropping his pistol. Behind him he heard Ace's weapon hit the floor. Kanji came out from behind the table to stand beside Nigel, a smile on his face. "Hey, tough shit," he said. "You can still watch the finale, though. Oughta be pretty spectacular."

Nigel indicated Ace. "Tell your friend here to stop whatever he's doing, Matt."

"Fuck you, man," said Ace over his shoulder as he continued to type. "I'm not your friend."

"A manner of speaking, old boy." Nigel smiled. "Now get away from that control panel, will you?"

Ace hit a key and swung around in his chair, his face bathed in sweat. "I'm into the system," he said to Matt in a voice hoarse with tension. His eyes flew to the clock on the wall. "Four minutes to launch. We've gotta activate, otherwise we'll lose the connection." He took the diskette from his pocket.

"No!" Takashi's voice cracked like a whip in the silence of the room.

Ace paused, diskette in hand, staring hard at him.

"Shoot me, asshole, and you'll also hit the console. That'll shut down the launch all by itself. That what you want?"

Takashi stared at him for several seconds. Then, without warning, he turned and fired at one of the technicians, hitting him in the chest. The man slid down the wall, leaving a bloody smear, and lay still on the floor.

Takashi pointed his weapon at the dead man's partner. "Another?"

"Christ." Ace's voice trembled. He raised his hands slowly.

Takashi smiled. To Nigel he said, "Get the disk."

Nigel stepped forward and plucked the diskette from Ace's fingers. "Lovely, thank you."

"Stop the test, Nigel," Matt said softly. "There's

still time. If Ragnarok launches, a lot of innocent people are going to die for no reason."

Nigel held the diskette delicately between long fingers. "Not for no reason, old boy. Purposely. Three years' work is coming to a climax out there. It's opening night, a new era in American high technology." He chuckled. "Don't want to disappoint our guests, do we?"

From far away a siren started up, peaked, and faded. Matt's eyes darted to the wall clock. Three minutes left. Just then he became aware of another noise, approaching fast from somewhere outside the building.

A helicopter.

Through the picture window he could see a camouflage-green Army Huey coming slowly toward the power station, its rotors whacking the air as it circled the building.

"Bloody hell," muttered Nigel. "They're coming to investigate the damned patrol car. What are we going to do?"

Takashi gestured with his pistol. "Go outside," he hissed. "Talk to them, keep them out there. Only a few minutes now."

Nigel nodded. Just then the telephone on the control console began to ring.

In the split second that Takashi's attention wavered, Matt moved. Grabbing Nigel by the arm he stepped back one pace, pivoted, and turned him halfway around, pinning his arm behind him, using him as a shield against Takashi.

The diskette clattered to the floor, and Matt

kicked it in Ace's direction. Kanji gave a low hiss and started toward it.

"Wrong move, Mr. McAllister." Takashi's lips were drawn back over his teeth. Nigel screamed as he saw the pistol coming up. Takashi shot once, hitting Nigel in the chest. The man slumped in Matt's grasp.

"Now you."

Takashi grunted in pain as Yuki's knee drove into his groin, breaking his grip. A split second later Ace's foot connected with the side of Kanji's jaw, driving him back against the wall. Ace snatched up the diskette and turned back to the computer console.

Matt dropped Nigel's lifeless body and launched himself forward. Takashi snapped off one wild shot before Matt's forearm hit his face, driving him back against the wall. He heard the pistol clatter on the floor, and then Takashi was behind him, his arm coming around his throat, locking him in an iron grip.

Matt pitched forward, dropping to one knee, bringing the *yakuza* up and over his back, slamming him to the concrete floor. He lay motionless, momentarily stunned.

Matt crossed to the console. Ace inserted his diskette, pressed ENTER, and looked up. "Cross your fuckin' fingers, man."

Columns of code raced across the screen, slowed, and finally stopped. "Frozen," Ace said. A wide smile split his face. "Odin's blocked. We did it."

"Matt!" Yuki's scream came from the doorway. Both men whirled to see Takashi dragging Yuki toward the patrol car. "Stay where you are, McAllister," he shouted. "Otherwise she dies."

With a squeal of tires and a cloud of dust the patrol car roared off, fishtailing crazily.

Ace moved up beside him. "What the hell we gonna do about *that*?"

Matt shifted his gaze from the speeding patrol car to Kanji's unconscious form, slumped against the wall. "Keep things calm and dignified in here," he said to Ace. "I'm going to have a word with the pilot over there." He pointed to the Huey, just settling onto its skids in a cloud of fine dust, thirty feet away.

Ace frowned. "You going after Takashi? Be careful; that sheriff's car's got a riot gun clipped to the backseat."

Matt walked straight up to where the Huey sat at the edge of the tiny parking lot, its rotorwash churning up whirlwinds of dust. The young pilot was unbuckling his harness, speaking into his mike as Matt approached, his pistol concealed down the side of his leg.

The pilot looked up, alarm in his eyes. Matt reached in, plucked the man's service automatic from his leg holster and threw it into the back of the helicopter. Then he yanked the astonished pilot straight out of his bucket seat and onto the ground.

"Christ, what—"

"Relax," Matt said, climbing aboard. "You stay here. I'll be back very shortly."

He buckled himself in, adjusted the controls, and pulled up on the collective, easing the cyclic control forward. It had been a few years, he thought, since he'd handled one of these.

The helicopter rose unsteadily into the air.

The Huey skimmed across the dry ground, yawing slightly from side to side as Matt wrestled with the antitorque pedals. He kept one eye on the instrument panel, the other on the dust cloud ahead of him, where the patrol car raced madly across the bare landscape.

Takashi was headed for the gate and the main highway, doing at least ninety over the rough ground. The _yakuza_ drove like a man possessed, the car bouncing and fishtailing as it hurtled along. Although Matt was closing the gap, he was doing it too slowly. In minutes Takashi would be out of the test range, on the highway. And although it seemed as if he could not possibly escape, Matt knew better. The man was a professional; he would do anything to survive, including killing as many people as necessary, beginning with Yuki.

Slowly, the helicopter narrowed the distance, until finally the Huey's shadow edged across the roof of the patrol car in a whirlwind of dust and sand. Takashi suddenly braked, slewing the car sideways. Taken by surprise Matt overshot. Working the cyclic and throttle frantically, he brought the helicopter back around in a tight arc, headed toward where the car sat immobile on the sand.

Matt came in low, his speed dropping. As he approached, the car door opened and Takashi rolled out, the heavy riot shotgun in his hands.

The first blast tore through the Huey's windshield, spraying Matt with glass and plastic, causing the helicopter to yaw dangerously. He recovered and brought the machine up and away to the side, but it was too late. He felt rather than heard a second blast, then a third.

The Huey shuddered and seemed to hang in the air for an instant. Thick smoke began to pour from somewhere overhead, and Matt heard a high screeching noise as the complex machinery of the swashplate assembly tore itself to bits. The helicopter tilted sharply and began to fall.

His last glimpse was of Takashi, shotgun up and firing, standing beside the patrol car. Then he hit.

The helicopter slammed into the earth with a bone-jarring crash, tons of metal collapsing in the space of a split second. His safety harness kept him upright in his seat, as all around him the skeleton of the helicopter imploded, buckling and folding up, fragments of metal and plastic flying everywhere, a long grinding screech building in intensity until it seemed as if his ears would rupture.

Then silence.

Matt glanced from side to side, moved his arms and legs, and found with amazement that he was alive and undamaged. The air lay still and heavy, the silence unbroken save for the pinging of hot metal. Then Matt became aware of the sound of liquid gurgling from a ruptured hose, somewhere underneath him. The radio gave a soft squawk and died in a tiny shower of sparks.

He unbuckled himself and slid sideways off his

seat, looking around vainly for a weapon as he levered himself upright. His pistol was nowhere to be found. Using his arms he painfully hauled himself up out of the seat and halfway through the cargo door, canted upward at right angles.

The *yakuza* stood fifty feet away, shotgun at the ready, holding Yuki with his free arm. As he caught sight of Matt, he began to fire, sending one volley of shot after another into the helicopter. Matt retreated inside the twisted metal of the cargo bay, hearing steel shot ricochet off the bulkheads. He felt blood flowing down the side of his face from a wound on his forehead, and tasted fear in his mouth. And then he became aware of the thick odor of spilled fuel, rising up around him.

Takashi moved closer, away from the patrol car and toward the side of the helicopter, firing into the wreck. I've got to get out of here, Matt thought. The wrecked helicopter was a death trap. Fuel gurgled from the ruptured tanks onto the ground, spreading out in a dark circle around him. Takashi fired two more blasts, and then Matt heard a click.

Silence. Another click. Then a curse.

He's run out of shells, Matt thought. Without hesitation he was up, leaping from the wreckage, hitting the ground hard, rolling, up on his feet, and running.

Away from Takashi. Toward the patrol car.

Ignoring Takashi's shout behind him Matt sprinted to the vehicle and threw open the door. Ripping the keys from the ignition he held them up for Takashi to see.

Takashi had discarded the shotgun now, and held Yuki in a stranglehold, close in front of him.

Matt walked forward, keeping the keys in sight.

"I'll kill her." Takashi's voice was harsh and strained. "I can snap her neck easily."

Matt kept his own voice under control, willing his breathing to be steady. "You can kill her, but you'll have a harder time with me. Let's make a deal. Let her go, and I'll give you the keys."

As he talked, he walked slowly forward, circling away from the car. As he'd hoped, the *yakuza* backed up as he approached, closer to the downed helicopter.

"Throw me the keys."

Matt shook his head. "Let the woman go first."

Takashi hesitated.

"You'll never get out of here without the keys," Matt said. "And you won't get the keys unless you let her go. Kill her, and you die. Set her free, and you have a chance to escape."

"I do not trust you."

"Okay, I'll go first in that case. Here." This had better work, he thought. Pitching underhand he tossed the keys hard, into the cargo door of the Huey. "Now let her go."

Takashi turned, looking at the wrecked helicopter. Then he released Yuki, pushing her away. She stumbled forward and ran to Matt's side. The *yakuza* took a step toward the Huey, then another.

Matt stood quietly, his arm around Yuki, watching him. Takashi was still not quite where he should be, he decided. Keep him moving; don't give him time to think.

He felt in his jacket pocket and brought out a plastic videocassette box. Time to provide an incentive.

"Remember this? The videotape. What you were going to kill me for. Still want it?"

Takashi looked at him for a long moment. Then he nodded. "Yes."

Matt threw it toward the helicopter, close to the door. "There it is. Go get it."

Takashi hesitated, and then moved forward, toward the plastic box on the ground. Two steps, three.

Ready now.

"One more thing." Something in Matt's voice made Takashi pause and look at him.

He stepped forward, his Zippo lighter in his hand. He shook it once for luck, and flipped it open. Takashi's eyes widened in horror as he grasped the meaning of what was about to happen.

"Marty gave me this lighter," Matt said. "Works every time. Watch, I'll show you." He spun the wheel, and as the flame ignited, he tossed the lighter forward onto the ground.

Hellfire erupted as the pool of volatile fuel ignited, enveloping the helicopter. Matt leapt backward, away from the scorching heat, raising his arm against the glare.

The Huey's main fuel tank exploded with a roar. The concussion slapped Matt and Yuki to the ground as a giant fireball billowed thirty feet into the air and bits of jagged metal flew past them.

The wrecked helicopter was wreathed in a solid wall of flame now. Inside, Matt could see a fiery figure waving its arms helplessly, jerking and capering in the inferno like a demented marionette. Matt hugged Yuki down close to the ground as the Huey's ammunition began to go off. There were two or three intense bursts, like a string of Chinese firecrackers, and then nothing.

The fire crackled, the air heavy with the odor of burning meat, oil, and rubber. As Matt and Yuki watched, the flames began to die down, revealing a huddled, blackened corpse among the wreckage. A shapeless lump of fused plastic still lay in its clawlike hand.

Matt got slowly to his feet and watched the burning wreck for several more minutes. Then he reached into his jacket pocket and took out a videotape. Yuki's eyes widened.

"I threw him the empty case," Matt said. "I needed to move him nearer to the spilled fuel."

He walked to the patrol car, opened the door on the driver's side, and pulled the trunk release lever. He walked back to see Sheriff Simmons, Yoshi Itoh, and the pilot still wedged into the trunk like sardines, their eyes bulging. "Sorry about the rough ride, gentlemen," he said.

He helped the portly sheriff out and removed his gag. The man's eyes widened as he took in the burning wreck in front of him. "Say, what the hell—"

"Just a little trouble, Sheriff. All over now."

Yuki put her hand on his arm. "Matt, look."

He turned to see a line of helicopters on the horizon, moving toward them. "The cavalry," he murmured. "Just like in the movies."

He walked forward and picked up the Zippo lighter, Marty's gift to him. It was blackened and nearly too hot to touch. He turned it around in his fingers, rubbing some of the soot from it. Then he put the lighter carefully in his jacket pocket.

He took Yuki's hand. "Let's go get Ace," he said quietly.

EPILOGUE

They sat quietly at the edge of the water, their feet dangling over the rocks, toes nearly touching the mirrored surface of the lake. On the far bank the red *torii* of the shrine was a splash of vivid color against the more muted autumn golds and yellows of the trees.

To their left Fuji-san appeared to float far above the lake, only its upper third visible above the low cloud layer. The almost perfect cone was sprinkled with snow now, foreshadowing the approach of winter.

Yukiko finished writing on the flyleaf of the book. She sighed, closed the cover, and handed it to Matt. "There. The very first copy." Yuki pointed to the characters on the inside page. "This is your name,

Matt. The book is dedicated to you." Underneath, in her precise English script, Yuki had written: *With deep love, to a true hero and* tateyaku.

Matt took the book with both hands. "*Itadakimasu,*" he said. He turned it over. Yuki's picture was on the inside flyleaf. The front cover, which would have been the back of a book in English, showed a beautiful Japanese woman and a muscled, bare-chested man facing a band of evil-looking desperadoes. Behind them, mountains soared into the far distance.

Matt flipped through the book. "Let me guess," he said. "The heroine is an innocent young girl who leaves home and goes far away. She meets a hero and several bad guys, maybe an evil king or warlord, perhaps even a dragon. Not everyone is what they seem at first. But in the end the hero and the girl win out and ride off together into the sunset."

She looked at him suspiciously. "Did somebody already tell you the plot?"

Matt smiled. "Just guessing," he said. "Too bad I can't read it."

Yuki laughed. "Perhaps someday you will, Matt-san. If you stay here long enough, who knows?"

He shrugged. "*Nihongo wo oboeru no wa asameshi-mae no shigoto de wa arimasen.*"

Yuki clapped her hands in delight. "Very good! No, learning Japanese is not easy, as you say. But you have made wonderful progress. Soon you will speak like one of us." She turned serious. "Matt, what are you going to do now?"

He took her face in his hands and kissed her.

"Live one day at a time," he said quietly. "I have no reason to go back right away."

"What about the Senate committee—the one that asked you to testify? What about the medal?"

Matt skipped a stone out across the water of the lake, watching with satisfaction as it bounced eight times and sank with barely a ripple. "The committee can interview me on the phone if they want to," he said after a moment. "The medal's in the mail, according to Buttons. I've got no interest in eating dinner at the White House, in any case."

"And your Ragnarok book? Don't you want to be there when it comes out? They are already calling, asking you to appear on television talk shows and things like that."

He hugged his knees. "Buttons can do all that," he said. "After all, he wrote most of the book. I just added the last couple of chapters. Buttons said the advance was a quarter of a million, and they've started a second printing already, even before it's hit the stores. First technical report in history to become a best seller." He grinned. "So you're not the only successful author around here."

"Matt, I think you are going to become rich."

"Only if the book sells well. Anyway, I gave most of the advance away."

Yuki's eyes widened. "You did what?"

"Well, not gave it away, exactly. I set up a scholarship fund. Two funds, really. Buttons helped me do it. One is the Theodore Edwards Fund, for an outstanding student in political science."

"And the other?"

"The Martha Larsen Journalism Award. For the best piece of investigative reporting during the year."

Yuki's eyes were serious. "Do you still think of her, Matt?"

He took her in his arms. "I always will. Poor Marty." After a moment he added, "But wherever she is, she's got the satisfaction of knowing that her video was seen by half the people on earth." He drew her close, hugged her. "Knowing Marty, she's probably delighted."

He looked out across the water at the *torii*. "Rollie Chalmers, wherever *he* is, is probably happy too. TransCentury's business is booming. They've been flooded with orders in the last two months, beyond anything they ever imagined. Ace Emerson's the project manager now for Ragnarok; he says this is going to be worth billions."

Yuki nodded. "And the Dragon is dead."

"The Dragon is indeed dead," Matt agreed. "And Yoshi Itoh and Kanji Nakamura go on trial next month."

Yuki laid her head on his shoulder. They sat quietly, their arms around each other, looking up at Fuji-san with its mantle of early snow, listening to the silence of the lake.

"I would like," she said after a moment, "to go somewhere far away with you. Somewhere beautiful, where we could be all by ourselves. Not luxurious, but simple and private."

Matt thought of Toad Hall, perched up on the sides of the Monocacy River Valley. He remembered the stillness of the evenings, the crystal quality of the morning light through the trees. He thought of how the woods must look at this time of year, aflame with autumn.

He drew her close. "I know just the place," he said.